Duello by Moonlight

Ilarion let loose of the woman abruptly, and she staggered back in terror.

Biagio Marsanti put out a hand and ripped out his long evil blade. *"Per Bacco!"* he snarled. "You ill-guided fool! I'll shred that face of yours so that no woman will ever want to see it again, by sun or candlelight!"

He cut with his sword and the sound of its slashing whistled through the air.

But where Ilarion had stood was now an empty space.

Then, with grace and gaiety, he lunged in, his sword a needle of flashing brilliance. It caught Marsanti's blade and ripped it from his fingers, sent it flying with a high screech of steel.

Donna Dorotea screamed as it clattered at her feet.

Then Ilarion whirled, leaping for the window.

For an instant he poised above the moonlit street. Around the corner swept armed horsemen, summoned by Marsanti's cries. Ilarion laughed and brandished his blade.

Then, legs straight out, he jumped.

THE BORGIA BLADE

A Gold Medal Original

by

Gardner F. Fox

GOLD MEDAL BOOKS

FAWCETT PUBLICATIONS, Inc., NEW YORK

THE BORGIA BLADE

I

He drove in and out of the torchlit room, his long blade a slash of red fire before him. His feet slapped the wooden flooring as he executed a flanconade or slid into the rhythmic movement of a *balestra*. The torches in the iron wall sockets glowed down on his frayed leather jerkin, on his length, and wide shoulders, painting him in crimson against the black backdrop of the empty fencing school.

"So!" he snarled. "So this is the way of your *circolazi-óne*, Messer Jacopo!" And his thick wrist turned and the naked blade slid through the darkness; the gleaming point barely touched the brick of the wall, and fell away.

His name was Ilarion, and Jacopo Balisandro, who owned the fencing school, always added, with a wry twist of his loose lips, *della stalla*. Of the stables. Even the plump and laughing Tea Panchesi, who served the men-at-arms and University students at the corner tavern, joined in the good-naturedly hallooed "Ilarion! Ilarion *della stalla!"* when he trudged by, a broom or a pail of slops dangling from one big hand, reeking of the horses that carried their masters to the fencing hall.

That was the way they knew him when the sun shone down on this little corner of Rome in the eighth year of His Eminence, Alexander VI. The city was thronged with hard-faced *condottieri* and swaggering foreign soldiers, for all Italy was rising, from Calabria in the south to Piedmont in the north, to serve the bull banner of Cesare Borgia, and fight against the French.

Half the world appeared to move on Rome in this late summer of 1500. Holy men in brown cloth frocks tramped the Via Flaminia and the Via Appia beside knights and nobles in armor riding powerful war horses. Lovely women in silks and brocades swayed to the curvetting of sleek mares, or jostled in the bouncing coaches which scattered the bare-footed farm women from Tuscany and Campania.

The blue waters of the Tyrrhenian Sea were thick with carracks, narrow galiots from Africa, and the long, many-oared galleys from Genoa and Venice. France sent its *coquets*, and Spain its galleons. For this was the Jubilee Year, when the Holy Door of St. Peter's was thrown open, and the pilgrims came from Flanders and the Levant, from the Danube and the plains of Granada, to worship in the square before the great cathedral.

In the daylight hours, Ilarion the stableboy went on about his chores, unaware that the world was erupting all around him.

But by night, creeping on naked feet from his stable pallet to the empty fencing hall, Ilarion was a different person. His hangdog gloom was gone, and his blue eyes glittered as they stared at the humpbacked, long-legged figure of ugly old Jacopo Balisandro slashing the empty air with one of his many rapiers, executing counters and *doppio circolazióne* that no eyes but those of the hidden Ilarion had ever seen.

He would lie there in the shadows, not daring to breathe, for if the one-eyed Jacopo saw him, it would mean kicks and cuffs. Only his eyes lived as he lay there following the rhythmic patterns of that cunning blade.

And when the old man shuffled off to his bed on the upper floor, an ornate four-poster that rumor said he had looted from a Ferraran palace in the Venetian campaign of '83, Ilarion came off his belly. He took down one of the

6

old man's swords and practiced the thrusts and movements he had observed so studiously.

For all the years he could remember, Ilarion had slaved for the old maestro, cleaning the stables and the hall. When he could, he stole away to visit fat Fra Matteo at the church beyond the campanile, on the Via Malatesta. It was Fra Matteo who taught him to read and to scrawl his name across a bit of parchment. And sometimes, after he had stolen through the moonlight into Tea Panchesi's pallet to spend the night with her, it was Fra Matteo who gave him absolution and a mild scolding.

He could never have told why he lost sleep to watch the old man in his solitary fencings. Sometimes he tried to put his thoughts into words, as when Tea lay with the moonbeams silvering her, looking up at him, questions pouring from her generous mouth.

"It changes him, the sword! To see that bent old body stamp into the *molinello!* To see his hump and his gnarled middle disappear when he uses the *filo!* If the sword can do that for him, think what it might do for me!"

That was why Ilarion *della stalla* forgot his sleep and his straw-colored pallet, and slashed the thin air with a sword until the dust rose from the floor plankings to choke him.

And that was why, on a crisp night in early September, when the door opened silently and a man and a woman crept in on soundless feet, they stared at his torch-reddened blade and intent face, and sensed something of the fire that burned in him.

It was the woman whose tiny white hands beat applause when he lowered the blade to suck air into his tortured lungs.

Ilarion heard the sound, and he whirled about.

He knew they had stepped off the streets to snatch an intimate moment, where kisses and the play of hands in stolen caresses might pass unseen. No sheltering doorway was safe from invasion during the fiesta proclaimed to celebrate the conquest of Forli by the Duke of Valentinois, Cesare Borgia. Attracted first by their own flesh, and then by the hiss of his blade and the stampings of his feet, the couple had spied on him.

"Why, it's Ilarion!" said the man, waving a pomade ball close against his thin nostrils. "Balisandro's stableboy!"

"Stableboy or not, he can use a sword," retorted the woman. She came forward a step, and the torchlight gleamed on the pearls set in her thick blonde hair and on the jewels that were sewn into the red satin of her cloak, Her eyes glowed brightly through the slits of her golden domino, and her wet red mouth was twisted in an excited smile.

"Did you ever see such a wrist, Paolo? His blade is a part of his arm!"

The man who leaned across her naked shoulder was a raffish dandy in violet doublet trimmed in ermine. Tight lavender hose, slashed in yellow, clung to his legs. A purple mask hid his lean face with its tight lips. The fingers of his left hand were lost under the cloak that she held to her as they stood in close embrace.

"Beatrice," he said, yawning. "You and your enthusiasms! So the fellow can wield a sword. I know any number who can do the same thing!"

"But not like this one! I have seen Bevilacqua, and Bevilacqua is a tyro beside this boy!"

The woman shrugged loose from the fop's hand, and came toward Ilarion. Her white hands, jeweled rings flashing fire from their slim fingers, were lifting the satin bodice that had slipped with the man's strokings. Ilarion caught a glimpse of her bosom, pale as mare's milk, before she fastened the crimson bodice.

His cheeks flushed, Ilarion was aware that she watched his eyes. Her laughter rang softly under the smoke-blackened beams of the hall. She fussed longer than was necessary in settling the jeweled front of her rich gown, affording his probing eyes disturbing glimpses of her. Her mouth twitched in amusement.

"Paolo, why not try him out? See if he can use that long blade against a man as well as he uses it against a shadow's arm!"

There was challenge in her bold eyes as they stared deep into his, challenge in the lift of her fleshy shoulders, in the sway of her hips. Ilarion touched his dry lips with his tongue. If old Jacopo chanced on him like this, talking to nobility . . .

He croaked, "Gracious lady, forgive me. I must—"

The dandy in the violet satin doublet came out of the shadows. "Relax, *giovane!* When the Countess Beatrice commands, oafs like you obey. Come! I'll make it short. It'll be over and you safe in your bed before you know it."

He whipped a blade from the wall rack and bent it, listening to the steel's clear *spanng* as he released it. His dark eyes looked bored as they turned on Ilarion. There is no emotion in him at all, Ilarion thought. To him, I'm like a table or the floor beneath his feet. Anger stirred in him, a hot, pulsing thing which shook him. Easy, easy, he told himself. Old Jacopo will wallop you with his olivewood club if you don't let him disarm you.

But the woman was watching, and a devil stirred in Ilarion as he slid his right foot forward into position. The fop touched his blade an instant, fell away, and came in. Ilarion retreated slowly, his point in tierce, moving only to counter the dandy's lunges.

They stamped toward the wall, where the torch flung red fire across their faces. The dandy was sweating as he pressed the attack. A film of moisture stood out under the black curls framed in the velvet, pearl-hung cap. His black eyes had lost their boredom, and glowed with sullen rage as Ilarion's blade parried his every attack.

He came in high, to be met with a parry in prime. He came in low, to find the stableboy using a bind in quarte, turning his blade as easily as he might a wench's slap, and thrusting forward in the *fianconata*.

"*Per Bacco!*" snarled the fop, slipping in the fury of the disengage.

The woman laughed from the shadows of the arch, and her laughter was a warm, hot thing in Ilarion's ears. "He's playing with you, Paolo! I told you he was better than Bevilacqua!"

The mockery in that voice made the black eyes boring into Ilarion's blaze in hot rage. Suddenly Ilarion knew, with a queer wrench of his belly, that the dandy meant to kill him. He could never let this stableboy live to tell the world that the Countess Beatrice del Gallina had witnessed his humiliation. For a moment Ilarion considered taking the man's blade in his arm, hoping a simple blood-letting might suffice. But one look into those eyes changed his mind. Blood-letting was not enough. The fop hated him, and wanted a kill.

Ilarion lunged. His blade slid past the other's frantic guard, a darting length of steel. The point cut into the velvet purse that dangled from Paolo da Rienza's girdle of golden links. A dozen coins went flying across the floor. A small cameo, with the face of a woman carved into its ivory and cabochon, fell to the floor, and rolled away.

Paolo da Rienza snarled his rage and came in fast, breathing heavily. Ilarion moved his wrist, down and up, catching the fop's blade under the *quillon* of his own. His wrist circled so swiftly that not even the woman's bright eyes could follow it.

Paolo da Rienza cursed savagely as he felt his sword yanked viciously from his numbed fingers by that bind. It flew upward, toward the dark beams of the ceiling, and dug into the wood, humming.

Da Rienza snatched at a slim dagger in his belt, lifted it. He poised on the balls of his feet, and launched himself at Ilarion.

"Paolo!" cried the woman, and came into the torchlight, bringing heady perfume and a rustle of satin skirts with her. She came close to Ilarion, looking up at him with eyes that were brighter than before.

"Paolo, you fool!" she breathed. "Can't you see he's what we need? Admit it! Marsanti does not know him. He will never suspect!"

"Marsanti?" The fop turned a blank face toward the woman. In a daze, scowling behind his purple mask, he slid his stiletto into its sheath. He licked his thin lips. "Biagio Marsanti would make mincemeat of this stable-boy. It was just pure luck he disarmed—"

"Oh, Paolo. You are eaten alive with jealousy! This boy can go a long way with that sword of his. Only old Jacopo might be nimbler with a rapier. And Jacopo is so old. So ugly!"

Ilarion drew a deep breath as the woman smiled at him. Her fingers touched his arm, and crept upward until her long, tinted nails scratched lightly at his cheek. The countess smiled at what she read in his face. Without removing her eyes from Ilarion, she said, "Paolo, I have decided! Go to Messer Balisandro. Buy the boy's bondage! I'll talk to him—explain what I want him to do!"

Paolo da Rienza snarled, "Buy his bondage? The old fool won't sell him! He—"

Beatrice, Countess del Gallina, stamped her tiny foot. "Hurry, Paolo! Gold will speak with better effect than your clumsy tongue! Offer him gold—much gold! He will sell the boy—to me!"

The dandy turned and strode into the shadows. Beatrice laughed softly, shifting on her satin-shod feet. Her feverish eyes caught at something deep inside Ilarion, even as her warm fingers caught his hand and drew him

10

under the shadowed archway, along the cobblestoned outer loggia. When she pressed his shoulders against the frescoed wall and leaned upon him, he dared not meet her eyes.

"So?" she asked archly. "You're a coward only to a woman? You are a very good-looking boy, Ilarion, with your yellow hair and blue eyes. You might go far, you and that sword of yours."

"But, madonna," stammered Ilarion, "I'm only a stableboy. To do what you suggest is to attempt what is impossible!"

Her laughter was like the tinkling of the fountain waters in the Piazza de Crocífero. "La, Ilarion! Life is for living, for snatching pleasure while pleasure can be had! A man takes what he can, now! His birth—be it in a ducal palace or a stable—is not held against him! Not if he can offer the world something! And you can offer it a sword!"

Her eyes mocked him through the slits in her golden mask. The perfume which dizzied him, as she shook her golden curls, was like a hypnotic incense.

Her full mouth pouted. "I need someone who can fight!"

"Messer Balisandro," said Ilarion, with a frown, recalling the fierce one-eyed fencing master, "is far greater than I. He could help you. If you paid him, that is. He will do anything for gold."

"Poof!" whispered the countess. "Poof, I say! That hump-backed monster! I shudder to think of him. But you—young, strong—yes, even handsome, you devil!—you would make a lady a fine champion."

"Anything in my power, madonna," he stammered.

"There is a man—a fiend, say—who has a painting of me. He is an artist, who duels better than he paints. He will not yield up his canvas. Not for gold; nor from threats. A strong man could take it away from him, slit it from its frame in his studio, wrap it beneath his cloak, and bring it to me."

She leaned against him, and through the thin stuff of the red satin cloak he could feel the yielding softness of her rich white bosom. Her eyes and her smiling lips warmed him, sent a wild shock through his lean body. "Such a man would be well rewarded, Messer Ilarion!"

The woman gave him no time to think. She drew back a little and fumbled in her cape, bringing out a tiny silk purse. It was heavy with gold florins. She pressed it into his hands. "Give this to old Jacopo. Make him teach you much about the sword! Remember, even the great Hercules once cleaned out stables! And now, my cape!" She held it out to him, a billowing length of red satin trimmed with sable. Moonlight glimmered on the soft flesh of her bare shoulders, and painted dark shadows. She watched where his eyes roved, and she smiled.

She whispered, "You have not asked me what I wore when Messer Marsanti painted that portrait of me, Ilarion. Have you no curiosity?"

"What were you wearing?"

She slipped loose and ran toward the yard, out into the full moonlight, lifting her skirts so that slim ankles appeared. Her voice floated back to him, and he had to strain to catch the words in the soft laughter.

"I wore very little, Messer Ilarion! I wore—nothing at all!"

He stood there a long time, hearing Paolo da Rienza leave by the front door, and the snick of the bolt as old Jacopo shot it home. He thought of Beatrice del Gallina, and of how she must have looked, posing for the Marsanti painting. Lifting his head, he stared at a shaft of moonlight that probed into the shadows of the hall, coating an object on the floor with pale fire. Curious, Ilarion moved into the fencing room and bent to pick the bauble from the floor. He remembered a moment in his duel with Paolo da Rienza when his swordpoint had slashed the fop's velvet purse. From the corner of his eye, he had seen this cameo fall. Now he put his eyes to it, and caught his breath.

Some unknown artist had captured a woman here forever in ivory and cabochon, and Ilarion felt his heart leap in his chest as he stared down at slanted green eyes and hair the color of a Roman sunset. Breathless, he recalled the books that Fra Matteo had given him to read and study. There had been the *fablieux* of *La Castoyement d'un Pere à son Fils* and the *Ordene de Chivalerie,* together with other writings of the jongleurs and the troubadours, and the ballads of the love courts of Provence.

Steeped in this tradition, it was easy for him to dream also of the immortal loves of Beatrice de Portinari and Danti Alighieri, of Laura de Noves and Petrarch, and to imagine some of their fire in himself. That he could fancy himself in love with a woman whom he saw only thus in

12

ivory and cabochon was an idle fancy—yet it gave him pleasure. He stood for long moments filling his eyes with the beauty etched forever on the cameo, lost in a magic moment.

And then a bitter smile twisted his lips. Such a dream, such a noble love, was not for a stableboy! He sighed, and put the cameo down so old Jacopo could find it and return it to Paolo da Rienza. But his fingers lingered on the ivory, as if caressing it, until the moonlight faded from the window.

After a while, he stumbled drunkenly along the stones and into the dark, empty stable. He was lighting a little brass oil lamp when he heard old Jacopo entering the chamber. His great white head swung forward on immense, sagging shoulders. From under the jagged white brows a black eye glittered brightly, cruelly. The loose wet lips drooled spittle. A black square of silk hid the raw, empty eye socket that was a memento of the Ferraran campaign.

Jacopo came into the room slowly, sliding crabwise on his great legs that were like gnarled logs in tight plum hose. His voice was biting.

"So! The stableboy grows ambitious! Too ambitious to work any longer for poor Jacopo Balisandro. He has a new master! Or should I say—mistress?"

The *contessa's* perfume clung to Ilarion. It made him bold. He said, "They paid you well. Too well."

"You *scorzone!* You scullery boy! You—"

Ilarion held out the silk purse and let it jingle. Old Jacopo lowered his huge arm and licked his lips. Ilarion threw the purse and it landed with a sodden *thunk* on the little wooden table that held the oil lamp. The old man stared at the purse, and his black eye asked a question.

"For you, Jacopo."

"Messer Jacopo to you, stableboy!" the old man snarled. His powerful fingers lifted the purse and tore at the drawstring. He poured the gold coins into a huge palm. His lips drooled as the coins clinked, and he wiped them with the empty sack.

"For old Jacopo, eh? All these ducats?" His laughter cackled. "Whose gullet do I slit?"

"I'm paying you for lessons—lessons with the foil. But not the lessons you teach fops like Paolo da Rienza! Lessons in the art of fencing that I see you teaching yourself

13

when the world sleeps. When you are alone in the hall, and none watches you but me."

For a wild moment he thought the old man would rip at his throat with his hooked talons. But the coins in his uplifted hand recalled him to his senses. He put the coins back into the purse, and slid the purse into his belt.

"So, then. You spy on old Jacopo, do you?" His great lips twisted. "Who gave you the gold, Ilarion? The Countess Beatrice? She must think you a good playmate."

Ilarion moved, but the old man scuttled aside into the shadows like some monstrous spider. His laughter boomed out. "Finicky, are we? Can't abide the truth, can we? Well, how is she, boy? As good as Tea Panchesi? Or haven't you found that out, yet? What've you promised in exchange for a crazy dream?"

Ilarion growled, and the sound of it brought the old man out into the light again. "No need for temper between us, boy. I'm not one for denying a strong youth the pleasures a fine lady can teach him! You want lessons, do you? So!"

He stalked slowly around Ilarion. His black eyes studied the lean middle and the wide shoulders that had outgrown the tight leather jerkin. He noted the hard calves and the long legs in the tattered hose. His palm slapped at Ilarion's chest.

"You're solid. Good arms and legs. Strength enough. And wit enough, too, judging by the night's happenings. But the sword is a jealous mistress, Ilarion of the stables. It needs something more than muscle to handle her."

Ilarion snarled, "I could have blooded Paolo da Rienza a dozen times tonight. I've lost sleep too many nights watching you fencing the shadows, old one. I remembered what I saw."

Jacopo grinned, white head bobbing. "Ai, I'll wager you watched me. No wonder Da Rienza was in such a fury tonight, demanding your bondage, forcing me to name a sum! You must have learned something, at that!

"So you spent your nights watching old Jacopo? No wonder you were so slow about your chores. Ah, well," he clinked the coins in the bulging purse at his belt, then continued, "perhaps it wasn't time wasted."

"What about the lessons?"

"Eh? The lessons? Old Jacopo grows talkative, does he? So be it. Come along. We'll learn quickly enough how much you know of the art of fence."

14

They walked from the little stable across the loggia to the high, smoke-stained arch of the fencing hall. Jacopo scurried into the darkness, lighting torches, thrusting them into iron brackets inset in the wall paneling. The torches flared brightly, reflecting red fire from the swords in their racks and the polished helmets and old standards hung here and there on the walls.

Jacopo snatched a rapier from the rack and made it sing as he lashed the air. His cackle echoed as he wrapped his gnarled fingers about the braided hilt.

"Lessons you want, is it? Lessons you shall have, my fine stableboy. *En garde!*"

He came in a rush and a stamp of feet, and for the moment Ilarion thought he saw raw, hot hate in the bright black eye that peered at him from under the shaggy white brows. But as Ilarion took his blade in tierce and slid it harmlessly away, the old man chuckled.

"Aha, so! You used your eyes well while you cheated on poor old Jacopo! Aha—now, so! Eh, well—keen eyes you have, Messer Ilarion *della stalla!*"

The humped old man, still powerful and agile despite the age-twisted limbs, moved in, his blade a blood-red smear in the torchlight. His feet in their leather sandals stamped and slid, shuffled and side-stepped. The arm, bare below the simple sleeve of his cloak, was like the bole of a thick oak. Untiring, it moved the sword here and there, in and out, feinting for clinks in the armor of Ilarion's guard.

He came in high, to be met by a riposte that sent him back three feet. He swept in low, body sweeping the floor, his blade stabbing out. "Ah, *peste!*" he snarled, as Ilarion's blade skipped by his nose, in a flanconade of quarte.

Grudgingly, respect began to dawn in the feverish old eyes. Old Jacopo knew caution as he maneuvered his sword. He swore under his breath a dozen times.

The blades scraped and clanged, loud in the still room. The pound of feet, the stamp of sandals in a swift attack, the harsh and labored breathing went on and on. The old man was as untiring as an ox. His iron body, which had stood to the rigors of *condottieri* campaigns in the past, did not betray him now.

And then, as dawn tinted the high windows a pearl gray, old Jacopo cried out, "Ala, Messer Ilarion—this is it!"

His blade winked, was lost in a flurry of movement. The point came to a stop an inch from Ilarion's flat belly. Under the shaggy brows, the black eyes glittered cruelly.

"I ought to run you through, stableboy! I don't because Jacopo Belisandro is a man of honor. I gave my word to Da Rienza, and old Jacopo keeps his word." The old man broke off to cackle shrilly, "Ai, though it means a loss to me here! The trouble I'll have to train a new slopsboy! Hee-hee! But one must indulge such a pretty mare as the *contessa*, eh?"

Ilarion put away his blade. He could feel that cold black eye following his every movement. *The old one could cut me to ribbons any time he felt like it*, he thought. His shoulders sagged, and then he heard old Jacopo's laughter ring out.

"Don't take this to heart, stableboy. You have talent. Ai, a bit of value to the world as a swordsman. But you treat your blade like a stranger. It's a part of you—like a long finger. Come, look!"

Ilarion stepped to the bent old man's side. He watched the ease with which Jacopo moved the sliver of steel. It slid and darted as if endowed with life.

"You see? Eh? Make it think for itself! Make it do the work. It takes too long for your brain to relay its message to your arm, and your arm to your wrist! The blade itself must find the opening and—fa!——it drags you along with it.

"In time, you will know that feel, the quiver of the steel running into your hand as though your blade is telling you. 'Now! Now is the moment for the lunge!' Or else, 'Parry! Parry the blade that slips by me!'"

Almost reverently old Jacopo put away his sword and brooded at Ilarion. He growled, "Practice! Always, it takes much practice to make the blade into the extra finger. But you will learn. Already you are better than— Well, no matter. Now, off to your pallet with you!"

Ilarion saw him lift the leather bag of gold florins, saw the loose lips twist as the black eye lighted greedily. Gold and cruelty, those were the old one's gods. He would be taking the sack now to the black tile under the statue of the Venus in the loggia, where he kept his treasures. He would fumble about until he undid the mechanism that lifted the tile. Many times Ilarion had watched when Jacopo thought him asleep in the stable room. Often had he himself sought the secret of the tile, when

his body ached from the kicks and blows of the club
that Jacopo had wielded. But always the secret of the
mechanism had eluded the clutch of his hunting fingers.

Ilarion shrugged and turned away. He went out into
the yard and stared upward at the stars. Much had happened to Ilarion *della stalla* since those stars first winked
down this night. He wondered, as dawn brightened the
world around him, what other nights and other days
would bring.

He stumbled into the stable. He tossed his jacket from
him and lay naked to the waist, gulping in the cool morning air. After a moment his eyes closed, and he dreamed.

The *Contessa* Beatrice was posing for Ilarion in his
dream. Posing in a mist, through which he could catch
disturbing glimpses of her rich, creamy flesh. And he was
painting her portrait with a sword.

II

ILARION WALKED SWIFTLY along the Via Lata, in the
cool of early evening. He was no longer the stableboy in
leather and homespun woolens, but a young dandy in
slashed maroon velvet trunks and doublet, ornate with
crimson satin. Scarlet and white hose were taut on his
legs, and a red velvet cape swung to the rhythm of his
strides.

He felt different, more vibrant, in these garments pur-
chased with the gold that the *contessa's* maid had slipped
into his hand when she had come to the cortile by the
fencing school.

Ilarion showed his teeth in a grin, and set his velvet
cap at a more rakish angle on his thick-maned yellow
head.

For days he had awaited Beatrice del Gallina's call.
Hour after hour, he had worked and slaved with his mops
and pails, pestering gnarled old Balisandro into giving
him lessons with the long blades that glittered on the
walls of the hall.

The old man would snarl, *"Gran Dio!"* as he demon-
strated the footwork that went with the *appuntata*. "It is
ruining me, this contract I have made to teach you to use
a foil, you clumsy scullion! No, no! Not that way. This
way—"

But despite his rantings and his mumbled oaths, the one-eyed humpback taught him. He made his right hand and arm into an untiring ally of the blade in his fingers, taught him to think with his brain in the hilt of his sword, to let the singing steel whisper to that brain and obey its dictates.

Only yesterday, after their evening meal of cold lamb and slices of rich Parmesan cheese, with wine to wash down the coarse hard bread, the old man had told him grudgingly, with a sneer, "There is not much more I can teach you. You are better than any in Rome, already."

The old man thought a while, with his large white head cocked on the bend of his wry neck. His black eye grew harder, glittering with the fierce pride that drove his twisted body. The flat of his hand slapping the bare tabletop made the winecans dance.

"In Rome? *Diavolo!* You are better than any in all Italy, from Piedmont to Calabria! And that means you are the second best swordsman in the world!"

Ilarion had grinned.

The old man jabbed a long, gnarled finger out at him. His thick white brows came together until they touched under his brown, furrowed forehead. "I am the greatest, slopsboy! Do not forget that. Greater than this Biagio Marsanti your *contessa* prates of, greater than Bevilacqua! Yes, and greater than Achille Marozzo, who writes a book on the art. *Dio mio!* A book on fencing! Whoever heard of such a thing?"

And that night they had gone into the hall and lighted the torches, and for three hours they fought each other with blunted blades. When they were done, Jacopo hurled his blade from him so that it clattered against the wall.

"*Per Bacco!* It is done! The greatest work of Jacopo Balisandro! I have made you—me, Jacopo Balisandro!—from a lazy stablelad into a great swordsman. I have made you—" The old man paused, choking. His great frame began to tremble. He shook soundlessly for a moment, and then wild, almost mad peals of laughter rose up from his throat to the wooden beams that crossed the ceiling above.

Ilarion stared. Has the old fool lost his mind? he thought. He watched him wipe the tears from his eyes.

"It is a private little joke," he told Ilarion. "You would not appreciate it."

And now, after those hours and days of work and fenc-

18

ing, when he despaired of ever hearing from the countess again, her French maid was here, thrusting the heavy bag of golden coins into his palms! Ilarion wanted to shout, to dance a gaillarde. His happiness bubbled inside him like a lid dancing on a steaming pot over the fire.

In an excess of emotion, he caught the woman and whirled her, laughing wildly. She had long black curls that jiggled on her white shoulders, and a mouth that was wine-red in her pert face.

"Give over this play! I've brought you a message, I tell you! Her Highness wants you to get her picture tonight—"

He kissed her gaily, and she arched against him, her own lips yielding to his hunger. Life was strong in young Ilarion *della stalla,* and he let the woman feel his strength until her tiny fists hammered at his shoulders.

"*Dieu!* You'll crush me, stableboy! Let me go now! La, now stop! The countess will pay you well for your work. She wants that picture very badly!"

"Where does this Marsanti live?"

"On a side street off the Via Lata. An artist's studio, built into a house with brickwork and leaded windows. Two statues of Hercules front the door. His address is in the pouch of gold. She leaves the manner of entrance to your wits. But it must be a careful entrance. No one must know what you do, or that you work for Her Highness. If you have trouble, use your sword—though saints pity you, if you must! I have seen Biagio Marsanti with a blade in his hand!"

The Marsanti home stood on a street off the Via Lata that ran onward to the Porta da Popolo, through which Cesare Borgia had marched his army after his conquest of Forli. It stood almost under the shadows of Castello Sant'Angelo, its brick walls weathered with sun and rain, its leaded windows dull in the moonlight.

The street was quiet. With a bound, Ilarion was at the top of the fence, reaching a hand to the ornate balustrade that ran the width of the house below the rows of windows. Then he was swinging upward, sliding a leg across the sill.

From somewhere inside the house, a woman laughed with mockery in her throat. Ilarion froze. Dimly the moonlight came into the room, and he could see an un-made bed, and garments thrown carelessly across its sheets. Another burst of laughter brought him inside, to stand tensely, craning forward, listening.

There was only silence in the house now, and he moved past the bed. He went on silent feet out of the room and into the hall, where a flambeau shattered the gloom.

The studio door opened to the push of a hand, and he was inside. He blinked a little at the blaze of a dozen bronze floor lamps, that made this corner of the room bright as sunlight.

A Savonarola chair, rich with crimson brocade, stood under the slanted windows. A lounge, curved at each end and deep with cushions, stood against the wall, where in-built shelves housed tall glass jars which were gay with red, blue, and yellow powders. Other jars held the oils that Marsanti mixed with his bright powders to form his colors. Two discarded palettes had been flung atop a pile of trash and slit canvas trimmings.

At the far end of the room, where the light of the floor lamps did not reach, paint-splashed canvases leaned against the bare plaster wall. There were dozens of oils here, leaning this way and that, some flat on the floor, others propped against the litter of casual chairs and tables that formed a wall for this impromptu storage space.

Ilarion went into the dark shadows and hunted among the paintings. He muttered impatiently over a group of religious oils, whose pink-fleshed angels and cherubs had a decidedly secular appearance. Ilarion went on, into the blackest shadows. He exposed a gilt-framed nude of a woman seated in the Savonarola chair, and another of a woman stretched on the lounge. He turned the next canvas, and his breath rasped in his throat.

Even in these shadows, he knew that face! This was Beatrice del Gallina.

Marsanti had caught her features in the brilliance of a shaft of sunlight. Her yellow hair was bound in a pearl fillet, and her blue eyes challenged the onlooker as she glanced back over a creamy shoulder. She lay on red velvet cushions, exposed from tiny white feet to the seed pearls in her hair. Shadows were draped like black satin across her rich body.

"*Gran Dio*," Ilarion whispered, staring. His hand shook as he fumbled at his dagger. Its thin length slipped into the canvas. Guided by the frame, Ilarion moved it down and across until the canvas came free, tumbling into his fingers. He thrust it under his cloak and turned.

The mocking laughter that he had heard from time to

time was loud now. Ilarion froze. A man and a woman were entering the studio, the man leaning close above her shoulder, the woman shaking her raven tresses and laughing richly, deep in her creamy throat. She wore a cloth-of-gold gown with a square bodice, a necklet of pearls gleaming above the wide expanse of bosom discernible in the fashionably deep cut of her bodice. Pearl rings were on her pale fingers, and a cap of pearls sat like a pool of milkdrops in her black hair.

"La, Messer Biagio!" she caroled. "You'd applaud my disrobing, if you dared! I come only to sit for my painting. Nothing more!"

Biagio Marsanti was a tall, thin man, with the gaunt look of the epicure. His dark eyes blazed hungrily, full brows above a bold, hooked nose, and his wide mouth was sensually full. He appeared to quiver in the lamplight as he thrust his arms wide on either side of his body.

"Madonna, you torture me! So many nights I have gazed on your loveliness, transcribing it to canvas! To mix oils, and dream of the whiteness of your skin! The jet of your hair! To see those limbs, those tender arms!

"Just once, I beseech you! Just once to adore with my lips! Madonna Dorotea, I implore you!"

Her laughter teased him. Her dark eyes, over the jeweled fan she held to her mouth, were luminous with merriment. "We grow eager, Messer Marsanti! Flatteringly so!"

From the black shadows where he stood, not breathing, Ilarion saw the woman lean forward and whisper into Marsanti's ear. The artist straightened eagerly. He caught her hand and covered it with kisses.

"Never have I painted as I shall paint tonight, gracious one!" He turned and went to the door. For a moment he stood there, and his eyes glowed as he stared at the woman. He sought the doorpull then, fumbling behind his back, and went out, shutting the door behind him.

Humming softly, the woman moved to a steel mirror beyond the Savonarola chair. She put her fingers to the fastenings of her golden gown and loosened them. Still humming, she lifted out her arms, and then slid the rich gown to the floor, revealing her clinging silk undergarment, through which her back and legs were visible, as in a mist. She undid that, revealing a white linen smock jagged with lace, tight about her waist and hips. Ilarion was very still.

The woman was standing now before the mirror, her brocades and linens pooled on the wooden planking at her feet. She turned this way and that, her lips smiling, seemingly unaware that a man stood in the dark shadows of the far end of the room and stared at her. And then she spoke.

"Do you like what you see, Messer *anonimo?*"

Ilarion started so that his leg banged against the empty gilt frame at his feet. *Per Bacco!* Were there others in the room, too? His hand went to the hilt of his dagger, and slid it from its sheath.

"I see your face, back there in the shadows, *signore!* Suppose I tell Biagio Marsanti that you spy on me? He would make mincemeat of your pretty face! I have only to call him."

She tilted her head and watched her reflection ape her movements.

"Well? You have not told me! Do you like me—like this? Am I something of which you have dreamed?" The woman preened herself before the glass.

Ilarion knew, now. There was no one else in the studio. Just he and this Madonna Dorotea. She had seen the reflection of his face in the mirror, and had mistaken him for someone else!

Like a cat, he moved. On silent feet he came forward, face hidden from the mirror by the angle of his advance. His arms went out. His hands closed over the woman's eyes.

With Countess Beatrice he had been uncertain and shy, not because she was a woman, but because she was a countess, and knew him. This woman, with the linen and velvet of her robes pooled on the floor of the studio, was a noblewoman, too; but she did not know him. She probably thought him of noble blood, like herself. The thought gave him confidence.

At the touch of his hands, she stiffened.

"You are not—not the man I suspected!" she whispered. "Who are you? *Chi?* Who?"

For a moment he wondered how to divert her question. But then, he recalled Fra Matteo's teachings—and the lyrics of the jongleurs and troubadours. Here was a chance to test their flowery eloquence! He called now on his memory, culling words from the ballads which the old friar had rendered into the Italian and read to his avid pupil. He spoke of her eyes and her hair, and the

22

soft cream of her milky skin. He painted her as Bertrand de Born had painted Maenz de Montagnac. A languid smile grew on the woman's mouth, and she shivered against the flame that his words had lighted inside her.

As his mouth touched her throat, he sighed, "Now you know me for an admirer, Madonna Dorotea. Always I see you from a distance. I could not resist the temptation to admire you from a position of better vantage!"

The woman yielded slightly, arching her throat against the advance of his lips. "Your hands are rough! That is how I knew you were not—not the man I thought you! His hands are softer even than mine! Your name? Your family?"

"To tell you that, I would betray friends who whispered to me where you went tonight."

She turned, staring curiously at him, her warm black eyes touching his lean cheeks and full mouth, studying the crisp hair that framed his forehead. She curled a long black filigree of her hair in her fingers as her mouth twisted humorously.

"You fooled me," she admitted. "I thought you a Ferrara, with those cheekbones and that Florentine yellow hair! You're no Ferrara—at least none I know. And yet—"

"I'm a nameless admirer," he pleaded, thinking of Marsanti somewhere outside the oaken door.

She let him draw her closer, smiled when she felt him tremble. She did not know that he was concentrating on the footsteps beyond the studio, listening to their pace, gauging the impatience of the artist.

"I had to slip in, to see you!" he told her. "To see you, to breathe in your perfume, to touch your skin. . . ."

He used flattery as he used the foil, this Ilarion of the stables. It came easily, unbidden, to his tongue. If he could convince her of these lies he whispered, he might stand a chance to slip from the atelier, to drop the dozen feet to the cobblestones outside, and get away with the painting.

He bent his head and his lips caressed her. For a moment he fought the rising tide of hunger, using his hands to hold her away, and then the dam of his suppression broke, and his arms pulled her against him.

Neither heard the oak door swing in. Neither saw the rigid, red-faced artist framed in the doorway, his eyes protruding with apoplectic disbelief.

"Hail"

It was no word that Biagio Marsanti shouted. It was an explosion of pure sound, rearing up from the outraged depths. He came across the room, bounding effortlessly.

But Ilarion was awake, now. His arms let loose of the woman whose lips had moistened his own. She staggered back into the mirror, and almost fell. Beneath her thin brows, her black eyes were hungry.

A large table covered with paints and brushes, with props and a discolored oil jar, stood between the oncoming Marsanti and the somewhat dazed Ilarion. Biagio Marsanti put out a hand and ripped up the long table that lay there.

"Messer Marsanti," began Ilarion. "I—"

"*Per Bacco!* You rash, ill-guided fool!" snarled the artist. "I'll shred that face of yours so that no woman will ever want to see it again, by sun or candlelight!"

He cut with his sword, and the sound of its slashing made the air whistle. But where Ilarion had stood was now an empty space, for the sight of that bared blade recalled Ilarion to his mission. It cooled the blood that had fevered his body. It made him think of Jacopo Balisandro.

His own blade whisked from its scabbard, touched Marsanti's, and disengaged. He lunged, and the artist retreated—but only for an instant. He was in again, his sword a needle of flashing brilliance before him.

"Your right cheek, you milksop!"

It was rash of Marsanti. The touch of that blade on his own, and the ease of its disengage and thrust, should have warned him. But he, like Ilarion, was not in secure control of his emotions. It made a man feckless, such emotion. It almost spelled doom for Biagio Marsanti.

For Ilarion did not give ground. He made the blade in his hand work for him, sliding Marsanti's sword down its length with a thin high screech of steel, and then his right arm was uncoiling, sending the other back a stumbling five feet.

Ilarion moved in on the attack himself with a *file* in quarte and a flashing, deft counter to Marsanti's low thrust. He swept into the deadly *pattinande*.

Marsanti opened his dark eyes wide. Only Bevilacqua, and perhaps Achille Marozzo, who was writing his treatise on the art of the *duello* in his little hall in Bologna, knew those swift, grim swordstrokes. A touch of fear began to crawl with icy legs up Biagio Marsanti's spine.

He yelled. As he fought furiously to stay that sharp blade from his flesh, he screamed, "Help! Eh, help me! A burglar in the house! He is killing me! Eh, help!"

The humor of the moment made Ilarion bare his even white teeth. He cried out, "And the *contessa* said I had reason to fear you!"

He came in with his sword a thin circle of flying steel. It caught Biagio Marsanti's blade and ripped it from his fingers; sent it flying toward Donna Dorotea, who was frantically wrapping camisole and gown about her pink flesh.

Madonna Dorotea screamed as the blade clattered at her feet. Then Ilarion was whirling, evading Marsanti's bull-like lunge, and leaping for the leaded windows.

As he ran he snatched up his cloak, which hid the up-rolled canvas of the undraped figure of the Countess Beatrice. With cloak and canvas in hand, he leaped for the low sill.

He poised an instant, seeing the moonlit street below him and the armed horsemen, summoned by Marsanti's cries, that were sweeping around the corner and heading his way.

Legs straight out, he jumped. He struck the cobblestones with his body limp, and he rolled. He thudded up against a street fountain whose waters splashed over the wide stone rim of its marble bowl.

A trooper in haqueton and steel cap swung his horse toward him as he lay on the cobblestones. His sword flashed in the moonlight. Then the others were joining him, spurring their horses forward, crowding in until Ilarion found himself hedged by a forest of equine legs.

From the open studio window, Marsanti was shouting. "A thief, who tried to kill me! Two scudi to the man who brings him down! I am Biagio Marsanti!"

Their very eagerness gave Ilarion the chance he needed. They hemmed him so closely there was no room to wield a blade. He hurled himself upward. His hand closed on the bull-decorated jerkin of a rider. A quick tug, a fumbling of his foot for the stirrup, and as the trooper slid away, Ilarion appeared in his saddle.

Ilarion was no mean horseman. For years, in the stables attached to the house of Jacopo Balisandro, he had ridden and tended the stallions of the wealthy Roman youths who flocked to the old swordsman for lessons. A pressure of the knees, a yank at the reins was all that he needed. Perhaps the horse felt his mastery in the sure, deft ease with which he acted. The horse reared high, whinnying, pawing out with sharp hoofs to hold his balance.

The hoofs widened the space before him. And then Ilarion was backing the hoofs with the cold steel of his blade, slashing at arms and faces.

"*Andarsene, amico mio!* Let's go!"

He was twenty feet away before they knew it, bent low over his animal's neck, taking the long mane in his face, a hand on the thick, warm neck. He coaxed with his voice. He rode with his legs easing the weight of him in the saddle.

He was through the Piazza Montanara and over the Ponte Sant'Angelo before they were after him, swords waving in the night, their voices making the air ring. Windows swung open. Voices called out into the night, asking of the moon what madness was this that woke the people of Rome?

"A lover," Ilarion shouted back at them. "Taken in surprise by a jealous husband!"

The good citizens of Rome reacted in varying ways. Some slammed shut their windows, mumbling over the morals of the present generation. Others sought for slop-pails and emptied them over the passing troopers. Still others leaned from their windows and pointed the way that the flying Ilarion had taken.

Ilarion pulled the animal around and sent him up an angling street. His eyes hunted anxiously. There stood the high walls behind which, in the quiet confines of the monastery garden, good Fra Matteo was wont to tell his beads. Ahead stood the towering bulk of the Porta da Popolo with its twin towers. And beyond the towers, in the shadows of the monastery walls, stood the corner wineshop he sought.

As the horse ran on, Ilarion slipped his feet free of the iron stirrups. He swung out and away, slapping at the animal's rump as he fell. He scrambled up quickly, ran toward the heavy vines that clung to the red brick wall of the wineshop. With practiced ease, he put his fingers on the vines, and climbed.

A bedroom window yawned above him. His hand caught its sill and lifted him. He moved up and tumbled into the dark room, just as Borgia's horsemen swung by the towers and straightened out for the chase.

He heard a gasp from the woman in the tumbled bed. He turned his head and showed his face. "Be quiet, Tea!" he told her, to forestall the loud screech beginning in her lungs.

III

TEA PANCHESI glared from beneath the tumbled mass of dark red hair which spilled about her face and splashed in thick ringlets over her smooth-white shoulders. Who was this fop with the expensive cloak and those long legs in slashed crimson hose?

The man by the window shifted his position. She saw his face clearly for the first time, framed in silver moonlight under the yellow hair tumbling from his rich velvet toque.

There was amusement in his voice when he spoke. "Well, Tea? How long do you have to look? Don't you know me yet?"

"*Dio mio!* You!"

"Sssst! Not so loud."

"Where'd you get that cape? Those velvet trunks? That cap? Hey?" She tossed the linens back from her wide pallet, forgetting that she wore only a thin shift. She spoke softly, crouched on the edge of the bed, staring at him where he knelt close by the opened window.

"Hai! Those are fine clothes for a stableboy! A velvet doublet and silk hose! Velvet trunks and a cape to match. Hai!"

She drew in breath with such force that the thin garment tightened dangerously across her bosom. She put a hand to her thick red hair and pushed it back, away from her wide eyes, as he snarled, "Be quiet, Tea! Those are the Duke's men below, hunting me!"

"The Duke's men? Why would they be interested in a boy who cleans Signore Balisandro's stables?"

She came to see for herself, bent above him, one hand on his shoulder. The street was bright in moonglow. The men in leather boots and bull-blazoned haquetons were dismounting. One of their number was cantering into sight with a riderless horse. At sight of him, a shout went up.

Tea asked, "Why are they hunting you? What've you

done? If you get me and my father in trouble with the Borgias—"

His hand quieted her, fingers to her lips. He held her tight, smothering her frenzied twistings with strong arms. Outside, the patrol was moving from door to door, pounding with daggerhafts, crying out, "Hai, inside the house. Wake up. Wake up!" Ilarion caught a handful of Tea's thick red hair and tugged until her face came away from his.

"I'm on a secret mission for a woman! *Una illustrissima!* Now be quiet, or you'll give me away!"

Tea Panchesi listened sullenly. This stableboy sounded as if he spoke the truth, and *il Gran Dio* knew she had no wish to bring the rage of the Borgias around her head! She rubbed her white arms, shivering.

"All right," she agreed. "I'll go below when they knock on our door. I'll help my father put them off. But what do I get out of it?"

Ilarion sighed and removed the purse the *contessa's* maid had given him. He pushed it into Tea's palms. With a hand she weighed the golden coins, even as a dagger's pommel pounded the wooden door of the tavern below them.

Tea Panchesi turned to the bed and lifted a crimson robe, wrapping it around her thinly clad body. Her eyes brooded at him. She opened her mouth to speak, but her hand tightened on the heavy purse instead. Then she tiptoed on bare feet to the hall, where her father was grumbling into his beard.

"Sons of a harlot mother! Must they knock down my door in the middle of the night?"

Nicolo Panchesi waddled down the wide wooden stairs, hand clinging to the carved rail. He shouted, "I'm coming, I'm coming! *Peste*, control yourselves!" Tea followed behind him.

The door opened to a man-at-arms with the red feather of an officer on his steel cap. He was corseleted in polished steel, and his poniard was naked in his hand.

"I seek a robber and a thief! A man who broke into the studio of Biagio Marsanti and stole money!"

Tea Panchesi gasped. She held her robe more tightly around her full body as the officer looked over her father's shoulder at her. He swept his steel cap from his curly head.

"A thousand apologies, *signorina!*" He bowed. "This

28

man is a dangerous criminal. He must be captured. I have sent word to His Magnificence, the Duke Valentinois, concerning him. His neck will stretch in a noose when we find him."

Her father growled, "Well, go find him, then, and don't be waking honest people up out of a sound sleep! I have a hard day's work ahead of me!"

Tea called out, "Come back when you're off duty, captain. My father has some fine Falerno."

The officer bowed his thanks, and the door closed on him. Tea Panchesi snatched up her robe, and her bare ankles scissored up the wide stairs. She felt anger burn in her. She crept into her room and shut the door, leaning her shoulders back against it. Her green eyes blazed and she spoke with contempt.

"So! A thief and worse! Now show me what you stole, that brings the Duke's men down around our ears!"

He let her lift the canvas out of his rolled cloak, and spread it. She caught her breath at sight of the *contessa* stretched out on the cushions. She whirled on him, a finger pointing.

"Is this what you risked your neck for, you fool?"

Tea eyed the painting more closely. There was something to be said for this one with the yellow hair and the creamy skin, lying there like a wanton. All that bare skin and golden hair, and the blue eyes in which Marsanti had caught a lurking devil.

Ilarion said eagerly, "She promised me fame and fortune, Tea! She said my sword could win it for me! This is just the start. I'll be rich, some day. Rich and famous. She told me so!"

He plunged on in his enthusiasm, not seeing Tea's twitching lips and mocking eyes. She interrupted his torrent of words by throwing back her head as her raucous laughter rang out. It brought a flush to the cheeks of Ilarion, disturbing the dream with which he had walked the night.

When she could, Tea Panchesi gasped, "Fame and fortune? Rich and famous? You utter idiot! You know what she'll do when you bring her the painting? She'll have a hired cutthroat slip six inches of steel in your heart! That's the fame you'll get! *Peste!* What an innocent you are!"

Ilarion shivered, suddenly realizing that Tea might be right!

The Palazzo Gallina had been built by Francesco del Gallina upon his return from Florence in 1427, to house the beauty of Aldebella san Sorel, whom he had just made his bride. Its central staircase was of yellow African marble, its bronze doors the handiwork of Lorenzo Ghiberti. Mosaic tiling ran between its fluted columns, and porphyry statues of pagan gods stood in its court.

Ilarion *della stalla* moved silently through its arches in this dark hour of early morning. The only sounds were the soft play of fountain waters, the occasional sputter of a wall torch, the distant voices of late revelers parading through the city streets, and echoes of his footfalls.

Twice had he slipped by patrols galloping in clattering haste along the narrow streets. Once he had stood like a carved statue, under an overhanging rooftop. The next, he lay flat on his belly behind a gurgling fountain while men-at-arms thundered by within five feet of his prone body.

Sweat stained his velvet doublet as he moved through the colonnade toward a bronze door hung with silver roses. He paused to drink in the cool, early morning air, then moved on until his knuckles rested on the door.

He rapped softly with the silver clacker. Faintly he could hear the swift pad of feet. The door latch lifted silently, and the door swung wide.

Ilarion grinned at the white face of the waiting maid. Her cheeks were pale with her nightlong vigil.

"Follow me," she whispered.

They went along a corridor hung with rich Flemish tapestries, and up a narrow stair sided with a wrought-iron railing. She swayed ahead of him, past a painting by Romano, and a row of gold masks inset in the stuccoed walls. She pushed open a door, and stood aside.

His heart began to thud. The scent of perfume and incense reached out to him as he stood in the shadows of the hall. He lifted the rolled canvas. It was his passport to the wide bed that he could glimpse through the open doorway.

The maid laughed softly, reading his eyes. She caught his arm a moment, holding him with her quick, nervous fingers. "You'll do better to remember she's a woman, and forget she's a countess!"

Her hand shifted to his shoulder, and she pushed him into the wide, long room. Her soft laughter came following, mocking him, until the door closed on it.

Candles glowed softly in the corners, and along the wall, where a rich tapestry hung from groined ceiling to the marble-tiled floor. A massive table crouched below the tapestries on four legs, carved in the forms of rearing lions. A chair beside an ormolu table was rich with red brocade. Beyond, framed against the far wall, stood the great bed, its linens luminous in the gleam of a bronze floorlamp, the twisted figures of its posters seeming to writhe as the shadows hurled by the oil lamp shifted and danced.

The *contessa* stood before a great steel mirror, in a maroon velvet gown, trimmed in ermine. The candlelight touched her smooth white shoulders where they lay bared above the wide bodice. She put out a white hand brilliant with rings, and came toward him, moving languidly, allowing his eyes to feast themselves where they willed. Her teeth flashed as she smiled a welcome, and then her hand was on his, and she was looking up at him with questioning eyes.

"Madonna, the picture—"

She took it from him and tossed it into the shadows. Her smile was provocative.

"You did it! You bested Messer Marsanti! You must tell me of it, every moment!"

He told her of the studio, and his search among the canvases. He said, "Marsanti discovered me there. He came at me, snatching a sword from a table. I disarmed him, caught up the canvas, and leaped from the window to the street."

The countess laughed softly. "We are modest, Messer Ilarion! Biagio Marsanti is reputed a splendid swordsman. You dismiss him with a few words. Tell me every stroke, every play of the steel!"

He grinned. "He was wooden. No imagination. It was nothing."

Beatrice del Gallina looked curiously at this tall youth who lightly shrugged aside an encounter with one of the leading swordsmen in Rome. He was not boasting. The *contessa* lived by her wit, and knew the truth when she heard it. An only daughter of the old Count of Gallina, she had been wed at sixteen to the *condottieri* captain, Bartolomeo Cadone. Enriched by his war-won wealth, she was left a widow when he conveniently died, in his fiftieth year, at their summer villa at Parma. She moved in court circles, bestowing her wit and beauty where it could do Beatrice del Gallina the most good. Friendly with Lucrezia Borgia, she deemed herself almost as powerful, and played dangerous games, moving men against women, soldiers against merchants, striving with flesh and brains to wrench security from the world.

Beatrice del Gallina let her eyes admire him. She had a weapon in this stableboy and his sword, a weapon to be forged in the furnace of her passions, to be used where and when she willed it.

She put a hand to his cheek, stroking it with her long nails. She whispered, "You must be worn. Rest here. Let me bring you more wine. Some cakes, perhaps?"

She was close to him, soft and warm under the daring gown which freed her body's lines to questing eyes. Her mouth smiled. Ilarion recalled the waiting-maid's words to him: "Remember, she's a woman!"

The confidence that had grown in him at his success with Dorotea del Andriola blossomed now with the *contessa*. What had worked once this night, would work again. He thought back on his varied readings, and on the suggested conduct of a lover with his beloved, which had so occupied such troubadours as Rimbaud of Vacqueiras and Montaudon. From memory, he could recite their advice, and so he acted on it.

He put a hand under the armpit of Beatrice del Gallina and brought her in against him.

He put his lips to the corner of her mouth, gently, then slid his mouth aside, to the warmth of her throat. She was surprised, leaning into him as his lips roved across her white shoulders, and upward to her ear where it lay hidden in the nest of her yellow hair.

"You are wine and food to me, madonna," he murmured.

Her lips opened to make reply, and it was then that he kissed them, boldly and hungrily. She stiffened against him, then went soft.

A wine goblet fell and rolled across the tiled floor.

A man chuckled.

Beatrice stiffened, legs flailing, trying to roll from the arms that held her. But Ilarion had no intention of permitting this woman to move from his arms. He held her where she lay against him, and he looked across her bare right shoulder at the man who stood framed in the doorway.

He was tall, this intruder in the rich black cloak whose

somber hue was relieved by a golden collar of St. Michel. Tawny hair fell to his broad shoulders, and a neat beard framed a wide, smiling mouth. The eyes that regarded Ilarion and the countess were bold, and at the moment, swimming in amusement.

Ilarion *della stalla* had never seen Cesare Borgia.

"You intrude, *signore*," Ilarion said dryly.

"My apologies, then. I come on a State matter. If you would only let the *countess* go, as she so fervently wishes—"

At the sound of that rich, mocking voice, Countess Beatrice cried out sharply. She pushed herself free, tumbling from Ilarion's arms. "Your Highness! Magnificence!"

Cesare Borgia gestured with his long fingers, fingers that could bend an iron horseshoe or stroke a woman's flesh with equal ease. Amusement was still in him, but his eyes were held by the tall stableboy rather than by the disheveled excitement of Beatrice del Gallina.

"Your love has caused some alarm in Rome this night," he smiled. "He not only disarmed the good Signore Marsanti, but fought off a dozen of my officers, and led them a fine chase through the streets.

"To cap that, he disappeared into thin air, somewhere between Marsanti's studio and your bedchamber. He intrigues me, this young man."

Beatrice del Gallina glanced at Ilarion, and her eyes were bright. She accused softly, "So! I knew there would be more to your story than what you told me!"

The Duke of Valentinois laughed softly, adding, "Perhaps your charms drove all other thoughts from his mind," he said. "Or perhaps it was the charms of Dorotea del Andriola, whom he so cavalierly disrobed and made love to, while he hunted for your canvas."

"*Dio mio!*" she hissed.

Cesare Borgia explained, "The Duchess of Fianti and the Countess Beatrice are not exactly the most amiable of friends."

The thought came to Ilarion, as he stood with a jealous woman on his right, and the most powerful prince in Italy before him, that no words of his could be effective at that moment.

"You disrobed her!" hissed Beatrice del Gallina.

Ilarion said dryly, "She did her own disrobing. She mistook me for another."

Cesare Borgia moved across the room, walking slowly, as though he were in his own palace. His bold eyes regarded Ilarion with searching intentness. "There is a resemblance, at that. In the dark corner of the studio where you stood, a woman even more perceptive than the good duchess might have been confused."

"You made love to her," hissed the countess.

The duke went on, after a brief glance at the furious Beatrice. "She said you toyed with Marsanti. She said you were a better swordsman than Bevilacqua."

Ilarion shrugged. "I am the second best swordsman in all Italy." He spoke wryly, not boasting.

Borgia lifted his brows. "Oho! And who might be your master? Who is this paragon with a blade that is better than you—you who defeated Marsanti, and some of my finest officers?"

"Messer Jacopo Balisandro, Highness. The fencing master by the *Via Malatesta*."

"Balisandro? Balis—oh, yes. The old soldier who fought in '83 against Ferrara. I've heard of his hall. It's quite the fashion to receive lessons from him. And you? How is it that you've been taught so well by the old bandit?"

Ilarion grinned. He liked this tall, restless man with the tawny hair and the bold eyes. He looked straight at a man, did this *gran signore*, fists on his hips and a tiny smile curving the corners of his mouth.

"I spied on him while I was supposed to be sleeping in his stable, on a straw pallet. I practiced what I saw him do. The gracious lady here saw me fence, and bought my bondage from the fencing master."

Cesare Borgia looked at the countess. He sighed. "He is no more, then, than a stableboy?"

"He is a pig!" said Beatrice del Gallina.

Valentinois laughed. "*Va bene!* Good enough! I would not have it changed. What did his freedom cost you, *illustrissima?*"

The countessa moved her plump white shoulders expressively. "Paolo da Rienza did me the favor. But he is mine, the boar!"

The Duke of Valentinois lifted a fat, swollen velvet purse from his girdle of gold plates. He tossed it across the room so that it landed on the table where stood the long-necked salver of *fior d'arancio*, a white Sicilian wine.

"There is more than enough in that to attend to the matter. I'll buy his freedom from you, in turn. I have need

34

of swords like his, at Rimini and Faenza. And now, if you will forgive me . . ."

Beatrice del Gallina cried out at sight of the long poniard naked in his hand. She shrank back against the trembling Ilarion who found himself awed by the proud bearing and impressive ease of this man who was lifting the canvas of the unclothed Beatrice and holding it up to the flickering light of the many candles.

The Duke sighed. "Lovely flesh, lovely woman. A shame to spoil either. *Macche!* Perhaps it can be done more subtly, so that a binder of petrarchs will be able to repair the ravages of my steel!"

The thin blade slipped through the edge of the canvas, slicing quickly. A bit of folded vellum tumbled into the candlelight. Dropping the canvas, the duke bent and retrieved it. He spread it wide and his bright eyes scanned the sheet. A smile came to the lips between the neat beard and curled mustache. He glanced up, pleased.

"Only this day I learned of this from a servant who works at Fossate. The wretch loosened his tongue under the screws, as Alexander's sword loosed the Gordian Knot. He babbled on and on, and I sent a dozen of my best officers to the studio of Biagio Marsanti.

"There they fell before this—this second best swordsman in all Italy! Arriving in the city late, I came at once to your *palazzo, madonna mia.* I recognized that, somehow, you had forestalled me, in your eagerness to serve my cause."

Ignoring his irony, the countess moved with swinging hips to the walnut table, where she filled a silver goblet with wine, and drank. Across the cup's smooth rim she stared at Borgia, studying the smile in his eyes and on his lips. Knowing men, she was sure that what she said now would be forgiven her.

"I learned of—that paper—some time ago, Your Highness. I pondered whether to bring you news of it or—"

"Or find a means to acquire it yourself, after which you might approach Orsini or Colonna! If they did not bid enough, you'd come to me. Luckily, you found Messer *della stalla!* He could get this paper for you. He could best Marsanti, and Marsanti, and his sword, was the biggest stumbling block in your entire plan."

The duke laughed. "Eh, well! I admire a bold stroke. Especially one that can be turned to my benefit." His eyes scrutinized Ilarion, and he nodded.

His long fingers slid the vellum out of sight in his rich, gold-slashed, black velvet doublet. The poniard clicked into its jeweled sheath. And still he stared at Ilarion.

"Someday," he said suddenly, "Rome and Venice. Florence and Milan will be no more. Instead, each of them shall be part of a great nation, a nation that will stretch from the Alps to the boot of Sicily. No longer the lion of St. Mark, or the she-wolf of Sienna. Only one banner, over one throne.

"I will sit that throne!" His eyes blazed. His hypnotic voice enthralled the ears, and in the dim candlelight, he took on greater stature. He moved about the room as he spoke, his eyes studying the nymph and shepherd emblazoned on the hanging. His hand smoothed the lines of a Carystian marble urn where it stood beside a carved oak chest.

"The French aided me against Forli. I still need Yves d'Alegre and his French lances, but others are joining me. Already two Spanish gentlemen, Juan de Cardova and Ugo da Moncada, and their retainers, are at Nepi. I have negotiated a loan from Milan. Men are coming from Switzerland and Gascony, to be joined by my new friends from Rome. The Contis and the Farnese espouse my cause. I have been spending much time, training these men into an army that will sweep everything before it."

Borgia lifted a silver maiden from the black wood table where she posed her loveliness. He turned the statuette in the light, admiring its lines.

He said, "Sforza is done in Milan. I have word that he is to be sent to France in exile. That frees the soldiers of Louis the Twelfth. I will welcome his men to my bull banner. There is much good fighting ahead of us. I intend to make the Romagna mine, first. After that—*chi sa?* But there will be riches for those who serve me. You understand that, madonna?"

He looked at Beatrice, but his words were for the ears of Ilarion *della stalla*. Borgia smiled. "That is what awaits a man who claims to be the second best swordsman in all Italy. You will dispatch him to me, *contessa mia?* After you have rewarded him?"

His black cloak swirled as Borgia moved back into the shadows of the room. Then he was gone through the doorway, as silently as he had come.

Beatrice del Gallina put down the goblet. Its solid silver base, patterned in damask sworls, made a loud click in the stillness. Staring across the room, idly turning an emerald ring on her finger, Beatrice brooded.

"He could make you rich and famous, if he would," she said soberly. *"Dio mio!* What he couldn't do for you! He's taken to you and your sword. It isn't everybody that can beat twelve of his men. He picks good men for such a job as he sent them on tonight!"

As she touched the silver flacon on the table, her eyes caught sight of the bulging sack of ducats that Borgia had thrown so carelessly on the polished table. Catching up the crested velvet bag, she poured out the coins in a golden shower. They clinked and rolled across the tiles like gilded wheels flashing in the lamplight.

"Flesh and gold, *Messer della stalla,"* she murmured. "The spirit of our times! A woman for your bed and money for your purse. Use both cleverly and—*chi sa?* Who knows how far you may go? I told you that sword could win you things!" The *contessa* stared at the floor, shining like a golden carpet with its spilled ducats. Her face sobered.

"Just as I emptied that sack, so a man can empty the cornucopia that holds his fortune! So fast, it frightens you! Alive one moment—in a grave, the next. There is no security in this world, none at all!"

For a brief second, the fright that shadowed her days lay revealed in Beatrice del Gallina's staring eyes and pale cheeks. There are those to whom nothing is secure, neither money, nor beauty, nor sanity. They must strive for more and more, to make secure that which they already have. Beatrice del Gallina had lost a mother and a father and a fortune, when little more than a child. And two years after her marriage, her husband had died at Parma.

The countess shook herself. With a trembling hand, she refilled her goblet with wine, and drank it swiftly. Color flooded her cheeks.

She turned her eyes to him, and abruptly, her face lost its brooding stare. Brightness came into her eyes, and her white hands clenched.

"Boar! You stallion! You undressed Dorotea del Andriola! You made love to her! And you knew you were coming here, to see me!"

Ilarion stirred. He tore the web of his dreamings from his eyes, and moved his hand in a placating gesture. "Madonna Beatrice, I—"

"None of your lies! I won't hear them. Oh! The—the shame of it!" The countess fed her fury on injured pride. She stood quivering, shaking, tiny white hands clenched into angry little fists. Her eyes were fever-bright with the rage that ate at her.

"*Diavolo!* That a stableboy would do such a thing to me! Da Rienza would go to Cathay for a chance to be where you are, here in my bedchamber. And then to hear that tale of—of—"

She launched herself at him, lacquered nails reaching for his face, tripping over the hem of her long gown. A lock of her yellow hair slipped from the pearl cap. She sobbed and swore through her writhing red lips.

He caught her wrists as she clawed at him, and held her tight against him, with her arms bent behind her. He could feel her warm and soft as she surged against him, and the heavings of her bosom as she fought furiously, trying to free her wrists.

"*Gran Dio!*" she spat. "A stableboy, that I let into my bedchamber! You've come from Dorotea del Andriola to me! You pig!"

"I had to bring you your painting, madonna! *Per favor!* I don't understand this anger. The duchess took off her clothes for Marsanti, not for me! She was posing for his brush."

Pouting, Beatrice del Gallina chafed her wrists. Her shoulders swung petulantly. She glanced at Ilarion from the corners of her eyes. La, but the boy was handsome, she thought. Strong and lean. It would be a pity to waste the night.

She said, "You are sure you did not caress her? Whisper *parola d'amor* to her?"

"*Madonna mia!*" Ilarion threw his hands wide. "Having seen your portrait as Marsanti caught you, on those red cushions, with the promise that I'd see you later this night—what woman would tempt me?"

"Words! Just words!"

He put his hands on her shoulders then, and drew her back to him. Her yellow hair, escaping the pearl net of her cap, was fragrant against his cheek. "You are lovely when your eyes blaze with anger, *illustrissima*. But you are even more beautiful when your eyes melt and swim in the tears of love."

The countess laughed softly, her back still turned to him. "You have a nimble tongue, Messer Ilarion. It says

38

things I want to hear. But you are in no position to judge my loveliness. You've never seen it!"

Ilarion lifted his hands and caressed her shoulders gently, holding her still closer.

"No!" she breathed. *"Caro mio!* A moment, please!"

Her hand pushed on his chest, and her eyes were gently mocking. "Go you, my strong stallion! There is my bed. Rest yourself! Remain at your ease—and watch!"

He walked backward, slowly, his eyes caught and held by the light that swam in her laughing blue eyes. When his knees struck the edge of the big bed, he sat down abruptly.

Beatrice del Gallina allowed the heavy brocade of her gown to slip a little, as she unfastened the rich velvet of her detachable sleeves. Her memory went back to her wedding night with Bartolomeo Cadone, and that rough *condottiero's* frenzied awe of her pale body. She had not experienced such teasing enjoyment in years.

Her arms came free as the sleeves fell away. She pushed at the shoulders of her gown, pressing them down. Sly fingers deliberately fumbled over the ribbons of her thin undergarment and camisole. As she slid out the final ribbon, she bent to lift her heavy skirt and straighten a jeweled garter.

Beatrice del Gallina fancied she could hear his heavy breathing, but she did not look at him. La, let him stare as she disrobed for his eager eyes! She posed a moment in her disarray, and lifted her hands to her thick, yellow hair. She hummed a madrigal that was popular in the ducal palaces, then lowered the gown and her undergarments to her waist.

Bending, she removed each garter. On the bench where she had given Ilarion her kisses, she rolled down her stockings.

She stood, then, a necklet of emeralds like green fire on her throat, jeweled rings flashing on her fingers. Arms above her head, she pivoted slowly, letting the lamplight play across her body.

Lost in the hypnotism of her own loveliness, she turned and ran to the bed.

She was five feet from the big four-poster when she halted abruptly, as if frozen. She screamed, but no one heard her.

Ilarion *della stalla* lay sprawled on his back across the bed, sound asleep.

IV

Tiny dolls were running over his chest and middle. They were living manikins, with the dark, lovely features of Dorotea del Andriola and the blonde ripeness of Beatrice del Gallina. They laughed at him, dancing on his ribs, calling his name and promising endless delights if only he would waken.

"*Caro mio!* Do not dream any longer!"

"Wake up and play with us!"

The manikin that was Beatrice del Gallina danced on his chest, and the touch of her fragile feet was wildly exciting. He laughed in his dream, twisting, crying out that she tormented him while he lay defenseless.

From the air, the doll snatched a flaming torch and tossed it on his leg—Ilarion woke, howling.

The torch stung, even in his waking moments, and he moved convulsively, hearing low laughter. Looking down, he saw the *contessa* seated at the edge of the bed, bent over him. There was a fleck of blood at the corner of her mouth.

"I bit you," she told him. "Lazy slug! You have slept all morning, after snoring the whole night long."

She was disheveled and wanton, her thick yellow hair artfully disordered about her flushed cheeks. He lunged for her, but she whirled and ran. In his sleep, she had danced on his body. The dream lingered, and with it the hunger he had had for her. She ran laughing through the dark shadows of an oak cabinet and into the light of a candelabra. Ilarion came after her silently, on bare feet. He caught her near a painted screen, grasping a handful of her nightrobe, and tugged her back into his arms.

He whispered savagely, "You will not find me sleepy now, *contessa!*"

It was dawn when Ilarion woke, to find Beatrice stirring lazily beside him. A servant had opened the velvet drapes, and a shaft of morning sunlight splashed the bed to a yellow pool. Ilarion stared as Beatrice del Gallina sat up, stretching her long white arms. He found it hard to believe her the same woman who had been with him before they had slept from exhaustion.

The countess smiled down at him. Her stableboy had

been a revelation. She was grateful, and a little surprised to discover a tenderness in herself toward him.

"You must be careful, Ilarion, *cavallo mio!* I would not have you harmed. Not now! Paolo da Rienza hates you. Don't forget it, or lose sight of it. He will try and kill you, in some way or another."

Ilarion laughed his scorn. "That fop! I don't fear him."

Her yellow hair tumbled as she shook her head. "He won't meet you with a foil. There are other, safer ways to make a man die. Not cleanly, with a piece of steel in his heart. Poison! The corded garotte around your throat in an alleyway, when your wits are muddled with wine after a party!"

The *contessa* shivered. The murder of Alfonso of Bisceglia, husband of Lucrezia Borgia, was too recent in court circles to allow an academic discussion of death. She rubbed her hands up and down her arms, trying to dispel the chill that had settled between her white shoulders.

They ate a breakfast of dried figs and cold meat, with bread hot from the kitchen ovens, over a tiled table on the loggia.

"Be bold at camp," she advised him, "You'll find many ways to line your purse with gold. But there are other things than the sword that can bring those same florins to you." She laughed at his blank look.

"News! Information! Where the Duke marches. How many men are under his banners. The disposition of his cannon, his lances. How he intends to use his arquebusiers. Anything and everything about his plans of conquest."

The greed that dominated her life showed in the eagerness with which she tolled off items on her fingertips.

"Any word of his alliances with the French. The names of the Roman nobles who fight for him, and those of them who share his confidences. All these mean money. I will get it for you, if you bring me the information that will buy it."

The noonday sun was almost overhead as Ilarion galloped out of the courtyard gate of the *palazzo* Gallina, and turned the roan mare the *contessa* had given him toward the Tiber. He clattered across the Ponte Milvio, hoofs ringing sharp and clear.

Ahead of him the Via Flaminia, the road the pilgrims took to Rome, flanked by low hills, stretched northward for over two hundred miles to the Adriatic.

Ilarion rode in a fever of impatience. He pushed the mare. He wolfed down a noonday meal the *contessa's* servants had prepared for him, begrudging the time it took. He drank deep of the cool waters of a brook, then lifted into the red Andalusian saddle.

He was halfway to Nepi by mid-afternoon, galloping past a copse of willow trees, when he heard the sounds. For a moment he thought them distant bells, and then his trained ear recognized them.

"*Diavolo!* They're swords!" he cried aloud.

He turned the roan and sent her straight for a grove of aspens that stood behind the weathered timbers of a roadside tavern.

There were a dozen men in the grove, cursing and stamping as they fought, knocking over the wooden tables and benches lining the little copse. Ten of them were rough bravos in tattered jerkins and ragged cloaks, pressing two *signori* backward into the jumble of furniture.

The mare came in a rush, with Ilarion bent low to her neck and her mane slashing his face. He reined her to one side, sending her hurtling into two of the cutthroats, angling them away from the others. A downward slice of his blade in the dying sunlight sent a third reeling, hands clutching his bleeding cheek.

Then he was out of the saddle. His blade was a thrusting needle, slipping through a clumsy guard and driving deep into a ruffian's chest.

He was an explosive fury, driving two of the purse-slitters before him. As one of the men sprawled across a fallen bench, spitting obscenities, he ran the other through the belly.

"Leo, look yonder!" he heard a deep voice bellow. "*Il Gran Dio* has heard my prayers and answered them. He has sent us the angel Gabriel!"

Ilarion leaped and dropped, left hand just touching the ground, his swordarm extended, slashing and cutting, blade darting like the tongue of an angry snake. He used the *finta de filo* to spit one of the cutthroats, and the *botta dritta* to slash the other. He turned and flung himself at two more.

Ilarion spat his scorn at them. "*Scorzone!* Filth! You want to use your swords? Use them, then—like this!"

They did not see his blade except as a flashing red blur, but one bravo caught at his bleeding middle with both hands and fell forward. The other took his point

42

in his throat and went sideways, his scream dying to a bloody gurgle.

The gentleman with the deep voice called out, "Let them go, Messer Gabriel! They are only ruffians seeking gold. *Per Bacco!* No need to slay them all!"

Ilarion stepped back at that deep bray, lowering his point. The six remaining bravos slipped and staggered in their anxiety to escape. One of the six went face down and the stouter of the *signori,* a man with curly black ringlets and a mustache set in a red-cheeked face, with the build of a wrestler and the voice of a hawker, planted a boot on his backside.

"On your way, you slab of lard, before Pietro Torrigiani regrets his words of mercy!"

Ilarion knelt and ran his blade through the ground. He wiped it clean with a napkin that lay under an overturned bench, and tested it. He became aware suddenly that both *signori* were watching him intently.

Pietro Torrigiani was a giant of a man, big and massive, with a powerful chest and a wide spread of shoulders. His genial face was split with a grin as he waved a huge hand.

"See how he cares for his weapon, Leo!" he bellowed. "Truly, he might be one of us, so tenderly does he cherish it."

The taller man smiled. He was in middle age, with gray showing in his dark beard and hair. "He is an artist with the steel, Pietro. He cares for the tool with which he executes that art."

Seeing Ilarion's face, Torrigiani laughed. "*Si,* it's you he calls artist, lad. If any should know one, it's Leo. Da Vinci! Leonardo da Vinci! *Peste!* Haven't you heard of him and his Last Supper? Or his dreams about flying men and boats that can move under the waves?"

Da Vinci chuckled. He was a tall man, lean, clad in the latest mode, in a red doublet foxed in ermine, with crimson hose above matching boots. His sword was decorated with flowers and thorns, its silvered hilt supporting a jeweled rose. Leonardo da Vinci was over fifty, but his eyes blazed with the fires of a youth, his ever seeking mind just reaching its prime. He said, "In his world, good Pietro, there is no time to spend on paintings and the names of their painters."

Ilarion stammered his apologies and Da Vinci laughed outright.

"He speaks truth. He's never heard of me. Well, it's refreshing, in a sense. But come! Let's finish our meal—and invite Messer Gabriel to join us."

Torrigiani lifted a pewter flagon and banged on an overturned table with it until two maids and a stout, perspiring innkeeper came running.

"Set up the tables and the benches again, good host! Have your servingmen clear the grove of these bodies. Then bring on the ham and the bread, and the chilled wines you've been saving for us in your cellar."

"Sit yourself," he told Ilarion, "and tell us what you do in Nepi. Wait until we eat, and we'll go with you."

"There's employment for a good blade in the Duke's army," Ilarion said. "I'm not rich. I can use some of the ducal gold as well as the next one."

A huge palm slapped the table so that the drinking cans jumped. "Well spoken! I like an honest man. It's not the gold that brings me to Cesare Borgia, but the need for excitement, for activity. Hai! And Leo here has dreamed of his war engines and great armored vans and bombards so long he seeks to find them an actuality!

"He has made maps for *Il Duca*, has our Leo. He has models of cannons in his studio in Rome that would make Vitellozzo Vitelli jump with delight!"

The red-faced artist broke off as the innkeeper and two maids came running. They bore big wooden platters heaped high with sliced meats and hot bread, with grapes and figs and apples. A servingman came after them, with an armful of bottles whose wetness guaranteed their chill.

Ilarion sat quietly as Pietro Torrigiani tore into a leg of mutton, clasping it in his hands and attacking it with his big white teeth as if he were starving to death. He shoved bread and fruit into his mouth between bites, and washed it all down with enormous swallows of cooled *barbera*.

Da Vinci ate sparingly. He seemed more interested in the preparation of the food than in its consumption. He drew out the stout little innkeeper, learning that he kept his own pigs, and that his wife baked all their bread in the kilns beyond the meadow. The *barbera* came by donkey caravan from Urbino, once a week.

He talked of bricks and kilns, and the value of hot and slow fires. He was no man of one talent, this Messer da Vinci. His artist's eye looked at the world, and where his eye led, his agile mind followed. From talk of food

44

and fire, he went on to systems of drainage and irrigation. He was in the midst of an exposition of his plans for the waterways of the Lomellina and the plain of Lombardy, when his companion interrupted.

"Let be, let be," growled Torrigiani, slamming the table with a fist like a slab of ham. "Must I listen to all this learning while my poor belly cries for food? Ilarion, bring out your sword and place it so that good Leo can see it. Perhaps it will frighten him into using his teeth and tongue for something other than chatter!"

Ilarion laughed. He had never been accepted as an equal before. It put a warmth in him that was like slow fire. He hunched forward at the table, elbows spread, eager to drink in this moment. It did not occur to him until later that it was his sword that had earned him this companionship.

Before they mounted, Torrigiani kissed both serving maids, and tossed a handful of *marchettos* on the table-top to pay for their fare. Then he had to shout at Da Vinci, who was standing on the edge of the meadow, discussing irrigation drains with the perspiring little innkeeper.

The sun was setting low in the west as they rode, but Nepi lay less than a league away. Now it was the bull-like Torrigiani who grew talkative, and Da Vinci who was silent.

"He dreams of the engines of war he will make for Borgia. Terrible cannon, worse even than the Tenerina! Perhaps he will build the flying things he sketches when he isn't drawing angels' wings and the faces of handsome youths.

"That Tenerina! What a cannon! It throws a ball almost a foot thick. It battered down Caterina Sforza's towers at Forli as I shatter a sand castle with my hand!

"But the she-wolf fought hard. I'll give her that! I was in one of the covered passageways, forcing a breach in the wall, when I saw her. In armor, with an ax in her hand, directing her men. More man than most of them, that one! They took her finally, at the Cadogna gate. After that, the spoils!"

Torrigiani slapped a hand to his thigh and grinned at his companions. "I'll never forget a redheaded wench I chased up the turret stairs and down again before I cornered her in a bedroom closet. *Iddio!* How that woman fought! But Pietro Torrigiani tamed her!"

45

Da Vinci said dryly, "If you want to stay alive to tame other women, you'd best let Ilarion teach you a few things with the blade. We came close to dying, back there, before he appeared."

"*Peste!* Now why didn't I think of that? Imagine not having to run from a dozen cutthroats or a jealous husband, ever again." He sighed and sat back dreamily on the high cantle of his saddle. "Well, lad? What do you say to it?"

"I'll teach you, gladly. In exchange for your knowledge of the world. I know nothing but the sword."

"Then first, lad, learn something of the man you rub stirrups with! This Da Vinci eats little and says even less —except when he's expounding his theories!—but he can paint like nothing before or since. Have you see his Regisole? Or his Annunciation? No, no! I keep forgetting. Here—look for yourself!"

Torrigiani reined in beside the older man, fumbling in his saddlebag. As Da Vinci closed a hand on his wrist, he shook him off.

"No need for false modesty, Leo. I'm your friend and so's Ilarion. Let him see your notebook." The big man drew out a sheaf of papers, bound in the shape and manner of a petrarch. He handed them to Ilarion.

Ilarion ruffled the pages. He stared down at the face of a pageboy, dreaming against a fluted column that overlapped a wagon on wheels that was covered by what seemed to be a wooden tent. The next page showed an architectural design obscuring the figure of a man with wooden wings strapped to his arms and back.

"He dreams a man may fly, does our Leonardo!" cried Torrigiani.

Ilarion knew nothing of art, but the power and the beauty sketched here by the pencil held his eyes. When he came to a page of horses running, horses leaping, he grunted. Ilarion *della stalla* knew horses. He recognized that these were not just pictures. These were living things caught for an eternal instant on parchment.

There was something of this in his face as he regarded Da Vinci. Torrigiani bellowed, pointing.

"You see? Even Gabriel admits genius when he sees it!"

Da Vinci made a gesture of dismissal, but he was pleased. He ran his slim fingers through his beard slowly.

"Ilarion, a great swordsman deserves a great sword. I

will fashion you one. I have done some such work for Ludovico Sforza."

Torrigiani slapped Ilarion's back with a vigor that almost toppled him from the saddle. "Some such work! You should see the hilts he decorated for the Duke! Entwined with vines and flowers. Graven with the silver wings of angels, with the jaws of the wolf!"

Ilarion said, "It isn't the hilt that matters. It's the blade. It must be tempered to give, but not to break."

Da Vinci smiled. "It shall be tempered as they temper blades in Toledo, of the finest steel obtainable. My word on it, Ilarion!"

A sword wrought by Da Vinci! A sword of the fabled Toledo steel, whose fame was reaching out through all of Europe! All his! A flush came and sat on Ilarion's cheek as he rode through the dreaming sunset.

V

A HEAP OF TUSCAN DATES lay piled on a golden salver, within easy reach of the hand that Cesare Borgia stretched to it. He popped a date into his mouth and chewed it silently as he regarded the tall youth who stood before him in his tent, with the lights and shadows from a torch playing across his chest.

The day had been a long one for Ilarion. He had moved in a whirlpool of events that left him no time for thought. A countess had bedded and fed him. His sword had saved the lives of Leonardo da Vinci and Pietro Torrigiani. He realized what that meant when he saw Cesare Borgia's welcome of the great artist, and heard the praises of armored *condottieri,* and felt their admiring eyes fixed on him.

Later, there had been a banquet spread on a table in the striped magnificence of the Duke's tent. He had listened in awe to Yves d'Allegre discourse on a charge of his lances, and to dark and sullen Vitellozo Vitelli when that artillery wizard had come alive as Da Vinci spoke his ideas on cannons and siege engines. Half in that daze, his elbow had been plucked by a page, who drew him into a small *tenda* where the Duke waited for him.

Ilarion wanted fame and fortune. He was discovering that he was already famous, and found himself, with the superb confidence of youth, accepting that fame with-out thought or reservation. I want even more, he told himself. I want all I can get. It's like a fire in me!

Borgia said softly, "You ate little tonight, stableboy. You drank even less."

"I only know the sword, your worship. If I fill myself with swill, I can't use it as I might have to. You said you had work for me."

Borgia reached for the dates. He took several of them into his palm, and jiggled them. "Good words, Ilarion! Words I wanted to hear. I'm not so much a great general, as men call me, as I am a judge of men. I pick a good man for a hard job. When they get them done right— *Dio mio!* Every tongue in France and Italy wags my fame."

This was a rare moment of frankness with the Duke of Valentinois. He appeared to realize the fact, for he shifted in his Savonarola chair, leaning his handsome face into the glare of the torches. His hand tossed the dates aside. He locked his long white fingers.

"I am honest with you. You ask why I choose a stable-boy to be my confidant? Because you can use that sword as no other man can, in all Italy. Because one man, with such a sword, is worth a company of arquebusiers to me."

The restlessness that burned in this man with the tawny hair forced him to his feet. He strode across the thick fur rug which covered the rushes spread over the bare ground. His long legs carried him easily, revealing a little of the physical power that was his birthright.

"There is a fortress at Fossate, built on a hill. In that fortress are three men. Those men are my friends, caught as they rode to keep a rendezvous with me in Rome. They possess vital information!"

"They may be alive. They may be stretched on the rack, or sitting with their thumbs in the screw. Too, they may be dead in their graves by this time.

"Dead, they cannot serve me. I must know if they are alive, and if they are alive, I must get them out of Fos-sate!"

Borgia slapped the oak tentpole until the shield and war ax hanging from it clattered and rang together. His face was dark, brows drawn together over his thin nose.

"That they are in Fossate I learned from the scrap of paper I cut from the painting of Beatrice del Gallina, after you rescued it from Marsanti. That paper was brought into the city by one of the thousand sell-souls who gather information as a means of livelihood. He sold it to Marsanti. Somehow the *contessa* learned of it and almost, by your help, got her pretty fingers on it. On that paper I learned where my three friends were, and why they were late for their appointment with me."

He paused and stood in the shadows, with the darkness across his face and throat. His voice seemed to come from a beheaded man, but its vibrant power shook the candle-flames.

"One man, or two, can get into Fossate! An army they would hurl back with stones and boiling oil. But two men—posing as sell-swords—could do it!

"Will you go on such a mission, knowing you may be going to your death?"

"It is why I rode from Rome today, Highness. To serve you!"

Borgia smiled. He came to stand before Ilarion, a hand on his shoulder. "Hold yourself in readiness then. I may not call you for a day or two. But when I do—be ready! Go now."

Ilarion was lifting the tent flap when Borgia spoke again. "One thing more. I reward well the men who serve me. If, by chance, you should bring those men to me alive, and with tongues in their heads with which to talk, I shall not prove ungrateful."

Pietro Torrigiani was waiting for him beside the huge wheel of a wagon that was laden with corselets fresh from the forges. His eyes studied Ilarion closely.

"So! Our Gabriel has speech with Il Valentinois. Secret speech! What's he planning for that sword, lad?"

"I ride on a mission for him."

Torrigiani grinned in the darkness, and rammed an elbow into Ilarion's ribs. "I smell adventure! Don't be so cursed sly, lad. Tell me, do you ride alone?"

As Ilarion looked at him, Torrigiani spread his hands. "A man can hope, can't he? You'll say a word for me, won't you? Tell him Torrigiani is your teacher in this evil world, and that you are my pupil! Together we could have a fine time. Where you go, things happen!"

They were moving between a row of tents before which a cooking pot stood suspended by chains over a wood fire. A man lifted a tent flap, and in the brightness of the interior behind him, Ilarion saw the insolently handsome face of Paolo da Rienza.

The fop looked up at that instant, and as he saw Ilarion, his face grew hard. Hate glowed like a living thing in his dark eyes.

The camp occupied a low, flat plain set below the village of Nepi. Borgia had gathered close to nine thousand men under his bull banner: French lances, French artillerymen, blond Swiss pikemen in blue and silver uniforms, his own personal guards resplendent in red and yellow, with his name splashed across their chest in silver.

The *condotti* of mercenary captains like Ercole Bentivoglia and Achille Tiberti swaggered through the camp lanes, carrying swords and maces toward the forges. Crossbowmen and Scottish archers herded in the meadows, their quarrels and shafts screaming at targets all day long. The October sunlight glittered on pikes and halberds, and on gilded pennons hanging limp in the windless air.

It was a rare, new wine to Ilarion *della stalla*. He walked through the press of men-at-arms, stopping to watch a slim *serpentino* being wheeled forward, or examining a suit of armor from the Missaglia workshops. Jacopo Balisandro had collected swords and daggers in his fencing hall, but Ilarion had never seen the like of those exhibited to him. He bought a slim dagger with a hilt formed in the shape of a slim dryad from a Milanese who told him it had been fashioned in the great armory forges of his native city.

It was then that Torrigiani came seeking him, to clap a hand on his shoulder and drag him eastward, where the greatest master of artillery warfare in the world had set up his cannons and falconets. Vitellozzo Vitelli, whose hatred of Florence was equaled only by his love for his guns, was sitting on the gun mount of a falconet, roaring at the sweating men who were dragging a culverine through the thick grasses.

Torrigiani drew Ilarion to one side, pointing. "There is the Tenerina! A giant among pygmies!"

The cannon was a nine-foot monster, cradled low in its slanting mount. At its sides lay a dozen triangles formed of its foot-thick balls. It gleamed in the sun, polished until its barrel glittered.

A glowing match was being touched to the culverine. The cannon leaped, shuddering and roaring. Smoke poured from its wide, round mouth. Far down the field a wooden hut, that was its target, jumped convulsively, spewing its shattered fragments across a field of bluebells.

"*Madre del Dio!*" whispered Ilarion.

"Ha! Wait until you hear the Tenerina belch! Wait until Messer Vitelli brings all his little darlings to bear on Faenza and Rimini! Then you'll hear something!"

Names ran in his ears all day. He met Achille Tiberti of Casena, and the Perugian, Gian Paolo Baglioni. The Scotch captain, d'Aubigny. Giamondo. Gian Paolo from Siena, with his *condotta* of lances, whose horse "El Savallo" was his pride in life.

They ate their evening meal with a group of Bolognese who served under Malvezzi. It was here that a Borgia page found them and led them to the Duke's tent.

The Duke was clad in Cordovan boots and a lynx-lined cape. Silvered spurs clanged as he strode to meet them.

"I've ordered horses for you. We ride at once to my sister's summer palace."

He slapped his gloves to his palm and whirled on a heel, giving no more information. But the page, his cloak emblazoned with the bull, gestured them to follow.

Two bay stallions stood tight-reined by a man-at-arms, who surrendered the reins to Torrigiani with a wink. Torrigiani laughed and called out to Ilarion. "Mount up, lad! We're in for fun, or I don't know my lord the Duke."

Stirrup to stirrup they rode out of camp, through the tents and stacked arms, up onto a road that twisted through the hillside. They galloped at breakneck speed, with Borgia setting the pace and pulling the others after him in his dust. They roared past the darkened houses of Nepi and along its deserted streets, and the thunder of their mounts shook the window shutters.

As they went beyond the town, the night seemed to disappear in a blaze of lanterns and torches. The summer palace of Lucrezia Borgia was ablaze with lights. Even at this distance, they could hear the gay strumming of clavichords, and the sharp laughter of women.

They swept by a float covered with flowers, on which sat a woman in a cloth-of-gold gown, who ceased from caressing a dwarf made up as the devil to pelt them with roses and thrown kisses.

"What a party this will be!" howled Torrigiani. "Lucrezia's farewell to her brother! Venus' good-by to Mars setting out for the wars."

51

A pavilion loomed before them. Men and women, wearing cunning masks in the forms of winged angels and the visages of apes, the brows of lions and the jaws of asses, swarmed in on the little party. Roses and orchids, forced in the hothouses which were a part of the palace gardens, bloomed on twisted vines above their heads.

Torrigiani bent with a shout to lift a woman, seeking her mouth. Her palm rang sharply against his cheek.

"You wear no mask, *signore mio!* No kisses to a man who lacks a mask!"

Ilarion put a hand over his face, covering it. He forced his bay into Torrigiani's mount, shouldering him aside. He bent and hooked his left arm about the yielding waist of the woman.

He cried, "I wear a hand mask, madonna!"

Her mouth touched his, and for a moment he held her there against him, bent low in the saddle, bathed in her perfume, and hearing the delighted shouts of the onlookers ringing in his ears. And then he was moving on with the others, hearing the woman shout after him. "Seek me later, *Messer il mano!*"

The party was dismounting and moving forward to be introduced to the pale, lovely Lucrezia Borgia. She seemed almost a child, fragile and white, with emeralds bound in golden wires set in her hair. She was recently a widow, but her gown was green and netted with tiny golden chains.

Ilarion watched her bright eyes follow her brother Cesare and he thought, She worships him. A hand was pressing into his back and he found himself standing before her brooding eyes, bowing slightly.

"My blade, dearest Luce," said the Duke. "The Borgia blade—who'll win me many things before I've done with him. Ilarion *della stalla!*"

He kissed her little white hand. Above his bowed head, she whispered, "Be a good blade, Messer Ilarion! Guard your master well."

Someone tugged at his elbow and a black mask was thrust into his fingers. His eyes studied it, noting that it was a crescent of black silk, stiffened by hidden wires. It covered his face from hairline to mouth, forming twin ebony horns above his head.

"You look like a devil in that thing," commented Torrigiani, from the protection of a white domino hung with pearl pendants. "So live up to his reputation, lad!

Me, I've business at the tables where they cool the wine."

The music of the violas and clavichords drew Ilarion. He stared at the figures moving in a stately dance. The men were richly dressed with gaily colored doublets and varicolored hose. The bare shoulders and full curves of the women were exposed above dresses thick with jewels and gold-and-silver threadings. Laughter rang loud through the torchlight that glowed and dimmed in the shifting winds.

He found himself clasped and turned by a woman whose scarlet gown was hung with hundreds of seed pearls. Her eyes were bright as fire behind a rose-petal mask.

"A black luna!" she cried out. "Young moon god! Take me up into the sky with you. I'm tired of the ground!"

He lifted her in his arms, holding her so that her head hung down. He lifted his head and covered her powdered shoulders with kisses.

All around them men and women drank and played, sheltered behind the anonymity of their masks. This was their saturnalia, their carnival. Theirs was a world where pleasure sat enthroned. A woman with her gown torn in front ran across the lawn, screaming with laughter, not bothering to shield herself. Behind a tree, a voice cried out thickly, passionately.

A hand caught at Ilarion's shoulder, wrenching him from the woman in his arms. "They play at statues in the lower gardens, lad! Come on!"

He recognized Torrigiani's voice, but it took him a moment to free himself from the spell of his pounding blood. The woman adjusted her voluminous skirts and grasped his hand, breathing harshly.

"The statues!" she whispered. "I've heard of them, but I've never seen them."

Her warm hand clasped his, and tugged. He ran with her across the grass, which was covered with bits of tinsel and cake and the spilled dregs of wine. They halted on a slope that overlooked a *camperello* where a number of tentlike silken structures, draped.in large lavender veils, had been erected. As they came up, one of the veils was being removed from the first of these three pages in crimson doublets.

When he saw what the falling veil revealed, Ilarion choked. His eyes glittered as the woman leaned against him, breathing faster.

53

She murmured excitedly, "Leda and the swan!"

The Leda was a reclining woman, clad only in a mask. A man was bending to her, a swan head nodding majestically above his naked shoulders. The audience watched, enthralled, for many minutes, as the statues acted out the little tableau.

The pages moved to close the curtains, and then went on to the next tent. The figures of Tarquin and a nude Lucrece came to life, with Lucrece struggling, performing the little drama with furious realism.

They followed in swift order, these libidinous performances, and on the grassy slope of the hillside men and women watched, feeding their senses. Occasionally a woman would cry out against the surfeit that lay pent within her. But mostly they watched in breathless silence.

It was between Pan and two fawns, and the theft of a lovely Helen from Menelaus, that Cesare Borgia appeared beside Ilarion. A smile twisted his lips as he observed the tableau enthralling Ilarion.

The woman broke from Ilarion's caressing fingers. "Excellence!" she gasped. "We did not see you."

"I could scarcely compete with that for attention. Not tonight! But I must steal your black moon, *madonna mia*. Your pardon!"

They went swiftly from the crowded hillside, moving across the lawns toward a little arbor where Lucrezia was holding court. As they walked, Ilarion could hear laughter rising from the men and women grouped around Borgia's sister.

He caught enough of their words to realize that they were speaking of him. A woman with vivid red hair was regaling them with an account of his activities with Dorotea del Andriola and Beatrice del Gallina. The laughter broke off at their approach.

Taunting eyes watched him, laughing behind a scarlet mask. This was the woman with the red hair, whose words had caused the laughter. She spoke again, and he heard her laughter ring out. It was impish, clear as the tones of the campanile bells that rang above Fra Matteo's monastery gardens.

She stood with a group of court ladies. She wore a crimson brocade gown embroidered in silver webs, hung here and there with rubies. The low slashing of her garment exposed her white shoulders that lifted like the corolla of the lily from her dress. Her rich auburn hair was set with a cap of seed pearls. Beneath the mask, her mouth was generous, tilted at its corners. What Ilarion could see of her face was pert and elfin.

Lucrezia gestured at her as she turned to face her brother. "Giula has been telling us something of your blade's adventures. It seems that he is as popular with the ladies of Rome as he is dexterous with a foil."

The Duke arched his brows at Ilarion. "My sister's friends are winged demons who fly from Rome to Nepi as swiftly as the hawk. How they learned what you did only the night before last—"

"My lord Duke," said the woman in crimson, "a story like this flies on its own wings! Besides, by brother is at Nepi."

Ilarion felt her eyes on him, felt shaken by the merriment he read in their green depths. He fancied they were swimming in mockery. But there lay something deeper than that behind her gaze. He read it, but he could not understand it.

Madonna Giula's smile grew wider. She touched her closed fan to Ilarion's cheek, patting it. "I understand that you are as commanding over women as the moon you represent, Messer Ilarion."

She stepped closer; from the valley of her bodice a new French perfume lifted to his nostrils. She smiled teasingly and put the heel of her little shoe to his toes. She stepped down hard, still smiling sweetly, tapping her fan on his mouth. There was anger now in her green eyes.

"My lord Duke says you are a stableboy. Actually, of course, you are nothing of the kind!"

Ilarion showed his surprise by widening his eyes. The woman saw it, and smiled. She nodded.

"You cannot fool Giula *la rosso*. Your hair is Florentine yellow, as mine is Milanese red! You look like a Ferrara with those high cheekbones and that long straight nose, and the bold eyes of you. But for your ability with the ladies, I should assume you one."

She waited, breathless, for the rage to kindle in his eyes. The others waited, too. Cesare Borgia had caught his breath at mention of the Ferrara name. His eyes narrowed, and he regarded Ilarion with new vision.

Ilarion grinned. "You want me to be angry, don't you, *Madonna la rosso*? How can I be angry when there's no room for it? Your wit has filled me with admiration."

Giula spread her fan with an angry flip of her wrist

and waved it just below her chin. Her green eyes were hot with injured pride. She had been so confident of provoking more laughter with her tongue that her failure stung her with added fury.

She had opened her mouth to speak again, when a page came running across the lawn. The court turned to watch him speak to the Duke, noting that Borgia's cheeks grew pale at his words. Borgia apologized, and went striding swiftly ahead of the messenger. Lucrezia Borgia went after him, and drew with her the men and women of her group. They left Ilarion and Giula *la rosso* alone.

Her fan moved a little faster as she correctly interpreted the eyes shining through the slits of his mask.

"You are a wicked, wicked man, Messer Ilarion."

"And you are a lovely woman, madonna! I find only one flaw in your beauty."

Her fan stilled for a moment, then resumed its metronomic march. Her elfin face was tilted upward, regarding him steadily. But curiosity had replaced the anger in her green eyes.

"What is this flaw that only those wicked eyes have the cleverness to perceive?"

"Your mask, *illustrissima!* It hides the perfection of your features."

Her hand swept up, and the crimson panel came away. Her eyes were slanted green emeralds under thin red brows. Her nose was tilted, fragile. The wide mouth gave character to the pert face of a pixie. And then he knew her. Her face had been limned on the cameo his blade had ripped from Paolo da Rienza's purse!

"There is no need of masks between us, Messer Ilarion. Masks are only to cover the blushes of those who engage in love this night!"

He stared down at her, stricken dumb. For once in his life, Ilarion *della stalla* could recall no instance of conduct or speech in his readings that would aid him. The words that had served him so well with Dorotea del Andriola and with Beatrice del Gallina were forgotten. The green eyes of this elfin girl, that sparkled at him so mockingly, the red flame of her pearl-hung hair, and the bow of her rich red mouth were distractions that hypnotized him.

Giula *la rosso* felt something of this as she stared into his worshiping eyes. The corners of her lips twisted in a smile, and her fan fluttered.

56

"I have revealed myself to you, Messer *silenzio!* It is your turn to let me see your features!"

Mechanically, his hand went up to the black luna and stripped it away, while he stood stiff and awkward as the girl cocked her head to one side and surveyed him.

"A nice face. Brown as a nut, and with something of a falcon's look at the nose and eyes!" She giggled, and her green eyes watched him over the lace rim of the fan. "Your ears are not as long as the donkey's, but like him, I find you speechless."

He flushed, and the hot blood loosened him a little. He touched his dry lips with a tongue. His eyes were glued to her face, and realizing this, Madonna Giula strolled around him, surveying him from side and back, thus effectively removing herself from his vision.

"You are very lovely, madonna," he said at last, huskily, when she stood once again in front of him.

The sincerity in his voice touched Giula *la rosso.* For an instant, she was ashamed to mock him, but the memory of his conduct, before she had removed her mask, restored her teasing smile to her lips.

"Pooh!" she said softly. "You sound like a calf lowing for its mother! Is it thus you wooed Dorotea del Andriola? And Beatrice del Gallina?" Her fan swung back and forth, and her laughter rang out behind it. "True, they are cows, but even so, you must have shown more fire with them than you have thus far with me?"

Stung, he started forward as if to catch her in his arms and hold her against him, and plumb the depths of him to bring forth words that would spell out the feelings that ran through him like liquid fire.

Giula *la rosso* mistook his intention. She read the heat in his eyes, but imagined that the lips that were struggling to find speech were shaping themselves for a kiss. She stepped back, and her eyes widened. Ilarion knew—with sudden instinct—what it was that he had read in her green eyes, besides their mockery. It was fear. Fear of a man.

The knowledge emboldened him. He smiled, and let his arms fall. "You need have no fear of me, madonna. Rather would I cut off my hand than cause you any alarm!"

Her head went back, and anger blazed in her eyes. That he had discovered the truth in her added to that anger. Secretly, she admitted to herself that she liked the tone and manner of this nobleman in disguise, but she would have offered her flesh to hot pincers before admitting it to him.

"You dare to imagine that I'm afraid of a kiss?"

He was abject before her. Realization was coming to him that he was only a stableboy, and this redheaded witch was as noble as Borgia or the *contessa* herself. When he protested against this supposition, she flared again.

"Ah! I'm not afraid of a kiss, then! You imagine me a wanton like those others with whom you disported yourself!"

He protested strongly, almost angrily. "Madonna, I beg you! I regard you as a woman above all others. As a goddess!" He told her of the cameo he had seen in the fencing hall, and the strange weakness that had come over him at sight of her, such a weakness as might have beset Petrarch at sight of Laura, and Dante Alighieri at sight of his Beatrice. He pleaded so passionately and so honestly that Giula *la rosso* forgot herself and listened, her lips parted breathlessly, an answering fire kindling in her at his words.

When he was done, she murmured, "You don't even know my name!"

"I know you, madonna! A name is only a word to distinguish people. No troubadour ever coined a name as lovely as your reality!"

She examined his eyes, and found in them the same fever that glowed in her. She folded her fan and held it tightly in her fingers.

"I am Giula da Rienza, of Milan. My brother is Paolo da Rienza. He's with Borgia's army. Perhaps you know him?"

VI

PIETRO TORRIGIANI WAS BELLOWING at him from the marble steps of the palace as Giula da Rienza whispered her name. Ilarion saw the big artist lift an arm and wave it at him, but his mind was numb with shock.

Something of this Giula felt. She moved back and her eyes searched his face. "*Che cosa?* What is it? You do know Paolo! That's it, isn't it? And you—hate him?"

His smile was crooked. "Say, rather, he hates me."

He told her something of their little duel staged at the hall of old Jacopo Balisandro. She listened, eyes fastened to his lips, her full lower lip caught between her white teeth.

"Paolo was ever a hothead! Him and his pride! I shall speak with him. I'll pour oil on the angry waters of his pride!"

Ilarion thought of Beatrice del Gallina's warning. Poison—the garotte—an assassin moving at his back to strike, along a dark street. Giula *la rosso* clutched his arm fiercely.

"You don't think I'll do it! Or if I do, that my words will have no effect. But I will. I will! If only to prevent him from doing something stupid, like fighting you."

Torrigiani pounded up to them.

"For the love you bear your mother, Ilarion! The Duke wants you! Riders have come from Venice and Florence with bad tidings."

He made his apologies to Giula da Rienza and left her looking after him, her green eyes thoughtful.

Borgia was pacing the library, tapping a folded paper against his knuckles. He whirled at their entrance, close to a large amillary circled with thin silver bands. His eyes were hard under grim brows.

"Are you ready to ride? Now? This moment?"

"Everything I own is on my back, Highness. There's nothing to keep me."

Borgia scowled at Torrigiani. "You've been tutoring my blade, I understand. I suppose you'd like to sample the wines of Fossate with him?" Borgia went on grimly, as the artist grinned, "It isn't to pick flowers in a field that I'm sending you on this mission! It's to find three men and free them! To bring them to me in good health. You may die, doing it."

A shadow grew across the doorway, stood for a moment, then moved back. Borgia, who was facing the arras-hung door, looked up. He saw only the shadow of a cabinet moving fitfully as a breeze touched the candleflames. He went to a sycamore desk inlaid with alternate squares of mother-of-pearl, and lifted two small velvet purses.

"You'll need gold. It's in here, a purse to each man, in case one dies. Word has reached me from the Doge in Venice that he regards my wars in the Romagna with cold eyes. Florence is close to Faenza. It too, worries over me."

His voice rose in power. He was a man with a dream,

this Cesare Borgia. "Let them fear me! I want them to know my power. No weak man can unite Italy! And Italy shall be united, to take its rightful place as the most powerful nation in Europe. I'll do it if I have to ride through their cities with lance and cannon!"

His voice lowered, he went on, "I'll pray you're in time, before the Doge sends poison to Fossate, to rid the world of three men with important information for me."

Ilarion drew his cloak tighter around his shoulders, against the chill wind off the Apennines, as they went out into the courtyard where a groom held their horses. On this side of the *palazzo*, the sound of the revelers was faint, lost in the hiss of torches guttering in their metal sockets and in the clang of grounded halberds as the guard went its rounds.

The thunder of their mounts' hoofs rang loud on the cobblestones for a moment, then faded as they galloped under the stone archway and out onto the road to Fossate.

Behind them, a man in plum velvet cape, with a doublet slashed to reveal a lavender lining, came out of the blackness of the stone stair and stared after them.

Paolo da Rienza had only discovered that Ilarion rode with Borgia from his camp an hour before. He had almost killed a stallion to reach the summer palace. At once, he had sought audience with the Duke, to demand that he—or some other noble of his rank—be sent on this errand, instead of a stableboy. Approaching the library, he had stepped back just in time to avoid being seen, only his shadow on the floor betraying his presence.

"It was a close call," he told the man beside him, a Piedmontese captain of cavalry, thickset in bright corselet and morion. "If he'd seen me—but, no matter! He did not. He does not even know I am here. It leaves me a clear field of action."

The fop remembered his pomade ball that dangled at his wrist. He waved it under his nose, sniffing gently. His thin lips twisted cruelly.

"Ilarion insulted me before Beatrice del Gallina. Knocked a sword from my fingers! A lucky stroke—and look what it's won him. He bedded 'Trice, or I don't know the signs. He's Borgia's pet. The Duke calls him 'my blade.' *Dio!* It's sickening! A stableboy, who's watered and curried my horses a thousand times!"

60

The captain thought philosophically that if Da Rienza were one-half the man the stableboy seemed to be, he wouldn't be standing here in the cold night air smelling his perfume ball and snarling his hate and jealousy. But he was paid to act for this *signore,* and not to think for him. He shrugged his big shoulders.

"Let me ride after them. I'll slip a swordblade between their ribs, take the gold Borgia gave them—and the world will deem it a highway robbing."

Da Rienza laughed hollowly, then said, "Do you think for a moment I'd stand here talking to you if that were a solution? You stupid fool! You'd stand no chance against him! He's a wizard with that blade!

"No, no! There must be a way to take advantage of the instructions I overheard the Duke give them. But it isn't the sword, Andrea. Believe me!"

Captain da Marolla had his own opinion of the swords-manship of Paolo da Rienza. Fortunately, he kept that opinion to himself. But it was there, and it betrayed him into thinking Da Rienza as poor a judge of swordsman-ship as he was an exponent of it. He told himself, I'll match swords with this stableboy, and you'll eat those words, signore mio. But he maintained a heavy look on his face, and waited.

Da Rienza said presently, "There must be a way! Some way! Borgia told them they rode to Fossate. The *contessa* herself told me there are men of Borgia's imprisoned there.

"Now suppose, Captain, that someone were to arrive in Fossate before these two riders. Suppose further, that this someone were to alarm the authorities about their coming. It should be a simple matter for the forces of Fossate to capture two lone riders.

"Of course," he added with a sly smile, "the authori-ties would pay a man well for such information. Many ducats, undoubtedly."

Da Marolla started. He grinned heavily under the peak of his morion.

"I'm as good as on my way, *signore!*"

Da Rienza put forth a languid white hand. His eyes burned hotly, and the captain winced at what he saw in them.

The fop said, "A few lies to those authorities will not harm your cause, Captain! You might let drop a hint that those riders are officers high in the esteem of the Duke."

The captain growled, "It'd mean the rack for them!"

Da Rienza laughed softly. "The rack, or the screws, or that Spanish segment of hell, the bastinado. Naturally, the stableboy will have no news to give the authorities. But by the time they learn that, this Ilarion *della stalla* will be whimpering to die!"

Da Rienza became brusque. "Into the saddle, man! Remember, too—what Fossate pays you, I'll double!"

Captain da Marolla galloped out through the stone arch with visions of wealth and the things that wealth could buy dancing before his eyes.

The inn stood by the side of a dirt road that twisted between hills thick with olive trees. Its thatched roof overhung brick walls stained black by age. Beyond the hospice was a stable almost as large as the inn, for this was a way station for travelers from Venice and Padua.

Ilarion saw the inn first, pointing and shouting, ramming a toe into his mare. He clattered forward over a bridge that spanned a deep gully, standing in the stirrups and throwing laughter back over his shoulder. Half a mile away came Pietro Torrigiani, trudging on foot, his boots and doublet layered with fine dust, leading a limping horse.

"By the bones in my mother's hands," he muttered into his beard. "For nearly an hour I've walked like this, ever since my Pegasus twisted a foreleg in a ditch!"

Ilarion was dismounting and waving an arm back at him from the cool shelter of the overhang. Torrigiani groaned. "Look at the ape laugh! Oh, my aching feet! He can't know how they pain, or he'd be shedding tears for my misery. *Dio!* See him now, how he grins."

Ilarion was stepping from the doorway, lifting a drinking can high. As Torrigiani watched from the heat and dust of the roadway, he put the snow-cooled *sassella* to his mouth, sipping, his dry throat appreciating the fruity flavor of the wine. The serving maid, a tiny thing with a full figure ill concealed by her smock, came to stand beside him, leaning a shoulder against him.

"Will your friend want some *sassella,* too, *signore?*" she asked softly.

"All he needs is a horse, *bella mia,*" he said. "I saw some stables behind the hospice as I rode up. Will you take me there?"

She shrugged, moving closer. Her eyes taunted him.

"You are a fine gentleman. Our inn boasts many things. Good wine. Fine horses. Even friendly maids!"

He grinned down at her. "*Va perdonno,* pretty one. Another time."

The maid wrenched away from him angrily, moving into the common room, where a wide hearth filled all of one wall. In front of it, a long table was flanked with wooden benches. Overhead a brass lamp swung on creaking chains embedded in the rafters that lined the ceiling. The maid swung her hips disdainfully and seated herself on a settle below a span of leaded windows.

Pietro Torrigiani stamped through the doorway, brushing the dust from him with his velvet toque. "I'll need a tin of wine to wash this dirt from my throat. A pity I haven't time for it. What about the horses, lad?"

Ilarion looked at the maid, who turned her nose up at him.

"You'll find them in the stables," she snapped.

There were three horses in the stalls. One was a black, the others, gray mares. Ilarion, who knew horses as he knew the sword, dismissed the mares at a glance.

"They lack depth in hip and legs. The black, now, looks like he has fire in him."

The innkeeper was crouched in the firelight from the hearth, roasting a pig in the red maw of the common-room's great ingle. He scowled at their entrance, but the sight of three golden coins on top of the trestle table brought a smile to his round face.

He was stretching a hand toward the coins when a velvet purse came sailing through the air, to land with a solid thump before his fingers.

"Take my gold, *Messer oste,*" said a voice. "I'll buy the black instead."

Ilarion whirled to find a heavy-set man in gleaming steel corselet and morion glowering at him. He had never seen Captain da Marolla, but he needed no introduction to the challenge that glittered in his eyes.

"You misunderstand, Captain," he said. "My friend and I are riding far. His mount turned a leg."

Andrea da Marolla shrugged. It was no matter to him, their predicament. He had his own mission, on which he rode. He needed an extra horse. He was buying it. That ended the matter.

Something of this he growled rudely. There was an anxiety growing in the captain to test the swordsmanship

63

of this stripling. The words Da Rienza had shouted at him in the courtyard of the summer palace still rankled.

Now he said, smiling disagreeably at Ilarion, "I'll take the black, and be gone. And host, put up some bread and meat for me. I ride at once."

Ilarion lifted the velvet purse from the tabletop juggling it on his palm, aware that the captain watched him with eager, hungry eyes. He wants me to throw his money in his face. But why? he thought. He threw it at the captain so that it hit his breastplate.

Andrea da Marolla was no diplomat. He had been trained under the *condottiero*, Bartolommeo Colleoni. His youth and early manhood had been spent in tents and on pallets hastily dropped under the looming uprights of mangonels and siege engines. His answer to the world was his sword, at whose use he fancied himself.

For a moment, he remembered Da Rienza and his warning. But Ilarion was here in front of him, with that why smile twisting his face. *Peste!* Wouldn't Da Rienza pay him well for the stableboy's death? His sword whipped out. He bent it, smiling.

"We have a means of settling our dispute, *signore*."

The innkeeper cried out sharply, and the little maid came running from an inner room. When she saw the big captain in his armor, and with his sword gleaming in his hands, she laughed shrilly.

Ilarion undid the tiestrings of his cloak, and kicked it away as it fell. His blade came out.

Like strange dogs, they circled each other, boots sliding over the hard-packed dirt of the tavern floor. With a cry, Da Marolla came in, his blade slithering through Ilarion's guard. His near success encouraged him. He stamped and shouted, and attempted the *circulazione e finta*. Again his point missed Ilarion by a hair.

Pietro Torrigiani stared. Ilarion was falling back, his sword a clumsy thing as it beat against the captain's blade. Here was no swordsmanship such as had opened the artist's eyes in the grove beyond Nepi. Ilarion looked almost frightened.

The captain roared, "Stand still, stableboy! Or I might miss and kill you. I seek only a bloodletting."

"You lie, *signore*," panted Ilarion, kicking a wooden chair out of his way as he moved backward toward the wall. "You want to kill me, I can see it in your eyes. Why?"

Da Marolla laughed harshly.

"It means gold in my pocket! Da Rienza sent me on to Fossate, to spoil your little plan courting favor with the Borgia. But why go to Fossate? What he wants done, I'll do here and now, and save myself the trip!"

"You hear that, Pietro? The captain seeks me to murder me. And after me, you! There must be none to ride to Borgia, to tell what happened to us!"

"Exactly!" growled Da Marolla, and swept in.

But where Ilarion had been standing with his back to the hard timbers of the inn, half cowering before the captain's flickering point, now he was moving sideways, and his *legamenta* was twisting Da Marolla's sword and moving it aside. The captain gasped at the change in the blade he faced.

The faltering was gone. The blade was hardening, stiffening. It grew cunning, elusive. It barely scraped the captain's sword, darting in, and then blood was running down his arm. It moved again, and a scratch widened on his cheek.

The captain fell back, swiftly, hopping awkwardly as Ilarion moved to the attack. That sword he faced was a demon! It mocked and taunted him. It fled from his beating blade, to come slashing in across a thigh, cutting deep.

"*Messer della stalla!*" he cried out. "You play with me!"

"I will not kill you, captain, as you would have killed me. A few wounds. A bit of blooding. So that you must take to a bed for a week or ten days!"

His blade slid into the *cavazione in tempo,* and eluding the captain's frantically beating sword, drove forward. This time his point protruded from the captain's right shoulder. Ilarion stepped back and ran his blade into the dirt floor.

The captain sagged over a wooden table. His blade lay at his feet as his left hand clawed at the fire running through his shoulder. His eyes were hot with pain and fury.

Torrigiani came forward. He tapped Da Marolla on his steel corselet. "Stay at the tavern, Captain. Come after us, to Fossate, and next time the stableboy's blade might miss and catch you—here!" His forefinger moved sideways across the captain's throat, hard, so that his fingernail left blood. His upraised eyebrows asked a question.

Da Marolla shrugged and looked at the waiting maid. His eyes ran over her heaving bosom, and the curving figure that was only partially hidden by her loose skirt. *Macche!* There were silver linings to all sorts of disasters, he reflected.

"Come here, little one," he sighed. "Help me to a bed. And bring my velvet purse with you. If your landlord won't take it, perhaps you'll have better sense."

Ilarion watched him go. He said glumly, *"Per Bacco,* Pietro! Who won this match—he or I?"

It was market day in Fossate. For hours, long lines of farmers and peddlers, their wares lashed to the backs of donkeys or piled high in wooden carts, had trudged in from the hills and fields. Girls led goats, whose fresh milk would be sold in the *gorgo.* Wagons were filled with cages of honking geese and bawling pigs to provide fresh meat for the city people.

Two *signori* in travel-stained cloaks moved stirrup to axle with a van that trundled over the cobblestones of the gateway. They moved on under the hanging eaves of the houses, leaving the wagons behind them. Spurring hard and shouting, they scattered barking dogs and yelling children.

Before them, looming high over one corner of the city, was the *rocca,* gray-walled and buttressed with four round towers. Pennons fluttered from poles set in iron rings.

The bigger of the *signori,* a man with red cheeks and a black beard, was growling, "That's where our prisoners will be. How we'll ever get into that pile of stone, though, is beyond my wits!"

Ilarion slapped dust from his cloak. "There'll be wenches in the marketplace. If we keep our ears and eyes open, we'll find a couple who are due back at the *rocco* by nightfall. Some wine, a few kisses—and perhaps we can slip back with them, to their pallets!"

They stopped for a bottle of *moscato* at the Ora d'oro, swaggered along the kidney stones to the White Hen, then moved closer to the great market square.

From the leaded windows of the Silver Lantern, they stared at the men and women and the bellowing hawkers that filled the square. A marble fountain, in the form of a cherub dispensing nectar to a thirsty maiden, towered above the cluster of wagons and milling people.

Torrigiani upended his goblet and morosely watched a a red drop of wine fall to the tabletop. Glumly he asked, "Must we go out into that hubbub?"

66

The door slammed open. A man with the city's crest worked into his stained jerkin stepped toward the bar, waving a hand.

"A dozen wineskins for the *rocca*," he shouted to the hostler. He was a fat fellow, overburdened with flesh and the sense of his own importance. He looked down his nose at Ilarion and Torrigiani, while he said, "Bring me the usual, from the forward part of the cellar."

The hostler ran with a pair of green bottles. He plunked them in front of the man, and added a drinking can.

"If your worship pleases, you might do better to drink in the other room. If you remember last time—"

The fat man sneered. "I carry my liquor as well as the next fellow, *oste!* I'm no sot to be tossed into the gutter! Still, my wife's out yonder, and—"

Ilarion rose to his feet, calling out, "Forgive this intrusion on your privacy, *signore!* But if you'll do us the honor of joining us in the next room, we'll forget the problems of wives, and consign them to the purgatory of forgetfulness!"

As he spoke, he was drawing out the velvet purse that was swollen with golden florins. Giuseppe Baltarone watched the coins that he spilled into a palm, and ran his thick tongue around his lips.

Ilarion said softly, measuring his man, "Naturally, we would not expect you to stand the cost of these noble wines. Our purses are plump, as your eyes can see!"

The fat man smiled greasily. His little eyes glittered above fat red cheeks. "You are more than generous, *signor!* Be advised, though," and he put a hairy hand on the belly that swelled his doublet, "that Giuseppe Baltarone is no mean wine-biber!"

Ilarion was joined in his mirth by the bellowing laughter of Pietro Torrigiani, who swung forward to clap an arm about the Baltarone shoulders.

"Confidentially now, it isn't only the wine we want to share with you! There are two wenches in the *rocca* whose acquaintance we desire to . . ."

The artist paused and winked. Giuseppe Baltarone chuckled in his throat. He liked these bold strangers, and more especially their gold. With both hands he snatched the tall bottles from the counter and lifted them.

"Good *oste,* prepare the room! Bring a side of lamb and some black bread! Fruit, too, and Tuscany dates!"

Torrigiani, nudging the fat man with an elbow added, "And some more bottles of this splendid *moscato!*"

The Silver Lantern was not crowded at this hour of the day. Ilarion discovered that the gold with which he paid for their fare was acting like a magician's spell on the *oste*. He came running with dusty bottles, to lead them through a swinging curtain and into a small room whose wooden rafters were dark with grime and grease.

They discovered Giuseppe Baltarone to be as able a trencherman as his words proclaimed him. He matched Pietro Torrigiani swallow for swallow, which he enlivened by discussing the amorous tricks of the maids and matrons in the *rocca*. From this he went on to guess the names of the wenches they desired to see. His chuckles shook his belly and the jowls of his plump cheeks.

"Felice is for the young one, eh? She's a toothsome morsel, but too high and mighty for me. I'll wager the lad knows how to handle her, though!" He paused to empty the contents of his drinking can down his throat, then refilled it with the white *moscato*. He grinned at Pietro Torrigiani. "You, now! Hmmm! Ah! *Peste!* None other than the blackhaired witch who keeps company with Felice. Eleanora Sascetti! Eh? Am I right?"

Their profuse admiration increased the Baltarone thirst. Bottles were emptied and replaced by the grinning *oste*. Ilarion, who drank little, found the hard-packed dirt floor of the room an excellent blotter, and dumped the contents of three drinking cans there until Giuseppe Baltarone grew too fuddled to care whether or not his companions matched his swallows.

Pietro Torrigiani plied the man with flattery, and kept pace with his cups. In a whisper, he told Ilarion, "The boor thinks he can hold his wine! I'll prove to him I'm a bigger cask than he!"

As the sun lowered beyond the town, the well-moistened Baltarone tonsils essayed a song. In this he was quickly joined by Pietro Torrigiani's rich baritone bellow. Both men proved keen students of the more ribald verses of the poets and musicians, and regaled Ilarion with their somewhat dubious knowledge.

When the *oste* came in with a lighted taper to touch its flame to the tall candles, Ilarion stood up. He swayed a little, as Giuseppe Baltarone regarded him owlishly.

"Felice awaits me," he explained. "And Eleanora grows hungry for my friend's caresses."

Giuseppe Baltarone slapped a tabletop with a hamlike hand. His lewd laughter rang out, and he slobbered apologies as he attempted to rise. Seeing the weakness of his drinking companion, Pietro Torrigiani went to his assistance, and when they both went rolling on the floor, it was Ilarion who lifted and set them to rights.

He was to find that the moscato had done its work well. No sooner was one of them bound for the door than his legs betrayed him, and he sank limply to the floor. In the end, Ilarion anchored himself between them, and they went swaggering through the streets of Fossate bellowing a most licentious *retroensa.*

Their voices brought the captain of the guard running as they tramped across the *rocca* drawbridge. The captain had been interrupted at the dice-cups when he was winning, and he had no time to spend on fools like Giuseppe Baltarone. Not even glancing at his two companions, he roared, "Get to your room, you buffoon! I only hope your good wife Fulvia breaks a broomstick on your head!"

The oaken gate swung wide to admit them, and now Ilarion began to worry about the drunken Torrigiani. "Hsst!" he whispered in the man's ear. "Try and sober yourself!"

The artist stepped back indignantly, and Giuseppe Baltarone fell face forward without his support. The fat man lay on the cobblestones, while his snores resounded from the brick wall of the keep. Pietro Torrigiani scowled down at him, then laughed.

"The pig! He fancied himself a drinker! I told you I'd match cups with him, lad!"

Pietro Torrigiani hiccuped loudly, then glanced apologetically at Ilarion. "Compose yourself. I'm sober as a Doge." He took a deep breath, and when Ilarion sought his eyes, he was amazed to find them clear. Seeing his expression, Pietro Torrigiani grinned. "Did you think you were the only one that could use the dirt floor as a mouth? *Peste!* The stage lost an actor in me when I chose art and soldiering as my life work!"

Ilarion caught his elbow. "Come! This is no time for self-praise! We've a job to do!"

They found a winding little stair that led from the court into the bowels of the *castello*. On silent feet, they moved along the narrow hall, and down more stairs, toward the dungeons. They met no guards, but they could hear the distant pacing of mailed feet.

Rats scurried across the floor as they hunted under the groined stone ceiling of the dungeons, peering into empty cells until their eyes ached. It was Ilarion who suggested that the prisoners, well-born *signori*, might be housed on a higher level.

It took them three hours, but at last they came to an oaken door recessed in the walls of a rampart tower. Through its rounded opening, set with slender bars, Ilarion could discern three men lying on pallets against the walls.

They came awake at his sharp whisper, all incredulity and eagerness, listening as he explained that Torrigiani would take a wax impress on the lock, then carve a wooden key with his artist's fingers.

It was slow work. Torrigiani whispered prayers and soft curses with impartial fervor. There was little light in this corner of the *rocca*, and without light, even his knife was clumsy.

It took too long. They both heard the mailed feet of the changing guard tramping the corridor at the same time. In the prison cell a man groaned. There is no cup so bitter as the one that is filled with hope, and then spilled from a man's lips.

His blade scraped its scabbard as Ilarion drew it. He said, "I'll hold them long enough for you to finish your job! Get to it!"

As Ilarion went racing down the corridor, Torrigiani turned back to his work. His knife moved more swiftly, and he choked back the prayers and the oaths.

To the five men carrying halberds, in the plain dark uniforms of the Fossate militia, the sight of Ilarion in the dim corridor, blade in hand, was like coming upon a ghost in a church. It paralyzed them with shock. They halted abruptly, gaping.

Their officer recovered his wits first. He leaped forward, crying out, "Borgia's bastards! They're trying to free the prisoners!" His sword hummed as it came out.

Ilarion moved aside. His blade lifted and thrust forward, and the officer lunged on without breaking stride. But he was dying as he hit the floor and rolled, with half his throat slashed away.

The halberdiers tried to bring their long staffs into position, but Ilarion was no ox to stand and be spitted. He dove into them, hacking at a hand, shouldering a man backward into another.

70

Ilarion soon learned that halberds were not swords to be parried and enfiladed. He took a gash on his upper arm, and a tear across his upper thigh before he ducked under a jab and spitted a man through the leg. It was close work with the long staves in the corridor, and one of the soldiers hurled his halberd from him with a curse, and drew out his sword.

This was an opponent Ilarion could handle. But even as he parried and thrust, the other halberdier sliced his ribs, leaving a torn garment stained with blood. It taught him caution. Ilarion backed slowly. His blade was a pointed thing that slashed and darted before the soldier's eyes.

And then Ilarion moved in, swiftly, on stamping feet. His blade encircled the halberdier's sword, and penetrated its guard. The man fell back against the wall, coughing against the wound that burned in his shoulder.

The other man threw his halberd from him and ran.

Ilarion's triumph was short-lived. Many feet picked up the echo of the fleeing halberdier's boots, and brought him to a halt. A score of soldiers under an officer came up the stairs, shouting.

They dove at him in a swirl of steel. Their boots stamped and their accoutrements jangled against the metal skirts they wore around their middles. Under the curving morions, their faces were gray, ashen. There was little room for anything but parry and thrust. It was hack and stab and step aside. The steel swords grated and screeched as they met and slid together until joined at their quillions.

Sheer numbers drove Ilarion back toward the oak door where Torrigiani worked, kneeling and sobbing prayers.

The door made a joint at the intersection of two corridors. Ilarion fought desperately, blocking one tunnel; but he could hear, above the curses of the soldiers and the clash of their blades, the sound of thumping boots moving up the intersecting corridor.

Ilarion gave ground, grimly. He made a shuttlecock of his blade, thrusting here into a gray face, there into an exposed shoulder. He made them pay for every step they gained.

"*Santa Maria benedetta*," groaned Torrigiani behind him. "It is still too large. It will not fit!"

The new soldiers swarming in from the other corridor were on top of him. He ducked a blade, and then Ilarion

71

was at his side, parrying and thrusting, and crying out, "For the love of heaven, Pietro! *Fa subito!*"

The artist used his knife, making two swift slashes at the wood. This time the key slid in, and the lock clicked, opening, as he turned it.

Torrigiani fell into the room, through the shadows of the three prisoners who were standing, staring. He got to his feet and began ripping at his clothes, removing them.

Ilarion was at the door, filling it so that the soldiers could not crowd past him.

From his middle, Torrigiani took a strong, slender rope. He said to one of the prisoners, a lean man with a dark growth of beard covering a wide mouth, "We'd hoped to spirit you out through the gate. But in case we ran into something like this, the lad at the door yonder thought we might try the moat."

In a moment the rope was knotted at one of the bifore, a tall window whose length was divided by a slim marble column.

"You first," said the artist, shoving a man forward.

They went swiftly. Soon only one remained. Torrigiani pushed him to the window, turning to stare at the doorway where only the scrape of steel on steel and the shuffle of sliding boots could be heard.

"Lad, come on!" he cried. "I'm fresh. I'll hold them!"

Ilarion had no breath to spare. This play of sword against blade, this thrust and circle, beat and feint, took all his senses. He was wounded in half a score of places. His arm was still steady, but he fought now with a numbness in his side, and his eyes that watched a dozen blades at once, ached with the strain.

He cried out harshly. "Go you, Pietro! I'll come when I can!"

Torrigiani would have argued, but he was a practical man. He knew that he could never hold those soldiers; perhaps not long enough for Ilarion even to squeeze past the column and grasp the rope. He went out the window, and began crawling down.

Ilarion fought on. His blade did not attack, now; it only fended off the thrusts that came at him, seeming to tire. The men-at-arms took heart at this, and pressed closer.

It was then that Ilarion made his move.

From somewhere inside himself, he summoned energy. He drove into the corridor, and the speed of his blade as it swung from defense to attack was blinding. Two men went down, tumbling in front of the others. A third sprawled over them.

It was the moment Ilarion needed.

He whirled and ran for the window. Three feet from it he left his feet and one hand caught the marble column. He swung around it and pitched over. He went down through the night like a stone.

He hit the moat with a force that almost broke his back. He plummeted down into the icy blackness, the cold water numbing him. He ached in both arms and legs, and his shoulder, where he had struck the oily water, was fiery with pain.

A hand clasped him, tugging upward. For a moment he fought, then yielded. He was dragged to the surface, beneath a drooping tree heavy with leaves. Pietro Torrigiani was knee deep in water, holding him.

"Mother of Heaven, he's almost dead!" the artist cried.

A voice whispered harshly from the shadows, "Slap his face! It may serve the purpose of arousing his anger, and so his will to live."

The man crouching in the shadows put a hand from the tree bole that curved outward over the water, and leaned down. His palm cracked against Ilarion's cheek. A moment later, he cried out sharply.

"*Diavolo!* That I should be alive because of him! A cursed Ferrara! I should have known it!"

Torrigiani was moving from the water now, hoisting Ilarion. "Give me a hand!" he called into the shadows. But the man was not there. He was moving away, and Torrigiani could hear his feet crackling twigs and rotten underbrush as he walked.

They came out of the moat, dripping. It was October of the year, and the early morning wind cut with the sharpness of a knife.

"*Peste!*" growled the artist. "I don't know which you drip more, water or blood! We'll have to get you to a warm place soon, or you'll be catching a chill."

They were on the east side of the ramparts, beyond the city walls. Above, the *rocca* loomed like some black monster. Around them was a little wood, that offered shelter from eyes that would be searching for them. Torrigiani set a fast pace. "The sooner we're away from here, the longer we'll live. The city fathers won't take kindly to this loss! Their prisoners gave them a good bargaining position with the Duke."

Ilarion nodded. His teeth were clacking against the cold. He could feel the pain of his wounds, now, as his strength flowed back. He loosed himself from the artist's hands and followed him along a path between the oaks.

They found the others in a little clearing. The man who had slapped Ilarion was glowering, his hands on his hips, his cape like the ruffled feathers of a fighting cock. He muttered oaths in the night, and then came striding.

"I've told myself it is best to wait! But I cannot. Back there in the water, I slapped your face, *Messer assino*. I should have slapped it harder. Like—this!"

His palm cracked with sharp venom against Ilarion's wet cheek. So great was the fury in him that Ilarion was driven back three steps.

Torrigiani called on the Angels, asking if he must be tormented by madmen, so close to the *rocca's* gates.

The man with the ruffled cloak cried out, "He'll want satisfaction for the blow! Know, Ferrara, that I am Galeazzo Gonzaga! Think back on what your kinsmen did to my cousin!"

Ilarion's right hand fumbled at his side, but his scabbard was empty. His sword lay at the bottom of the *rocca* moat.

Gonzaga saw his scabbard at the same moment. He lowered his blade, and his scowl grew blacker.

"Always, it is thus! Whenever a Gonzaga faces a Ferrara with a sword in his hand, the Ferrara finds a way out!"

Torrigiani was a slow man to work to anger, but he was angry now. He threw both arms around Gonzaga and held him. With his bull voice, he roared in the man's ears.

"Look, you *goffo!* See his face! Study it!"

Galeazzo Gonzaga was helpless. Some of his rage dwindled at the honesty his ear discovered in the artist's voice. And so he looked at Ilarion's wide cheekbones, and his yellow hair and blue eyes. His anger changed to puzzlement.

Torrigiani let him go. Gonzaga was contrite, offering his hand. "Forgive me. If you knew how Ferrara got my cousin with child, then poisoned her—"

"Ferrara, Ferrara!" said Ilarion. "That's all I've heard since I left the fencing wall! Are these men monsters? First Dorotea del Andriola mistook me. Then it was Giulà da Rienza. Now, you!"

74

Gonzaga peered at him with sharp, bright eyes.

"There's a resemblance. A strange resemblance, if no blood of theirs flows in your veins! Are you sure?" But at Torrigiani's bellow, he shrugged, and spread his hands. "I merely ask. If you say he is no Ferrara, it's enough for me. But he looks like one, devil take me. Enough like one to set my blood bubbling."

Ilarion said, between chattering teeth, "While we gossip, the *rocca* will have its soldiers hunting here!"

Torrigiani caught him by the arm. He bulled his way past Gonzaga and the other two *signori*. "There's a road not far from here. I marked it as we rode to Fossate. Come along."

They trudged the road for an hour, the sun rising at their left. They had gone three miles when the creak of wagon-axles halted them. A wide cart, drawn by a big dray horse, was moving toward them.

There was an old man on the high seat of the *careta*. He scowled when Torrigiani offered him the companionship of five men going south, and shook his head. He had met *signori* who wanted a ride before. He lifted his reins and chirped to the horse.

It was Ilarion who approached then, jingling what was left of the golden florins Borgia had given him. The old man's eyes lighted. Ilarion lifted the sodden purse and let a few of the yellow coins fall into his palm.

"Almost a year's profit from your wagon, old one. Take them all!" He replaced the coins and threw the purse up to the old man.

"Get in, then," the old man grumbled, admiring each coin as he lifted it out and felt it. "In the straw. But any noise, and I'll toss you out, gold or no gold."

There was no noise. Ilarion was asleep as soon as his back settled itself to the straw. Torrigiani and the others sat talking until the heat of the sun and the gentle motion of the cart made them nod. In a symphony of snores, the cart moved southward along the road to Nepi.

VII

Cesare Borgia opened his attack on the gray stone hulk of Fossate with a thunderclap from the round iron muzzle of the Tenerina. Its foot-thick stone ball hurtled upward, smashed through a wooden outwork, and careened onward in a shower of splinters to the street below. At that signal a score of culverines roared and shook. Falconets erupted rocks and stones from the opposite hillside, their wheels jerking in the recoil of their fire. Broken planks and shattered tile began falling in a steady rain into the city.

A thick arrowshaft from a hand-cranked *ballista* went soaring high into the sky, its point wrapped with globs of flaming pitch. It flew above the keep, and buried its point two feet deep in the wooden front of a building. A moment later red flames were licking upward toward the roof.

Beyond the *ballista*, huge catapults and trebuchets groaned and creaked as their cordings were wound tight. Gigantic stones, weighing upwards of five hundred pounds, went screaming in looping arcs over the dark stone parapets, falling onto rooftops and walls, shattering brickwork, crushing anything in their paths.

Round balls of fiery pitch fell like a rain of fire in the streets. The scream of crossbow quarrels filled the air, clearing the embrasures of defenders, for no man could live in the teeth of those tiny shafts whirling up from the plains.

The *chup-chup* of the squat mortars began to be heard. These little potlike cannon hurled langridge—bits of metal and stone—on a high trajectory over the walls, so that the defenders in the streets below were deluged by flying missiles that could pierce and kill a man even as he ran for shelter.

Looming high above the treetops was a wooden-ribbed, forty-foot-high tower, covered with hides toughened by brine, that could stop anything short of an arquebusier's ball. Men swarmed into it, carrying bows and quivers, arbalests and quarrels. Huge wooden wheels enabled the tower to be rolled flush with the fortress wall, drawn by hundreds of men protected by the curving shelters of huge mantlets.

On the road that twisted south of Fossate toward Urbino, a thousand picked horsemen sat their high wooden saddles, their tall ash lances forming a glittering forest above their helmets.

Here Ilarion *della stalla* stared out at the world from behind the lowered visor of his steel basinet. He was fitted in armor from the great Milan forges, from the collar of chainmail dangling from his helmet to the mailed sollerets on his feet. His well-rounded breastplate was fitted with a high pansiere and huge shoulder pieces. Metal cuishes gripped his thighs. Upper and lower plates, joined by a fluted elbow-cop, protected his arms. Under his tassets, a mailed apron was visible. Ilarion was not used to armor, or to the thickly quilted hacqueton over which the steel plates were fitted. He clasped his long lance in one hand, and his reins in the other, and he silently cursed the streams of clammy perspiration that came crawling down his body.

This waiting was what hurt the most, the older lances of the company assured him. "You sit and you wait while the bombards smash the gate and the chains that hold up the drawbridge. You think about what's coming. And then, when your insides have turned to jelly, they blow the trumpet!"

His armor was hot in the sun. The wooden saddle felt sleek and slippery under his thighs. The ash lance weighed a ton, and had a tendency to topple sideways unless he held it tightly, and when he did that, his fingers grew numbed and cramped. Now he discovered that his knee-caps were pinching him.

He tried to think back, to take his mind off his discomfort. When their cart had creaked into Borgia's camp, and Gaspare Torrella himself had doctored his wounds, he had gone with Pietro Torrigiani to receive Cesare Borgia's fulsome thanks. The Duke had listened carefully to the artist's description of the *duello* in the tavern with Captain da Marolla. He chuckled when Torrigiani revealed the ruse by which they had gained admittance to the *rocca* with Giuseppe Baltarone, and sobered over his description of the fight in the *rocca,* outside the prisoners' cell.

"I promised I would not prove ungrateful," he said at last. "You shall receive money, and advancement. For the money, a fat purse will do, with a few days off in which to spend it. You might find solace in Nepi, for the women there are every bit as toothsome as the madonnas of Florence."

Borgia paused, and his eyes grew thoughtful. "Soon now, I will make you a captain, Ilarion. But the time is not ripe. There is much about my army for you to learn. I have spoken with Galeazzo Gonzaga. He feels, as do I, that you would make a good lance, under Tiberti.

"Learn your trade of soldiering. We'll march next on Fossate, to teach the dogs a lesson. Conduct yourself well. Then, we shall see how a captain's feather looks on your cap."

Torrigiani puffed out his cheeks when they were alone. He said, "Ho! A captain, is it? Now why, lad?"

His words drained a little of the self-esteem that was filling Ilarion *della stalla* at the moment, and he grew hot, as youth will when its abilities are challenged. The Duke had agreed to a reward. He was merely fulfilling that agreement.

"But not so fast! Not so fast! To be a captain in Borgia's army is no mean achievement, even for a man twice your years! It means good pay, and a possible *condotta* of your own, in a few years."

The picture he painted overwhelmed the artist. He shook his head, grumbling in his beard. "There is something behind it. But for the life in me, I can't think what it is!"

Borgia had given them gold, and a few days' leave in Nepi. Hai! That had been a week end! Together, they roved the taverns, tossing the wines of a dozen vintners down their throats. And the women! *Nome del santo!* He never did learn how he got back to camp.

He sweated that week end out in the fields below Nepi. With a lance in his hand and his feet in the stirrups, he rode hour after hour, tilting at the targets they set up on wooden poles thrust deep into he ground. Even when his thighs ached from the pressure of the saddle, and his wrist was numb and senseless, he drove his mount at the white, swaying shields that dangled on cords from tall willow poles.

The news that Borgia was marching on Fossate came as a welcome relief. It would give him a chance at real fighting, with no more dry runs on helpless little shields.

But Pietro Torrigiani grumbled, "Fossate is no threat to him. He could pass it by as if it were a hog lying in the wallows. He wants to make an example of it, so his path against Rimini and the other cities of the Romagna will be easier."

When Ilarion looked his puzzlement, the artist leaned forward and tapped his knee. "You've never seen a city given to the sack, lad! Ai, I enjoyed myself at Forli with the baker's wife. But there were sights— Well, no matter! When Rimini hears about what happened at Fossate, they

78

won't be so eager to put up a fight. Mark my words!"

Now Fossate was before him, big and dark, at the end of the road where Achille Tiberti sat his horse, waiting.

The man next to him said, "Listen to the Tenerina! She's talking long and loud today."

"There goes the tower!"

Ilarion could see it, squat and huge above the forest, rumbling forward like some monstrous finger beyond the trees. Its wooden uprights were dark with bull-hides, its platform thick with arquebusiers and crossbowmen. The defenders were massing on the parapets to meet it, wheeling forward giant pots of boiling oil, and mobile *ballista*.

. Sheltered by mantlets formed by overlapping shields, a dozen squads were bringing up battering rams. In a moment the dull thud of their round metal heads could be heard, pecking at the reinforced gates. A huge tun of boiling oil was pushed to the edge of the wall above and overturned. Even from this distance, Ilarion could hear the screams of those caught in the steaming downpour.

The tower was joined to the wall, now. A score of fire-arrows had dug into it, and red flames were licking up its sides. On the platform, a wave of pikemen moved from the tower to the wall, meeting the city militia in a welter of bloodied steel.

A voice said hollowly from the shelter of a huge helm, "The Duke has them crowding in to fight his tower! Watch now!"

"Ha! He'll be bringing out the bombards he has hidden at the edge of the woods near the road. Look! Look!"

Gleaming cannons rolled forward, a score of men to each gun. They drew them with great, thick ropes, bent forward with the ropes over their shoulders, feet clawing for purchase in the ground.

Close to the edge of the dusty road that pointed at the main gate of Fossate, they halted. Men dragged the stone cannonballs in canvas strips, lifting and loading them. Matches flared. The cannons roared.

Ilarion watched with wide eyes. He saw one ball hit the arch above the main gate and rebound into the waters of the moat with a geyser-like splash. Another hit the upraised wooden gate, showering white wooden splinters. A third crashed full on into the chains that supported the upright causeway. Links snapped with a screeching of tortured metal. Part of the bridge swayed and toppled, hanging crookedly.

The bombards shook and belched smoke and stone. It took five more balls to smash the other chain. The wooden drawbridge quivered a moment and then fell, bouncing once as it hit the ground.

A trumpet flared, far down the road.

Excitement ran like fire through the lances. Men who had been lounging now sat upright. Eyes glowed feverishly behind lowered visors. Fingers wrapped tightly around lance-butts.

The forward ranks were moving as though drawn by a magnet. Ilarion rammed his long- roweled spurs into his armor-hung horse, conscious that his blood was hammering through his veins. This was war! This was what he had come from Rome to find. Conduct himself well, Il Valentinois had said, and he might become a captain!

The drawbridge was down. Beyond the drawbridge the oaken gate gave way, and now the galloping horsemen could see the streets of Fossate, and watch the men-at-arms frantically running to form a fence of flesh and steel against them.

Now the lances were driving across the fallen drawbridge, the heavy hoofs of their barded war horses drumming a rolling tattoo of thunder from its wooden planks. Their slim, metal-shod spears came through the open gate and men were going down, with lances sticking through their ribs, and screaming.

Here and there, a few men-at-arms hurled themselves upward with swords naked in the sunlight, but the huge espadons and maces that the lances wielded for close-in work stretched them quivering and bloody on the ground.

Ilarion was under the gate now, mingling with the others, his lance still untested in his hand. He could see a little of the blood-wet cobblestones, and the quiet shapes of men-at-arms who had gone down fighting, through the narrow slit of his visor.

An officer roared, "A score of you stay here, to keep the gate open. You others—after me!"

Ilarion tossed his lance from him, lifted his visor, and stepped out of the big wooden saddle. He shook his head to the cool breeze that swept in through the gateway. He put his helmet at his feet, and stretched, feeling the trickles of sweat inside his hacqueton run down his chest.

A lancer said, "The Duke is going to gut this place! *Peste!* I'd rather—" His voice broke off suddenly.

80

Ilarion stared dumbly at the gray-feathered crossbow shaft transfixing the man's throat, like an obscene leech fastened there to drain him. The man moved back one step, then sprawled on the stones with a crash of armor.

A quarrel screamed against Ilarion's shoulder-boss and ricocheted past his eyes. Other bolts whistled down, filling the air with a hail of slim, feathered needles. Five of the dozen lancers now sprawled before the gate. From a narrow stone stair built against the wall, grinning men-at-arms were coming. A swarm of Fossate's mail-clad militiamen poured from the streets.

They met, seven against a hundred, with a scrape and clang of sword against sword. The seven fell back a step. Now six men stood fighting for their lives. Another man dropped.

The thought came to Ilarion as he fought for his life, moving his blade in and out of the many that he faced, that once the gate was closed, Fossate would butcher Achille Tiberti and his horse, trapped inside the city. What was keeping the footmen and the archers?

He heard them as a mace whipped its knobbed ball, at the end of a flailing chain, down on his helmet. The sound and the shock exploded over the thump of mailed *sabbatons* on the drawbridge planks. He reeled, staggering, blinded and numb. His foot hit a body and he tripped, sprawling.

He did not hear the pikemen rush forward to engage the city militia. He did not see the militia fight for a few moments, then break and scatter through the city. The grim-faced Swiss mercenaries, in their blue-and-silver uniforms, went after them.

Ilarion lay like a dead man, across the body of a mail-clad man-at-arms.

It was much later that he stirred, rising from the welter of bodies. He gulped in air, kneeling among the dead and dying. And then, abruptly, seeing the torn throat of an unhelmed lancer, the bleeding stump of a militiaman's wrist, the awful stillness of men he had known, Ilarion was sick.

Shaken and gagging, he climbed to his feet. He found his sword, and mechanically cleaned it. In the distance, he could hear the faint sounds of fighting, the scream of a woman.

With his helmet in one hand, and his sword naked in

the other, he walked on into the city. He passed under a row of arches. Here and there along the walls lay dead in pools of their own blood. A woman, caught and abused by passing soldiers, sprawled moaning in a spray of afternoon sunlight.

Fire was eating a row of wooden-fronted houses down an intersecting street. The flames stretched upward like grasping fingers toward an orange sky. A group of shouting men-at-arms, flushed with wine, their mail stained with blood and hairs, careened out of a building, laden with silver salvers and heavy draperies.

Ilarion realized dully that the conquest of Fossate was over, and its sack was now beginning. To the soldiers who followed the *condottieri* captains, the sack of a city was an important part of their wage. The chance to loot a town of its art and jewels, its silver and its gold, was not to be passed over lightly. If a man was lucky at a time like this, he could buy himself a farm, and need not fight again.

And so Ilarion, who had learned what it meant to fight with Borgia's horse that morning, learned now what it meant to walk the streets of a city as it lay defenseless to its own rapine. He heard women scream until their breath bubbled in their throats. He saw a barmaid run from a tavern, with half a dozen soldiers close after her. He watched them catch her and drag her back into the tavern, whimpering and begging for pity.

He passed the Silver Lantern, and turned away, sick, from the sight of the plump little proprietor hung to a slowly twisting rope above the lintel of his door. Inside, where he had befuddled Giuseppe Baltarone with wine, drunken men were roaring obscene songs, waving drinking cans high over their heads, watching a woman shake her hips at them as she danced on a wine-wet tabletop.

In the *borgo*, the fountain was foul with blood. The dead lay thick where they had been caught between Achille Tiberti's lances and the long shafts of Borgia's Scotch archers.

It was here that Pietro Torrigiani found him, seated on an overturned bench, staring dazedly around at the bolts protruding from men's chests, at the throats slit and gaping, the hacked-off hands. The artist clapped him on a shoulder.

"Lad, you look like Paris, surveying the ruins of Troy! Put a smile on your lips!"

"So many dead! The *oste* at the Silver Lantern—hung by the neck in his own doorway!"

Torrigiani puffed out his lips, and made a face. "It's not pretty, this business of war. But Borgia set out to teach Fossate a lesson. He uses death and rape to serve him, does our Duke! The word of what happens here will go up and down the length of Italy. Malatesta in Rimini will hear of it, you can rest assured. So will Sforza at Pesaro! Such news will do Il Valentinois' work as well as another *condotta* of lances! They won't want this to happen to their cities!"

Ilarion shook his head. "But this isn't—"

The artist looked at him shrewdly. "It isn't what you pictured it, is it? Galloping on your war horse, scattering soldiers before your lance and sword! Carrying the bull banner with you, destroying *Il Duca's* enemies? Eh? You didn't think your Borgia hero capable of this? It hurts you, deep inside. Makes you a little fearful of your own neck—if Borgia were to decide that he could profit by your death!"

Torrigiani shrugged and spread his arms. *"Peste,* but I'm morbid today! Come, forget all this and help me find a good spot to do a picture. Il Valentinois told me to sketch in a background and— ah! Over yonder! Beneath the fountain, with the dead piled at your feet, your blade in your hand—*perfezione!"*

"Piled at my feet?" questioned Ilarion, staring. "What do you want with a picture of me?"

Torrigiani went stamping toward the fountain, waving a hand. "You shall epitomize the spirit of Borgia's army! *Capisce?* Standing as a conqueror among the bodies of the dead! Ha! If only I had a wench to pose sprawled below you, clinging to your knees!"

Ilarion said gloomily, "It wouldn't be right. I'm no conqueror. I lay like a dead man during—"

"Dio mio! One day you're a hero, the next a dub. That's war! Get over there, with your helmet under your left foot—so!"

As he spoke, Torrigiani drew out a sketch pad and a bit of charcoal. For an instant, his bright eyes studied the little tableaux in front of him and then his right hand was moving swiftly, surely, transfixing it to paper.

All around them, Fossate shrieked its agony to the flame-lighted sky. They could hear the screams and cries of terrified women, the moans of men caught and tortured. Once a group of drunken archers went by with three wenches in their midst. Torrigiani's hand shook as he watched them in the shadows of a tavern doorway.

"*Diavolo!*" he groaned. "How can a man concentrate at a time like this?"

Ilarion saw one of the women pause to set her ripped clothing in place. From under her tumbled brown hair, her white face stared back at him with frightened intensity.

Torrigiani sighed and put his pad and charcoal in his purse. "Come along, lad. Now's no time to stand and pose for your portrait! You've learned how war is made today, so learn a little more. Discover how sweet conquest can be, in a woman's arms."

Ilarion gaped at him. "A woman? Now? After this? I couldn't! You go on without me!"

Two women had paused and were watching them from under the shadows of a brick-faced house whose roof was supported by dark wooden corbels. One of the women was ripping loose her wide sleeves, baring soft upper arms.

Torrigiani watched her. His voice was hoarse as he spoke. "Go on without you? *Diavolo!* I will!"

He ran, and the women, seeing him coming, fled squealing down an intersecting street. Ilarion watched them go, and wondered a little at the sickness that lay in him.

The sory of Fossate spread forward from the timbered slopes of the Apennines as ripples in a pool into which a stone has fallen. Men whispered of the hangings and the torturings, and of the red fury of devouring flames that had brought Fossate's houses down in crashing ruin. Women gasped at the ravishings, and at the forcings of noblewomen and maids to the wills of brutal soldiers. All Italy listened to the tale, and shuddered.

· Cesare Borgia, with the army that had put Fossate to the sword and given its timbers to the licking flames, was marching once again. Rimini lay before it, and beyond Rimini, Pesaro: two plump fowls in the path of a stalking wolf.

Panic ran like a wind before the marching thousands. In Rimini, the common council spoke in hushed whispers of their city's lack of defense, and of the French cannons that had battered the walls of Fossate to rubble. In Pesaro, Giovanni Sforza was more complacent. He was no fool. He had begged Venice and Mantua for help that never came. Alone, he could not stand against Il Valentinois, and so he made preparations for flight.

While panic swirled over the city states of the Romagna, a scudding rain swirled across its fields and meadows, drenching Borgia's army as it moved away from the charred and gutted wreckage of Fossate. The roads were thick with oozing mud, through which men and horses waded, knee deep. Pikemen and archers staggered, struggling to maintain ranks as they marched behind the sodden pennons.

Miles in back of them, the Tenerina was sunk to its trunnions in a muddy bog. Bombards and culverines lay hub-deep, overturned and half buried in the thick Romagna mud. The chill October rain buffeted men and horses as they fought to drag the cannons upright, to set them on their wheels, for without cannon and bombards, even Il Valentinois could never hope to take a walled city.

And so, where walls and pikes could not stop Borgia, the rain and the flowing mud did.

With raindrops beating in thick sheets against his body, his velvet toque a sodden ruin over his forehead, Cesare Borgia gave an exclamation of disgust and surrender.

"*Iddio!* We'll stop at Deruta. It will take at least four days to extricate the cannon and get them rolling again!"

It took four days, as the Duke prophesied, to right the culverines and bombards from the rain-washed roads. But at the end of those four days, Borgia discovered that he did not need them.

The Council of Rimini sent messengers, offering surrender. And Giovanni Sforza of Pesaro was on a ship whose sails were aimed at Ravenna while a *condotta* of horses under Achille Tiberti stood before his city's gates, demanding that she yield.

Six days later, Cesare Borgia rode into Pesaro at the head of two thousand lances. The late October rains dripped from golden helms and steel lancepoints, from the *chamfrons* and *orinets* that decked the great war horses as they paced slowly down the avenue.

Rimini and Pesaro had fallen to the bull banner without the firing of a single arrow, without the use of even one cannon ball. In full panoply, their heads held high, these veteran troops marched with swinging strides to the music of their kettledrums. The red and white jerkins of the Swiss mercenaries were sodden ruins beside the wetly glittering breast-and-backs of the French men-at-arms. Silvered pikeheads moved below flapping pennons and banners that were emblazoned with the red bull of Borgia.

Ilarion rode with Achille Tiberti's horse, his armor freshly scrubbed and polished. He rode without a helm, his yellow hair blowing gently as the damp breeze caught it, his blood slamming to the martial music of the drums and trumpets. He stared out over the crowds that thronged the cobblestones, at women who threw kisses, and men who shouted at the colorful procession.

While Cesare Borgia took up his court at the Sforza palace, whose arched windows peered out from graceful arches set with marble traceries and Sgraffito decorations, Ilarion found himself quartered in a more modest fashion. He shared a room with Pietro Torrigiani in a timbered house with tiled gables. Its second story was formed with a semi-balcony fronting the molded pattern of its Gothic windows.

A maid-servant led them to a large room whose ceiling was slanted to the slope of the roof above. A big bedstead was set into the wall, its headpiece forming part of the wall panel itself. A wooden washstand, a big cypress-wood credenza and a press of willow, worked with a tongue-of-fire ornamentation, completed the furniture. Several tall candlestands lined the wall.

Torrigiani looked around and expressed his delight at their housings. "You stretch out, lad. I'll go down with milady here and bring up our gear."

The maid giggled when Torrigiani put an arm around her shoulders and led her from the room.

They ate in a big dining hall below stairs, and it was here, as they dallied over wine and slabs of creamy cheese, that a messenger from the Duke found them, with an invitation to attend the ducal victory ball.

Torrigiani looked up from he platter of figs he was munching.

"We grow great, lad! A ducal dance, and you're summoned to it! *Iddio,* but he's pushing you fast! I find myself wondering—why?"

Ilarion knew pulsing excitement as he went up the stairs to change his leather jazerin for rich doublet and new hose. Perhaps Giula da Rienza—*la rosso*—would be among the court ladies that rumor said had come to Pesaro to join Il Valentinois, led by the pale Lucrezia

86

herself. He discovered that eagerness made him clumsy, and so Pietro Torrigiani must come and tie the ribbons that decorated the dagged sleeves of his purple, ermine-trimmed gipon.

The artist stood back and surveyed him with a critical eye. "You'll break hearts tonight, lad!"

Ilarion tried to see as much of himself as he could, bending his neck and contorting himself into various positions. "There's only one heart I'm interested in."

Torrigiani grunted disparagingly, and sat at a little table where a bowl of apples had been placed. He took one and hefted it in his hand, then reached for his knife.

"There speaks a young man. When you get to be my age, you'll have better sense. Then one woman won't matter. It'll be any woman."

Torrigiani pared the red skin from an apple attentively after Ilarion closed the door behind him. For a moment the artist continued to peel the fruit, his head cocked to one side. Then he placed the apple and the dagger on the tabletop beside the silver salver and got to his feet.

From an oak cabinet rimmed with ivory inlay he withdrew a cylinder wrapped about with silk. Carefully he undid the silk and drew out a rolled canvas. Spreading it, he held it in both hands and studied it.

It was a study of Ilarion *della stalla* as he had stood in the square of Fossate, before the fountain.

"Why there should be so much secrecy about this, I don't know," he grumbled. "It's of a sort with everything else that concerns the lad. His advancement! His invitations to Court dances!

"I don't like it! Borgia wants to use the boy for some devil's purpose of his own. I can't understand it, or I'd warn the lad to shorten his stirrups and ride like the wind out of here. Borgia means no good to any man but Borgia. Now he's got his teeth in the lad, and the lad's so bemused by his own importance and so addled with love for that slant-eyed redhead that he can't think for sour wine!" He fixed the canvas to a collapsible easel among his gear, and stepped back to eye it dubiously.

"He got me to paint this thing by offering me so many ducats my ears popped. *Per Bacco!* He doesn't play at chess, this Duke, when he's willing to pay such sums for a picture of a stableboy. But why's he want it? That's what worries me."

He painted in the background, glum and scowling. After a few moments, he tossed the brush aside and stared at the picture with his hands on his hips.

"It isn't coming. I'll need the lad as a model again. His eyes and the set of his mouth elude me. I picture them in my mind, but I'll need him before me to set them right in oil. Ha! I only hope he lives long enough for me to do it. Borgia and his plots and schemes!"

He thought of Alfonso of Bisceglia, Lucrezia Borgia's husband, whose death was laid at the feet of the Duke of Valentinois. He thought also of the Duke of Ganida, who had been fished out of the river in a net with his arms tied behind him, dead from nine stab wounds from Cesare Borgia's dagger. These and other men had died when Borgia had used them, and had dreaded the power that their knowledge might give them.

He started as a knock sounded on the paneling of the wooden floor. With a sudden glance at the oil painting, Torrigiani lifted his cloak and threw it over the canvas, hiding it. He went and opened the door, wondering who would visit him at this hour of the evening. It was the chambermaid. "I've come for the platter of fruit, sir."

Torrigiani grinned and put a hand under her arm. "Come in, come in. I haven't finished it, yet. But now that you're here, you might as well stay. You're in no hurry, now, are you?"

She laughed. She was a saucy thing, with her milky throat and bosom showing in the round cut of her kirtle. Her brown eyes let him see her admiration for his big bulk and curly black hair.

When she saw the easel, she squealed. "An artist! Oh, *illustrissimo!*" She clasped her hands and tried to peep under the cloak that covered it. Torrigiani caught her arm to draw her away, but she shook free. She pouted, and swung her hips. "Let me see! You're painting some woman."

"You're the only woman I'd ever want to paint."

Her laughter was shrill, exciting. She let him draw her in against him, and her soft hips brushed against him as she wrestled playfully, dodging his lips that sought her mouth and cheeks.

"Messer, I beg of you—"

"Just a taste of those cherry lips! A taste, that's all!"

"No, you mustn't! If someone heard—"

Torrigiani did not see the calculating look that turned

88

her eyes as hard as agates as she led him on. He knew only that her loose kirtle had come undone, and that he was holding her close.

The backs of her knees were pressing into the bed that was thrust back under a roof eave. Her laughter teased him, maddened his senses. For a moment her mouth kissed his. And then she tumbled backward and lay smiling up at him from the bed, her skirts awry.

The Sforza palace was bright with the light of a thousand candles as Ilarion hastened along the great tiled floor of the gilt-walled antechamber. From the closed bronze doors that had been wrought by Ambrogio Borgognone, he could hear the strains of a stately madrigal and the faint susurrus of dancing feet.

He was passing a marble-topped table upheld by golden legs carved in the shape of crouching maidens when his eye was caught by a flash of bright scarlet. A woman was emerging from the concealment of a pillar of Phrygian marble marked with purple veins. Ilarion came to an abrupt stop. Some inner sense whispered to him that this was Giula *la rosso,* and he paused to drink in her loveliness, his breath catching in his throat.

She wore a dogalina that hugged her hips, and clung to her upper arms and the rounded curve of her bosom with a shaping tightness. The red velvet dress was cut square at its gold net bodice, displaying the shadowy cleft of her white bosom in modish revealment. Ai! He knew that pert elfin face, with slanted green eyes and heavy, languorous mouth, and the red hair that was gathered in a gold mesh that fanned across the nape of her neck.

"Madonna Giula," he whispered.

She turned, and now he knew that she had been waiting for him, but that her pride would not let her see him first. He came swiftly to stand before her, resplendent in his purple gipon. He took her hand and held it to his lips, savoring the smooth texture of her skin.

"I've dreamed of you, night and day," he said, and Giula *la rosso* shivered at the ardor of his blue eyes.

She tossed her shoulder in a shrug. The tease in Guila was never far from the surface, and it pleased her to give it full play. "Being a man of action, I suppose you'll be planning to make those dreams a reality."

He recognized her raillery, but a spirit of humility lay in him, and she read his hopelessness in the shrug of his

89

shoulders. He said glumly, "There are some men who can aspire only to dreams, madonna. I'm only a stableboy turned soldier. Gifted by an ability with the sword. You are noble. You can understand why dreams must be my only solace."

Giula da Rienza was aware that her pulse was pounding as she regarded this tall, golden-haired youth. She had been given to dreams of late, herself, and was surprised to discover something deep within her that responded to their vividness. Ilarion *della stalla* had come to her often as she twisted and turned under the coverlets, until she had hungered for physical sight of him.

She said now, breathlessly, "You speak of despair."

He smiled wryly. "Better despair than defeat, *madonna mia.*"

Her fan, red to match her costume, came open. She regarded him from behind its laced fringe as the fan moved swiftly. "Why either, stableboy?"

He started, and his blue eyes widened. Ilarion was conscious that his heart pounded behind his ribs. His tongue touched his lips. "It would be impertinent of me to think of making my dream come true."

"To the impertinent, all things are possible," she whispered, twisting and leaning a little closer, breathing fast.

Faintly, they could hear the music of the viols and clavichords from the ballroom where the men and women of the court were dancing. She was close and fragrant, and the speeding pulse of her blood caused her bosom to surge. It was a moment that Ilarion recognized. All he had to do was reach out, and madonna Giula would be in his arms, soft against him, and he would be tasting the moist pressure of her lips as he had dreamed of doing since the night in the gardens of Lucrezia Borgia's summer palace.

But where he would have acted with Dorotea del Andriola or Beatrice del Gallina, he stood frozen now, awed before this woman whom he fancied as cold and as chaste as the fresh snows of winter.

She regarded him shrewdly. "You are mistrustful, Ilarion. Of me?"

His stricken look made her soft laughter bubble up, restoring her good humor. She leaned to him, green eyes mocking. "They are dancing in the ballroom, Ilarion. A new and daring French dance, in which the man holds the woman very tightly!"

They paused outside a marble-trimmed doorway. Through its opening, the music of the *branle* swept to them. At Giula's bidding, Ilarion took her hand and went four steps to the left, then to the right. Feet together, they swayed, Giula da Rienza with her hands on her hips, Ilarion with his arms behind his back. He whirled her under an outstretched arm, then caught her waist to hug her in to him for a brief moment.

Ilarion discovered that his feet were not as clumsy as he had feared. They were trained to the swift movements of fence, and to shift from those to the steps of the dance took little effort. He moved around the antechamber, with Giula *la rosso* warm and fragrant against him. It occurred to him that he had never been so happy in his life.

"The music has ended, messer," she whispered, looking up at him and smiling.

He flushed a little. They were very close. His right arm was about her waist. Her hand joined with his. Almost unconsciously, he lowered his face and kissed her. Her mouth was sweet and warm. She clung to him a moment, frenziedly, then brushed her lips aside and pillowed her face on his chest.

Suddenly she said, "I am glad Dorotea del Andriola and Beatrice del Gallina are not in Pesaro, Ilarion! For their sakes! If they were, I'm afraid I'd go looking for them with a dagger in my hand!"

She threw back her head and stared up at him defiantly. "Oh, I'm well aware that you met them before you did me, but you'd seen my cameo! What manner of faithfulness do you call that?"

Ilarion was amazed at her sudden anger. He put his hands to her cheeks and kissed the tip of her nose.

"You'll have me believing that a mere lance in the Duke's army could dare to lift his eyes to you, madonna."

His tone was bantering, but she sensed the emotion deep inside him. Giula da Rienza was moved. With white fingers, she undid a thin silken scarf, a wisp of scarlet fluff, from her throat.

With her white fingers, she tied the scarf to the girdle of thin silver plates from which hung his dagger's scabbard.

"Wear it as my guerdon, Ilarion," she whispered. "As ladies once gave their knights favors to wear in battle, so I give this to you."

Ilarion was overwhelmed. He was only short months away from the days when he tended stables for Jacopo Balisandro, and this talk of knighthood and ladies' guerdons was heady stuff. It opened his eyes to the fact that he still walked in a world where anything might happen.

He kissed her hands, and humility warred with hope inside him.

"I'm only a soldier, madonna! A commoner. You're of noble blood. The cousin of a duke, granddaughter of a prince! I could never hope to win your love. But—but I'd die for a chance!"

He told her of the days when he had cleaned the stables and scrubbed the floors of Jacopo Balisandro's salle, and of the dreams he'd had of a better life. He whispered of the nights when he had spied on the old fencing master. When the Countess Beatrice del Gallina had come to the salle, she opened a door to him. Now that the door was open, and he had the opportunity of looking into the world of fine ladies and noble men, he realized he could never take part in it. Always, he must stand outside and watch, like a starving child staring in through the window of a sweetmeat shop.

He told her something of this while her fingertips caressed his cheeks and her green eyes moistened with pity, moving back and forth, studying his face as if she would engrave it forever on some corner of her mind. Her lips murmured little endearments and sympathy.

He poured out his heart to her between the columns of the antechamber, and Giula da Rienza knew that no other man could ever hope to stand in the heart that belonged fully, now, to Ilarion *della stalla.*

"Oh, my dearest," she whispered, "My own dearest!" She put her hands on his shoulders and strained against him, as if she could pass some of her strength to him.

And then the bronze doors of the music room were flung open. They whirled, hearing the faint tinkling of bells. One of Lucrezia Borgia's two dwarfs was dancing toward them, shaking his bells and laughing. Behind him came Lucrezia Borgia, pale and wan in cloth-of-gold gown with black satin lacings, her long blonde hair set in a coif of pearls. Cesare Borgia leaned on her arm, whispering.

"Beware, milord Duke! Beware I say!"

Cesare looked up, alarmed for the moment, as any prince will be at danger, for he lived in an age of the assassin's dagger. But his lips curved when he regarded the dwarf standing with spraddled legs before Giula da Rienza and Ilarion.

"Of what must I beware, fool?"

"Your master is here! See him, with his weapon that no man may escape!"

Borgia laughed, but his pride lay naked in that same laughter.

"My master? Who is this lord paramount? Not my blade, surely!" The jester turned a cartwheel, his deformed legs flashing in their green-and-white hose. He fell on his rump, his face loose and idiotic, and was rewarded by the laughter of the court.

"Not Ilarion the stableboy! Not him—but love! Cupid! Eros! He has feathered his shafts in their hearts! Ha, you see the lady blush? The man look foolish?"

Ilarion scowled, laughed, and stood silent, not knowing whether to show anger or amusement, and succeeded only in showing embarrassment. Madonna Lucrezia stretched out a pitying hand to him.

"My fool forgets that the victims of Eros are always blessed! They're not dead men slain by an arrow, but men awake to win the glory of their lady!"

The dwarf danced around Ilarion, pointing at his girdle where the scarlet scarf lay bright against the purple of his doublet.

"A gage! She has given him a gage! He is her knight—but stay!" The dwarf put his finger to his cheek and regarded Ilarion with eyes that were bright and malicious. With a shock, Ilarion realized that they glittered with jealousy, for within that misshapen body was a mind that knew agony at its own misfortune, who hated all others because of it.

"But wait, I say!" the dwarf cried again. "Is he a knight? Is he of noble blood, to win such a guerdon? Aha! I smell something!" He capered with his legs kicking high, and for the first time in his life, Ilarion wanted to pull a man's tongue from his throat.

"I smell manure! Phew! But why? Why? Because this is no knight! He is a scullery boy, demoted to the stables! What should he want with the gage of a noble lady?"

Before any could stop him, the dwarf reached out and snatched at the silken scarf. He had it almost free when Ilarion caught him by the little green silk doublet he wore and lifted him high. Jealous eyes looked into killing eyes, and the tiny caricature of a man knew what it was to face death. He licked his large, wet mouth with a thick tongue. "I—" he gasped.

Ilarion threw him from him, sick. The dwarf landed on his hands, turned a somersault, and went running down the long, tiled hall, screaming his mocking laughter.

Cesare Borgia said in the sudden silence, "I invited the court to listen to the latest improvisations of the divine Aquilano, Serafino Cimino. As punishment for your outburst of temper, Ilarion—I refuse you admittance to the library. For your anger, you shall be exiled to the garden with Madonna Giula. Perhaps there, she can remove the sting of our jester's words."

They stood together as the men and women of the court moved on in the wake of Cesare Borgia and his blonde sister. The dwarf had put a steel hand in Ilarion's middle with his mockery, and he could feel it squeezing until his misery became a physical pain. Madonna Giula shook him gently. "The gardens are beyond the loggia, *caro mio.*"

He let her lead him down the high-ceilinged chamber with its marble columns and gilded, carved abacuses that squatted under the weight of decorated architraves. The bright canvases that were fitted into the ogival arches of the groined ceiling, and the statues that flanked the walls, were all reminders to Ilarion that this luxury was part of Giula da Rienza's way of life. She was used to bronze doors wrought by a Borgognone, to paintings by a Da Vinci, to statues hewed from stone or metal by a Cellini. He fed his bitterness on his self-pity, recalling the straw pallet where he had slept for so many years, the smells of the wooden-planked stable, the coarse black bread and the cheese that he had eaten and then washed down with goat's milk.

They crossed the loggia where it was striped with moonlight falling between stone archways. Here Madonna Giula caught his hands and turned him, smiling. In the background, a little fountain splashed its waters.

"You are sad, Ilarion! After all I said to you, you wear the look of a boy whipped for stealing cookies!"

"I am regretting my birth, madonna."

"You were born a man! Sometimes I think that must be a very pleasant thing."

"Not when he's born without name or position! Not when he falls in love with a noblewoman whose blood is as old as the Borgias!"

He shrugged against the hopelessness in him. The taunts of the dwarf had opened his eyes to a truth from which Giula *la rosso's* pity and caresses had blinded him. He cried out bitterly, "I love you, *Madonna la rosso!* I dream of wedding you, but deep down I know that a commoner may never wed with a noblewoman like yourself!"

"Splendid sentiments!" cried a harsh voice from the walk behind them. "Sister, I crave pardon! You asked me to seek Messer Ilarion in friendship. I was not aware that he knew his place so well. The fact adds an argument to your own."

Paolo da Rienza stood in the shadows of a bush, touching his pomade ball to his nostrils. His eyes glittered.

"Paolo!" Giula cried. "You spy!"

The fop threw his hands wide. He looked to heaven for support. "It was warm inside. The air was foul. I thought of the gardens, and the cool breezes I would find here. Is that your definition of spying?"

Ilarion said stiffly to Giula, "It grows late. I have duties to keep me busy tomorrow. I beg leave, madonna." He bowed and kissed Giula *la rosso's* hands, sharply conscious of Paolo da Rienza's eyes fixed on him narrowly.

Moonlight filtered in through the leaded windows and onto the bed where Pietro Torrigiani snored in sprawling slumber. Beside him, a woman with yellow hair and dark brown eyes sat up, not bothering to shield her milky flesh from the candles guttering on a nearby table.

She crawled over the sleeping artist, to stand beside the bed. She paused irresolutely, putting out a hand to him.

"You are no mean lover, messer," she whispered. "Almost, for you, I would gather my things and leave now. But there is something I must do."

The chambermaid went on bare feet to the canvas and lifted the cloak. From the table, she raised a copper candelabra, holding it so that the flame lighted the picture. She caught her breath at sight of the face on the canvas.

"*Si, si,*" she whispered faintly. "It is he, the one who shares the room with the artist. There is no doubt of it."

She replaced the candelabra and began to dress, pulling on her cotton undergarments and lifting her arms, dropping the homespun brown kirtle over it. Sheltering the man from spattering tallow with the cup of a hand, she blew out the candles, one by one.

In the moonlight, she made her way to the door and opened it. On bare feet, carrying her shoes, she tiptoed down the hall. She paused to throw a cloak around her shoulders, then slipped into the street. She went swiftly through the narrow lanes and under the leaning houses. When she came to a grille gate set in a low wall about the palace gardens, she tapped three times.

Paolo da Rienza was there, in place of the guard, into whose greedy fingers he had slipped a dozen coins. Da Rienza caught her hands. His black eyes blazed at her.

"Well, girl? What did you learn? Did you see the canvas that Torrigiani carries with him, as a mother does her firstborn? What's on it, for the love of *il gran Dio?*"

"A man with yellow hair, *illustrissimo*," she panted, infected by his fever. "The young man who rooms with the artist."

"Ilarion *della stalla?* Eh?"

"I think that's his name. Yes! I heard the artist speak it, this afternoon when they brought their gear."

Paolo da Rienza loosed her hands, as his white teeth gnawed his lip. A scowl blackened his dark features. "Now why should Torrigiani be so secret about the fact? He could paint his friend, and who would care? But the fact that he's so careful about it! Not showing it. Cradling it like a child!"

The woman shivered beside him, recalling the fop to the moment. His long white fingers fumbled in his girdle and lifted out a small purse. He pushed it into her hand.

"Take this, *zitella*. You did well, this night. Come to me with more news of what the stableboy does, and you'll find me grateful."

The chambermaid turned and ran, leaving Paolo da Rienza alone at the gate, the puzzlement in his face drowning the hate that showed every now and then.

VIII

From Pesaro, Cesare Borgia marched on Faenza and Brisghella, to topple those cities of the Lamone valley before him. The rains that had delayed the army from Rimini to Pesaro came down in torrents across the Appenines, turning the roads into muddy quagmires, drenching troops and supply trains. Men marched in eternal fogs, buffeted by winds and lashed by a cold autumn rain that stung like hail, seeping into the chinks of vambrace and tasset.

While Cesare Borgia went about the further conquest of the Romagna, two men were meeting in the upper room of a comfortable inn at Forli. The light of a score of candles brightened the chamber against the dark sky and the rain that beat against its leaded windows.

A crystal beaker of *valtellina* reflected the candleglow in ruby tints as one man sat brooding over the great oaken table that filled a quarter of the room. He poured the wine into a blown-glass goblet and lifted it. He shifted in the brocaded chair and turned toward the soldier who watched him from the dark shadows of the hearthpiece.

"You failed me, Captain," he said, smiling grimly. "While I wait here for the Countess del Gallina, with information from Rome, I summoned you to explain it."

. Paola da Rienza turned now from the goblet of wine to a pomade ball, set in pearl-hung wires, that dangled from his wrist. Closing his eyes, he feasted his nostrils on the scented stuff. He went on softly, almost dreamily.

"I find it inexcusable. You disobeyed my orders. You fought with Ilarion *della stalla*. You lay wounded while he went on to Fossate and wenched his way into its *rocca*. You know the result of that!"

The man in the shadows was breathing harshly, his big fists clenched at his sides, his wine hose and cape a rich background for the burnished back-and-breast he wore. His helmet lay on the velvet seat of a curule chair with his sword and baldric.

Captain da Marolla could have broken the back of this fop who sat at his ease, sipping wine watching him with his cold, small eyes above the rim of the golbet. But Paolo da Rienza was a nobleman, and Andrea da Marolla had no desire to be hung alive on hooks for the birds to eat.

And so Captain da Marolla said, "I am sorry, *illustrissimo!* I honestly hoped to spit him on my sword!"

Paolo da Rienza smiled and turned the glass so that the candlelight gleamed red and dull in the *valtellina*.

"You cheated yourself of a small fortune, Andrea." He knew his man, did the fop. He recognized the greed that twisted his insides. This would be the last jab of a spur that would render him docile to his will. As the captain swore softly, Paolo da Rienza almost giggled.

"A fortune in gold florins from the city fathers at Fossate! Gold florins I would have doubled! Imagine it, captain! So much gold that even your muscles might have difficulty in carrying it! Gold that would buy you an olive grove or two, or a farm on a Perugian hillside. Gold that would bring you women and many servants!"

Captain da Marolla groaned. He did not need the softly spoken words of this dandy to point out to him the consequences of his rash act. While he lay under the sheets of the bed at the inn, with the serving maid Caterina to attend him, he had gone over his losses a thousand times. And each time he reflected on them, he added to his torment. With something like fear inside him, he had crawled into his saddle when he could, and chased Borgia's army from Fossate to Rimini, and to Pesaro, and thence to Forli.

Beyond the leaded window above the wall settle, he could see the rain beating in sheets, as it swept with appalling fury across the rooftops. He heard the pounding water slamming on the tiled roof, the gurgle of its passage down a drain. It seemed to wash away everything that life, at one time, had offered Captain da Marolla.

The pomade ball swung slowly, back and forth, with almost hypnotic effect. Paola da Rienza watched it, smiling. "I try to forget, but I find myself reminded of your stupidity. It frightens me, Captain. I say to myself, 'This man has failed me, and will fail me again!'"

"Highness, I will not fail again! My word on it!"

The fop looked up, and now the raw fury that he had kept concealed shone forth clear and strong. "Your word, you ingrate! You hulk of brainless flab! Muscle and skin, that's all you are! Your word—it's meaningless!"

Paolo da Rienza threw himself from his chair in a pet and walked to the window, down which the rain came streaming in wide channels. He watched it, heard the splash and splatter of the drops. In the distance, a vein of lightning ripped the black sky.

"I hate this stableboy! I want his life! But even more than that, I want the things his death may give me! Ah—I surprise you, do I?"

"Yes, Highness. How can one man's death—the death of a stableboy, at that!—gain what you seek, this power you mention? I cannot understand."

Paolo da Rienza struck his forehead with a palm. "*Santa Maria benedetta,* forgive me! I should realize that I speak with a lump of lard. I must use one-syllable words, to convey the meanings his wits are too dull to perceive for themselves! Listen, Captain! Listen well!

"Venice and Florence fear Cesare Borgia! So do Milan and Genoa! He runs like a maddened hound here and there across the Romagna, and where he runs, cities topple! He gains power by the moment! France rides with his bull banner!

"If it were but his army those cities had to contend with, they might unite, if only for the sole purpose of putting this upstart in his grave! But Borgia is blessed with the sight of the devil. He looks at you, and aims at me. He strikes here and there, and he hits where he did not strike!

"He uses men as no other has ever used men! He whips them on with his words, and when he has used them, he casts them aside as I would the parings of an apple!

"Now, he has chosen this Ilarion *della stalla* to be his tool! Pietro Torrigiani paints his portrait for the Duke. Why? Why? That is what I ask myself, until I am sick from the effort to think!"

Captain da Marolla licked his lips. He saw a chance to court favor, and he took it.

"I could take this artist, Pietro Torrigiani, with a couple of men. There is a torture cellar here at Forli. We could hang him on the rack. He would talk."

"You besotted fool! I don't think Torrigiani himself knows what the painting is for. He looks as puzzled as I feel. Nor does the stableboy. They're only tools. Borgia's tools! But there's an answer. I'll guess it yet!"

He went to the rich, oak table and poured more wine into his goblet. He savored it, standing there scowling.

"Borgia is aiming at something, with this picture. Something that will serve him in his sweep across Italy. If I could discover his target and remove it, I'd earn the gratitude of Milan, Florence and Venice. I'd be well rewarded. My family is old and noble. I might win a dukedom myself, if what I discover would lead to Borgia's downfall!

"I must make no mistake! I have sent riders to Rome, with documents for Beatrice del Gallina. She will learn what buzzes in the Borgia bonnet! She is powerful and accomplished at court. A word here, a word there, and she will understand. That is why I hope . . . Listen! A ducat that's her coach below!"

They heard the creak of wheels outside the inn. Paolo da Rienza went to the windows by the settle, and kneeling on the pads, stared out. He saw a coach whose black pan-

99

els were set with the golden crest of the gamecock, and liveried footmen clustered in the rain by its opened door.

A woman in black velvet, with a black lace veil hanging about her head like a shroud, ran on mincing feet for the shelter of the door.

Paolo da Rienza clapped his hands together. "She has come! The *contessa* has learned something! Now, Captain, we shall see the truth of my words!"

She came through the great Gothic door into the room, her taffeta gown rustling to the stride of her legs. The golden hair that clustered thickly under the black lace veil glimmered softly in the candle flames. Her shoulders and the upper slopes of her bosom were rich cream against the black of her taffeta gown. Beatrice del Gallina extended her fingers to Paolo da Rienza. The excitement that surged in her was contagious. He quivered as he kissed her hand, and even Captain da Marolla shifted in the shadows, clenching and unclenching his big hands. She turned to him, her eyes brightening at sight of his thick, strong frame and bulging shoulders. Her lips widened. "Your captain, Paolo? Is he with us on this?"

"If he won't use his own wits, and depends on ours," snapped Paolo, pouring wine.

"I'm sure he will." The *contessa* smiled, and in the shadows of the chimney-piece Da Marolla nodded earnestly.

Beatrice del Gallina sipped the wine, conscious of Paolo da Rienza's eagerness, and the impatience that made him restless. She leaned back and closed her eyes as he bent close, and asked, "You bring word? Of the stableboy?"

The *contessa* turned her thoughts to Ilarion, and to the night she had spent with him in her great bed. La, but the boy had been a revelation to her! There had been a tenderness and a softness in her toward him, that next morning when she waked to find him beside her.

But deeper than her fleshly needs, the countess knew a greed for gold, and the security that such gold could bring her. In that first flush of tenderness, she had warned Ilarion against Paolo da Rienza, counseling him to be on guard. Later, looking back on that morning, she was to realize how her senses had betrayed her mind.

The impassioned letters with which the fop had bombarded her defences taught her that Paolo da Rienza could point out a greater source of gold than the stableboy, even if he should prove to be the spy she hoped. And reluctantly, Beatrice del Gallina gave over certain dreams before this more substantial reality.

And so, with a willingness to sacrifice Ilarion *della stalla* that caused her no concern at her own heartlessness, Beatrice del Gallina used her influence with the men and women of the Borgia court, and what she learned from voices behind cupped hands made her blood run hot.

Gran Diò! What an opportunity this was! Venice and Florence and Milan would open their coffers to her white fingers when she brought them the fruits of what she and the fop had now met to consummate.

As Paolo da Rienza impatiently repeated his question. Beatrice del Gallina laughed softly.

"Through Ilarion and the painting of him done by Torrigiani, Borgia seeks to ally himself with Venice!"

Paolo da Rienza choked and clawed at the lace collar that rimmed the throat of his gold doublet. His face darkened with hot blood.

"With Venice! *Iddio!* If he does that, there'll be no stopping him! Florence will join with Venice, and Milan with Florence, in recognizing him. Behind his bull banner, with their support, he could march from one end of Italy to the other! And as he grows great, so will that slopsboy, Ilarion!"

Beatrice del Gallina smiled at the burly captain who stood in the shadows of the hearth. "That is why it is so imperative that we act!"

"God save me!" shouted Paolo da Rienza. "Will you be supposing that I haven't been acting?"

The *contessa* peeled off the lace gloves that patterned her white hands in a play of light and shadow. Her eyes glistened as she raised them, and her face hardened.

"Perhaps your aim has been misdirected. We can stop Borgia, no matter what his plan, if we kill Ilarion!"

Paolo da Rienza snorted. "I've tried to kill him! Ask the captain about what happened outside Fossate."

Captain da Marolla explained his stupidity, and the manner in which Ilarion had put his blade through his shoulder. When he had concluded, Beatrice del Gallina nodded briskly.

"He isn't an easy target. I've seen him use his blade. But in the heat of battle—if a crossbowman should put a bolt beween his shoulder blades, or between his eyes? You follow me? Now, Paolo that's up to you. You have men you trust? Who'll hold their tongues, kill for gold?"

"I have more than a few such men in my company," said Captain da Marolla.

"The amount I offer is ten florins," purred the countess. "But there must be no mistake this time. We may have but one more chance before Borgia acts. If we fail—"

The *contessa* shrugged. The hot eyes of Paolo da Rienza and the whispered curses of Captain da Marolla assured her that this time they would not fail.

Some days later, Cesare Borgia swung his army in a loose circle around Faenza. Tents went up to form an outer ring of silk and canvas around the inner ring that was the dark wall of the city. Men dug trenches and shallow dugouts to protect them from the cold wind almost as much as from the crossbow bolts and arquebus balls of the Faentini. Trops were dispatched the length and breadth of the Lamone valley, to the Marzano river and beyond, for food and kindling in this land that the Faenzese had stripped almost as clean as a hound's fangs. Overhead the thick, fluffy clouds foretold the coming of winter and its snows.

Falconets and mortars were rolled forward. The mortars were the first pieces to go to work. These squat metal cannon, resembling big cooking pots, rested almost on their backs as they belched their balls high in looping arcs. East of Faenza, Borgia set up his heavier pieces, the Tenerina and the serpentines. Basilisks and sakers added their iron throats to the bombardment. The cannonading soon became a constant thunder that shook the ground, hour after hour.

But Cesare Borgia had subtler weapons than his cannon. He summoned an arbelestier with instructions to tie a parchment around a bolt and shoot it into the castle itself. "In it, I commend their castellan, Castagnini, for his help," he told his captains. "It'll give them treachery to worry about, as well as my cannon balls."

How well Cesare Borgia could judge fortifications was proved some days later. On horseback, he rode with Achille Tiberti around the city, studying its bastions and cressalated ramparts. He dispatched a rider with orders for Vitelli to direct his fire against one section. Early one morning, while Borgia was at breakfast, the sound of shouting men came to him. Tossing his lawn napkin one way and the apple he had been paring another, he ran out to find a horde of foot soldiers racing pell-mell down the grassy slopes toward a great gaping hole in the Faentine wall.

Ilarion was on duty when he heard the shouting. Curious, he ran beyond the line of iron cannon staring toward the city. He saw the crumbling hole in the mighty wall of the *rocca,* and heard the frenzied shouts of the men-at-arms storming forward, crying, "A breach! A breach!" The Duke had given orders. There was to be no storming of the walls. Ilarion drew his sword and ran.

He tried to turn them, using the flat of the blade against their breastpieces, but these were bearded, hardened veterans who had looted Forli and Fossate. They had the smell of loot in their nostrils and the bit of rape between their teeth. They manhandled Ilarion, thrusting him back and to one side, and surged on, down the hill toward the ruin of the wall.

There was blood, hot and salty, at the corner of Ilarion's mouth, as he went after them. "Back there! To your lines or I'll spit you on my point!"

"Gut them!" said a voice at his ear, and then the Duke was in among them, and his rage was terrible. His big white hands, that could bend a horseshoe, were flailing at heads and faces. "Back, you gutter scum! To your posts, or I'll flog you with my own hands!"

His voice was a ringing bell in the October air, but the soldiers were drunk with greed. For an instant, Borgia went back on his heels, and steel flashed over him in the cold sunlight. It was Ilarion who caught him by an armpit, righting him. His blade slid forward and the man-at-arms who had drawn his dagger dropped it with his wrist sliced open to the bone.

Borgia was pale, but his lips were tight. He snatched his own dagger and struck at the faces that were surging past him. "Use your blade, stableboy! Point and edge!"

They fought there in the early morning, side by side on the bloody, dewy grass, until Malvezzi came roaring up with a score of his *condotti* at his heels. The men-at-arms gave way, and their charge was broken.

Borgia drew the sleeve of his apricot velvet doublet across his face. His eyes were black holes of swimming fury. "They'd have been cut down like sheep at the slaughterers if they'd got into that wall. It isn't so much their lives I'm concerned about! But they'd be the first trickle in a flood of men! They could have ruined my entire plan!"

He looked at Ilarion. "We saved my army this morning, stableboy. I won't forget it!"

He paced toward his tent, and Ilarion went back to his post, thoughtful. He had seen another facet of this strange man's character. He would kill his own men to prevent their being killed by an enemy. Ilarion supposed it was the mark of a good general, but there was something in the awful pride of the Duke that was terrifying in its utter contempt for human life. This is a dangerous man, he thought as he paced between the cannons. The thought dawned on him that it was to this man he had pledged himself and his sword. He had been something naïve, those months ago. He had believed what that rich voice said, and what it promised. Now, he was not so sure. If Cesare Borgia could gain anything by sacrificing Ilarion *della stalla*, he would do it. The conception gave birth to a strange, cold fear inside him.

Ilarion went off duty toward noon, and found Pietro Torrigiani sitting in the tent, waiting for him. Torrigiani said, "Come, lad. We'll go for a walk. I've your picture to finish, a few more lines around the mouth and eyes."

Ilarion came and stood at Torrigiani's shoulders, expressing his surprise at sight of the canvas. "I'd forgotten about that," he confessed. "Don't tell me you've carried it around ever since Fossate?"

"Not only that, I've been working on it. Well? *Como ti piace?*" He chuckled as Ilarion grunted, quite impressed.

Ilarion *della stalla* had never seen the angel's head that had been limned for all time in one of Leonardo da Vinci's notebooks. Perhaps Torrigiani had caught something of the master's fine use of line and tone, for the same flare of nostril and arch of eye was there, and his yellow hair seemed to swirl in a driven wind.

They found a little meadow out of sight of the bombards, and Torrigiani posed Ilarion to his liking. He sketched swiftly, strongly, pausing occasionally to peer closer at the set of his lips and the jut of his chin.

"The Duke himself ordered this," he said, after a while. "Why he wants it, I haven't the faintest idea."

His words hung in the chill air. Ilarion, so recently filled with ominous thoughts about the Duke, grew restive. He knew that common gossip credited him with the murder of Alfonso of Bisceglia, who had been Lucrezia Borgia's husband. Alfonso of Bisceglia. The Duke of Gandia. And someday, Ilarion *della stalla?*

He brooded while Pietro Torrigiani sketched on, and his thoughts were grim. He had a sword, but many men owned swords. He used a blade as none but one- eyed old Jacopo Balisandro used one. Perhaps that very factor, that had first drawn the Duke's attention to him, might turn that attention to disfavor. And those who fell out of favor with Cesare Borgia died.

For their return to camp, they chose a cow path that wound in and out of a grove of sycamores, past a little brook, and thence to a high knoll overlooking the city. They paused there to breathe in the late afternoon air, crisp with its hint of approaching winter.

As they were about to turn away, Ilarion cried out hoarsely, "Look, Pietro! *Dio in cielo!* What is it?"

A grotesque form hung in a noose high above the Faenza keep, turning and twisting slowly as the winds played with it. The dark body seemed somehow evil and ominous, hanging there above the ramparts.

"Faenza's castellan," growled Torrigiani. "One of Borgia's tricks, lad! He ordered a crossbow bolt shot over the wall, to land in the street beyond. There was a message on it linking the castellan to the Duke."

"If the man was a traitor—"

The artist snorted gustily. "No more a traitor than you or I! But Castagnini was an important man in Faenza. If Borgia could make the Faenzese suspect treachery, it would make his task simpler. You follow?"

"This Castagnini was not a traitor, then? He was an honest man that the Duke slandered?"

Torrigiani grinned, but his eyes were serious as they regarded the hard lines of Ilarion's face. "A clever trick, eh? One that Nicolo Machiavelli of Florence would appreciate! Your *duca* does not always look where he aims. He uses any method to gain his ends."

Ilarion felt the wind cut through his wool clothing. He gathered its folds tighter around him, shivering.

IX

SNOW FELL ON FAENZA, and on the fields and roads around it, in the latter part of November. From a few drifting flakes, the snow became a raging blizzard that coated the world in white. It buried cannon and tents and hid the rooftops of the city under glittering white blankets. Sentries shivered as the wind hurled eddies of blinding flakes into their numbed faces and between the chinks of their armor. Wet and cold, they tried to warm fingers by hiding them under their padded hacquetons.

The food supply lessened with the rising fury of the storm. Wagons bogged down in the great drifts. Hungry men, chilled and wet, returning from posts of duty, found the campfires empty of food.

From the walls, the Faenzese watched and gloated.

Discovering their advantage, the warm and well-fed city militia came out of their gates in terrible sweeps. Pikes and arrows cut deep gashes in the Borgia lines. Their mounted lances rode at the gallop through ranks of freezing soldiers whose arms were too numb to respond to the orders of brains that realized death thundered down at them from the storm.

Again and again, the Faentine soldiers struck. They hurled wedges of men and steel between outposts. For a few bloody moments there was grim slaughter, and then the Faenzese retreated behind their black stone walls. No man knew from which gate the attack would come next. The uncertainty began to unnerve Borgia's veterans.

The snow continued to fall, often covering the huddled forms of those who had been caught and cut to pieces by the city's pikemen. In a black mood, Cesare Borgia watched the iron discipline of his army begin to rust.

"*Iddio!*" he told the snow. "The Faenzese know my men are hit hard. I'll let them think they plan desertion. Perhaps they'll take the bait!"

And so as keen eyes watched men ride out of tents and away into the blackness, delight came to the people of Faenza. Half of Borgia's army seemed gone. This was their time to strike! Their lances came first, spurring hard, followed by the pikemen and halberdiers. In back of them, protected by standing shields, their crossbowmen sent out flight after flight of screaming bolts.

A blare of trumpets alerted the ducal camp.

Men who had moved away from Faenza in broad daylight, only to return under the sheltering mantle of darkness and falling snow, came running from the tents where they had been hidden.

On the frozen roadways leading out of Faenza to Rimini and Padua, men came marching back under the shouted commands of their officers. Silken coverings were lifted off quivers of long, steel-tipped arrows. Bows were strung under a snowy curtain. A thousand horses waited, unsuspected by the oncoming Faentines, their forest of lances wet with melted snow.

Men ran from the great fires and the warmth of tents and blankets, buckling on armor and snatching up swords and triangular wooden armshields, covered with rawhide.

To the Faenzese, with only the confusion of these camp-fires and tents before them, this was an opportunity to be fully exploited. More horsemen were sent charging across the city's drawbridge. Hundreds of their archers marched with hurried tread through the mushing snow.

Cesare Borgia waited until Faenza was committed.

Then his hand lifted and fell, and a company of arque-busiers swung into a square before the onrushing lances. Their glittering arquebus barrels lifted and steadied. A splash of flame ran to meet the city's militia, and in the flame ran tiny leaden pellets.

The pellets hit the lances and the archers and cut them down, tumbling them into each other.

Swiss crossbowmen trotted forward. They planted themselves in the wet ground, and the *tchik-tchik* of their snapping crossbow strings heralded the tiny quarrels that found holes in Faenzese gorgets and bosses, digging deep. Here and there, armored horsemen spilled from high, curved saddles.

And then these lances were on top of Borgia's crossbow-men, driving them as the wind scattered the snowflakes. But these were veteran soldiers, trained by the finest captains in Europe. In an orderly wedge, the crossbow-men retreated. They filtered backward, splitting into groups, fleeing with precision.

The Faenzese lances hurtled on, the ground trembling to their charge.

Too late, they found themselves faced with a rim of long, knife-bladed berdiches, and ox-tongue pikes. Crouched in the snow, the butts of their weapons ground-ed solidly, Borgia's Swiss mercenaries met the riders.

As Charles the Bold learned at Morat, so the Faenzese learned before the black walls of their city. They cata-pulted in upon that living hedgehog of pikeheads, and they went down. Horses screamed. Men, trapped in a weight of armor that could suffocate them, groaned and shrieked. Pikeheads screeched as they sheared through breastplates and chamfrons.

And now, to back up the *points de Suisse,* Borgia's arbalestiers covered the sky with crossbow bolts that whined and whistled, and dug into eyes and throats, and between the chinks of plate and mail. Horses lay kicking on the ground. Men squirmed helplessly against the quarrels that dropped from the air around them.

Faenza sent its own polearms forward, and Borgia countered with his arquebusiers, that he had held out of the battle for this moment. The matchlocks roared, and their balls went into the massed target of the Faenzese pikemen, where even the poorest marksmen could score a hit. As the arquebusiers reloaded their clumsy weapons and primed them, then lighted the bits of tinder in rope form with which they fired them, Scotch archers with their long yew bows completed the confusion.

A trumpet blared from the woods beyond the camp. A thousand horsemen in fluted armor, whose elbow pieces bore delicate spikes, and whose metal bodies crouched low over barded war horses, came down at the gallop to flank the Faenzese men-at-arms. They tore into their dismayed ranks with the shock of an explosion.

Lanceheads grated on steel breastplates. Wood splintered. Horses drove in among the Faenzese soldiery. War axes and thick, spiked maces swung down on steel caps and helmets. In a few moments, the fields beyond the city were dark with corpses and furious knots of battling men.

The drawbridge shook to the tread of marching reinforcements that hit these lances with the shock of a thunderbolt. Borgia deployed his Swiss pikes against these fresher men, and the tide of the battle swayed.

Faenza had struck hard and suddenly. For a little while, it seemed that they would cut a swath through the camp, and turn it in upon itself. But these were no green troops that wore the bull device on their jerkins. These were men hardened by Forli and Fossate and Brisghella. They reeled and gave ground, but they held just at the instant it seemed the Faenzese would sweep over them.

Achille Tiberti and his lances turned the tide.

They came sweeping down from a slope of ground behind which they had been hidden. They hurtled across the grassy plain, a thousand lances in order, like the teeth of some gigantic comb. The sun flashed from burnished helms and braguettes, from greaves and tonlets. Like a ·metal whip they hit the city militia of Faenza and cut it in two. Men screamed as the thin ash lances drove into them, impaling wriggling bodies. Men went down before the second wave, the thudding hoofs of the heavy war horses trampling over them. Trumpets blared and a sword fell, and a third line of horses swung down on the fleeing militia. Caught between those lances and the long shafts of the Scotch archers, the pikemen went down.

Achille Tiberti turned his lances, and sent them hurtling at the city's archers, crouched behind mantlets, loosing their shafts. The big wooden shields fell. The armored horsemen used their heavy longswords and maces, riding back and forth, bending from the saddle to whip a mace against an exposed face, or to send the edge of a great espadon shearing through mail and plate.

Ilarion fought with them, hot and wet behind his encasing armor. He had learned much since Fossate, at Brisghella and the other cities of the Romagna. He herded his strength, and he peered through the narrow slits of his salade at a world that shifted and changed from one moment to the next. He hacked at arms and shoulders. He drove his heavy horse in upon three archers, cutting two of them down. He gashed blood from a pikeman's mailed arm.

His sword arm lifted and fell until it grew numb. He could not know how the battle was going, for he was locked inside a suit of armor that shut him off from the rest of the world. All he knew was the shock of cutting, the jar of his armor as it took a blade or quarrel.

Ilarion heard the trumpets call with a gratitude that revealed the extent of his tiredness. He sat limp in the saddle, pushing up his visor to gulp in the cold, damp air with heaving lungs. He stared around him. Dead men lay in dark blotches on the mushed and bloody snow. Mounted men were moving past him, grim and somber in dark armor. Blood dripped from swords and maces in their gauntleted hands. He toed his horse forward.

He did not see a crossbowman, his bearded face dark and ugly beneath a steel cap, as he slipped a bolt into the arbalest's rack. Thrusting his foot through the stirrup-like iron to hold it steady, the arbalestier rested the piece on the bloodied ground, and cranked the windlass with both hands.

Ilarion made a splendid target, upright in the saddle, framed against the November sky, with his basinet open. A lock of his yellow hair was caught in the chinpiece and he halted his mount, fumbling at it, to free it.

The crossbowman lifted his arbalest. His hands steadied. Over the curved iron bow, he held Ilarion silhouetted against the clouds.

His finger tightened on the trigger. The cord twanged. A quarrel screamed as it raced across the field.

Had Ilarion been more familiar with the armor he wore, he would have taken that bolt between his eyes. But as he fumbled with the chinpiece to tug his hair loose, his clumsy fingers touched the pivot that held his visor aloft. It clanged shut an instant before the crossbow quarrel hit its curving metal cheek.

The noise deafened and startled Ilarion. The shock of steel on steel rang in his ears with the clarion effect of a bell. It took him a moment to gather his wits, and then, through the narrow eye-slit of his salade, he saw the crossbowman racing away. He drew his sword and plunged spurs into his mount's side. At the gallop he rode the man down, sword uplifted.

At the last moment the man turned, drawing a dagger, and Ilarion saw the bull design worked into the leather jerkin. With his blade, Ilarion sent the dagger flying through the air. And then his sword was turning and its flat length came crashing down on top of the man's steel cap. The man crumpled bonelessly.

Ilarion carried him, slung like a sack of meal across his crupper, and dumped him in front of a fire where Achille Tiberti's lances were peeling out of their armor.

Ilarion told his story to Achille Tiberti. The *condottiero's* scowl was dark, and his slim nostrils quivered as if the treachery he detected was possessed of an ugly smell. "I'll have the truth out of him," he told Ilarion grimly.

With two men-at-arms on either side of the crossbowman, he led them across the fields, away from the tents and past the rows of silent snow-draped cannon, toward the striped magnificence of Cesare Borgia's tent.

The snow drifted past his cheeks in fluffy flakes as Ilarion sat his horse and watched Cesare Borgia move out of his camp along the muddy road to Forli. It was early December, and the drifts were piling up in big mounds. Every road but this was blocked by Vitellozo Vitelli's cannon and grizzled men-at-arms. Along this road three thousand foot soldiers and lances moved steadily southward.

The hunger that had been an ache in the army encamped outside the black walls of Faenza was now acutely painful. The countryside that had fed the thousands of pikemen and archers, men-at-arms and lances, had been stripped by foragers. While the snow continued in a steady blizzard, there was no food to be found in arbors and vineyards, or stored away in earthen cellars.

And so Cesare Borgia lifted his siege.

He withdrew to Forli with an escort of one hundred and twenty-five lances and close to three thousand foot soldiers. The troops he left behind formed a ring of steel around the beleaguered city, for although he had lifted his siege, Borgia was undertaking a gigantic blockade to starve the city into submission by the time the spring rains allowed him to move his army.

His final act at Faenza was to invest Ilarion *della stalla* with the rank of captain of lances, entitling him to an annual stipend as long as he served under Borgia's red bull banner.

Ilarion was conscious of a sense of great relief as he watched the brown legs of the horses stepping through the snowy curtain. As whiteness rimmed helmets and gorgets to give the effect of enamel inlay on the steel armor, he thought, I'm free of him! The gloom that had encompassed his days here at Faenza was rising as a mist lifts off the Pontine Marshes at the first coming of the sun. For he had seen too much and too closely how Cesare Borgia went about his warfare. A man as intimately associated with him as was Ilarion, a man to whom Borgia gave his secrets and called him *confidente,* walked daily in the shadow of the assassin's dagger. He was aware that he brooded overmuch, but he was no longer the naïve boy who had stood in Jacopo Balisandro's fencing hall and been talked into thrusting his head in a noose by stealing an oil painting from under the noses of a dozen officers of Cesare Borgia's personal guard!

Army life matures a man. It matured Ilarion. He threw himself now into the blockade by which Borgia closed the gates of Faenza. He took daily counsel with the sullen, hollow-cheeked Vitelli. He rode miles on galloping horses, to check sentries and outpost groups of men-at-arms. When wagons came trundling through the snowy darkness, he was there to meet them with a dozen riders, to turn them toward the blockade campfires.

Later Ilarion was to realize that at this period of his life he felt guilt, and this dervish-like activity was an expression of atonement. As Pietro Torrigiani had pointed out, he was advancing too fast. A captain of horse already, and he not a whole year in the army! He tried, with any means in his power, to justify that advancement.

As he galloped through the December days from outpost to artillery crew, along roads thick with flurrying snow, and under the bare brown branches of dead trees, he would reach in under his leather jazerant and touch a red silk scarf. That scarf had been given him by Giula *la rosso,* and it was with her face before him that he rode on, day after day, like a possessed man.

News of Cesare Borgia filtered to his ears from cloaked riders who flung themselves from saddles to gulp down wine from bladder skins. From Forli, Borgia had moved on with his horse and footmen to Cesena, there to take up winter quarters. He had celebrated Christmas Day at Mass in the Church of San Giovanni Evangelista. He worked on into the early hours of every morning, did the Duke, on the schemes designed to win him all Italy.

Ilarion was dining with a captain of artillery on a raw January day when one of these riders came striding through the snow to him, extending a letter from Cesare Borgia. Ilarion read it with thudding heart.

The snow fell silently in little white puffballs, and the wind howled more strongly as Ilarion lifted his eyes from the parchment. Borgia was going to use him and his blade, and for that reason summoned Ilarion to Cesena without delay! One more task for the Borgia blade! One more task whose fulfillment would give Ilarion further knowledge of Cesare Borgia's secrets!

Ilarion felt a frantic urge to mount and ride into Abruzzi, and thence south to Otranto and a carrack that would carry him across the seas and out of the life of this man. But a sense of duty was too strongly instilled in his blood. He turned and moved through the snow toward the tent of Vitellozo Vitelli, to make his farewells.

His meeting with Cesare Borgia was brief. He found him ensconced behind a mountain of letters and documents, writing furiously. In the pale winter light that filtered through a window of the Palazzo Malatesta, Galeazzo Gonzaga stood with hands clasped behind his back, staring gloomily out at the streets of Cesena.

At Ilarion's entrance, the Duke looked up, and a smile came to his pale face, transforming it. He came around the edge of his desk, and Ilarion was quick to sense the change in him. His eyes were softer, almost respectful, as his hand caught Ilarion by the shoulder.

"Captain Ilarion! Vitelli has written of you in his dispatches. You've made yourself into a fine soldier. A fine soldier, of which any family in Italy might well be proud! But since you own none, I regard myself, along with St. Julian, the patron saint of taverns, inns, and stables, as your protector!"

Galeazzo Gonzaga came striding to grasp his hand and inquire of the blockade of Faenza. There was delicate red *braccheto* wine in crystal goblets, with fruit and sweetmeats, to idle away their gossip.

It was Borgia, with a glance at the work that remained on his desk, who broke off their conversation. He said, "Gonzaga rides to Rome, carrying an important painting. I've news that there are some who'd like to lay hands on that painting. Or, failing that, to kill you."

Borgia stared at him soberly. "You are a very valuable man, Messer Ilarion. Worth an army to me, if not more. I want nothing to happen to Gonzaga or to you, on this journey. Make haste. Avoid trouble. If trouble comes, attend to it swiftly. Then move on with all speed to Rome. There, you will put yourself into the hands of Galeazzo Gonzaga. As he commands, you act."

There was that in Cesare Borgia's manner that forestalled the protests that bubbled in Ilarion's throat. He had been advancing rapidly at Faenza, learning the trade of war. To be ripped from his post of command to ride with a man to Rome was a stupid waste. Borgia could have ordered a hundred of his men into their saddles for a powerful escort.

Ilarion opened his mouth to argue, but Galeazzo Gonzaga caught him by the elbow and swung him toward the enameled doorway. They bowed out, and whatever chance Ilarion had owned of securing Borgia's change of mind was gone.

X

THEY RODE THROUGH the swirling snow, wrapped in great woolen cloaks, the beat of their horses' hoofs thudding in the cold air. From Forli to Urbino was a distance of forty miles, and beyond Urbino to Rome itself, was another hundred and twenty. There were miles of frozen roads, for it was late January, and the trees were rimmed with frost, and great dangling icicles made the flanking woods a place of fairy carvings.

They pounded through Gubbio and down into twisting valleys dotted with the thatch-roofed huts of shepherds and farmers. It was a gray day, and great cloud-puffs scudded across the leaden sky. Ilarion was silent, his mind alive with the premonitions that rode him like witches on their way to the *Sabbat.* Glumly, he reflected that the worst of it was that he had no idea why he rode here, like a demon on a hell mission. That he had been selected to protect Galeazzo Gonzaga was a sophistry. Borgia wanted Ilarion *della stalla* in Rome. That was why he rode, but the answer to the greater question, the reason behind his haste, went unanswered.

"We'll be beyond Assisi soon," Gonzaga called from the depths of his chlamys. "We can pause there to eat. I'm as empty as a wallet of a Brother of St. Francis!"

Lanterns gleamed ahead in the darkness that swept from the Adriatic to blanket the Romagna. At the crest of the road that ran through Umbria to Narni they saw them, little globules of light in the approaching night.

They reined in at the inn, whose bulk was alive with yellow brightness, their horses throwing their heads and nickering, sensing the bags of oats that would be waiting in the stables. A door opened and a groom in leather apron and stained shirt came running. Ilarion discovered a ravening hunger in his middle, and his mouth grew moist at the warm smells of roasting pig and freshly baked bread that came through the wide doorway.

Gonzaga held the leather cylinder that contained the painting as he shoved through the doorway, pausing with the snow on his back to survey the big common-room that was lighted by a score of tallow twists thrust into iron candlestands. Three long wooden tables stretched from beyond the door to a great hearth and brick chimney, where iron spits and cooking pots stood black against the red-flamed interior. It was a large fireplace, where a man could stand erect. A bed of coals threw heat and a red glow into the room itself. The room was empty, save for a blowzy barmaid who sat on a joint stool, nodding sleepily.

Gonzaga grunted his satisfaction, and caught the big

114

woolen cloak as it slid from him. He tossed it on a bench and went to stand before the hearth, warming his hands. The leather cylinder he placed carefully at his feet, some little distance from the flat red hearthstones.

Ilarion came and watched a suckling pig that turned slowly above the coals. It was a compliment to his youth that he thought first of the hunger in him, rather than the danger that threatened his life. "Bring the whole thing to the table," he told the maid. "With a head of cheese, and a dozen fresh loaves. And two bottles of *barbera*."

They were halfway through the pig, and were attacking the round of cheese when they heard the clank of spurs and the sharp clang of a sword-pommel striking a back-and-breast. A dozen horses thundered into the yard. As the groom ran out, they could see men-at-arms dismounting in the light from the door.

The soldiers swarmed into the commonroom, hardened mercenaries with the bronze of the sun on their faces. They were a swaggering lot, throwing back their cloaks, stamping their boots, glaring curiously at the two men who ate so silently in one corner of the room.

"They wear no insignia," muttered Gonzaga, hunching forward. "They might be Borgia's men, or ordinary cutthroats who prey on travelers once the sun sets."

Ilarion tapped his hand on the hilt of his sword as it lay resting between his thighs, its tip to the rush floor. "*Basta la spada!* They won't bother us."

And then a big man with a black beard blustered his way through the curtain of snowflakes outside the door and paused there. Ilarion got to his feet, aware that Gonzaga was beside him, exclaiming in alarm, with fright for the unexpected. "Do you know him?"

"The last time I saw him, I put a swordpoint through his shoulder and left him in an inn some miles below Fossate. That's Captain da Marolla, who serves Paolo da Rienza. *Basta la spada*, I said. Well, mayhap the sword won't be enough!"

Captain da Marolla glowered for a moment, then pushed between some of his men to a table. He pounded on it with the earlobe-shaped pommel of an Oriental dagger, bellowing for food. The captain studiously refrained from glancing again at the two men at the far end of the first table.

"Now that is strange," muttered Ilarion, finding in himself no appetite and pushing the food away. "With so many men at his back, it would seem a good chance to renew a quarrel."

Gonzaga smiled. Knowing nothing of what had transpired between these two, he was lulled into a sense of security by the action of Andrea da Marolla. He put his hand restrainingly on the arm of his companion.

"Easy, Ilarion. *Peste!* I didn't know you were such a gamecock! Don't provoke a quarrel here, *per Dio!*"

But Ilarion would not be persuaded. He shook away the hand, and sat with his eyes fixed on the bearded face beneath the wide-brimmed chapels-de-fer that the captain wore. "I pick no quarrel. Paolo da Rienza paid him gold to betray me to the city fathers of Fossate. Me, and Pietro Torrigiani. He'd have succeeded too, except that the fellow fancied he could save himself the bother by crossing blades with me."

That brought Galeazzo Gonzaga awake to danger. His nostrils flared, and his eyes gleamed. "He'll have followed us to Rome, to slay us both! *Dio mio!* What's the matter with my wits, that I didn't perceive it myself? To slay you, and me, and take the canvas! Come, we'll go."

But Ilarion was in no mood to turn tail and flee. A stubbornness was dawning in him that locked his lips and put a hard gleam to his blue eyes. He was no stableboy now, to run when a man snapped his fingers, or stand when a word halted him. He was taller, and leaner, and the width of his shoulders under the ornate green jazerant revealed the swell of splendidly toned muscles.

He discovered a devil sitting inside him. For weeks he had fought the phantoms of his imagination. He had worried and puzzled over the ghost of Cesare Borgia's whims, had been a target for a brossbow bolt from a man who fought on his own side, had been chafed by doubts and fears as to the final disposition of the painting that Galeazzo Gonzaga carried. There had been nothing to fight, no target on which to vent the pent-up furies that had grown within him. He had a target now, this captain who sat big and bulky in his gleaming breast-and-back, wolfing the food before him.

Ilarion smiled, and the flat hardness of his lips made Gonzaga shudder. Ilarion said softly, "We'll take our time. We won't run like a hare at the first howl of the wolf. Ho, the maid! More *barbera!*"

Gonzaga leaned closer, and hissed, "Have you lost your wits? We ride on a mission of gravest importance! To dally now to satisfy a personal vengeance is madness!"

"Use your own wits, Messer Gonzaga! Is it chance that sends Captain da Marolla here? The arbalestier that Borgia racked said that Da Marolla paid him to kill me! Borgia sent out men to find Da Marolla, but they could not. He was in hiding. Now he appears with us in a tavern a dozen miles below Assisi. Is that by chance? Is it chance that a hunted man rides the roads of the Romagna with a dozen men-at-arms at his back?"

"*Madre di Dio!*" moaned Gonzaga, shrinking inside his fur-lined tunic of patterned red-and-white stripes. Nervously he clasped and unclasped his hands. "An assassination attempt! But why do they delay? Is it because this captain toys with us as a cat with a mouse?"

Ilarion shrugged. "He failed once. I'll risk a florin he only seeks an opportunity to guarantee him success."

Gonzaga slapped the table with a palm. "I'll test your theory, devil take me!" He stood up and with the leather cylinder in his hand, reached for his cloak. Captain da Marolla stood up too, lifting a drinking can in his hand. "Ho, the two travelers! I bid you drink with us, as befits strangers met on a road at night. Come, sit by my hand, here. Make way for them!"

Galeazzo Gonzaga bowed his head. "Our thanks, but we ride at once."

If there was anything to betray, Captain da Marolla betrayed it by the sudden fury that twisted his dark face. "*Iddio!* I give an invitation, and it's refused. I've been insulted!" And in one move, he hurled his goblet at the crimson-clad figure of Galeazzo Gonzaga. The winecup hit his chest and splashed his collar and throat.

For many minutes, Captain da Marolla had sat here, pondering ways and means of killing these two men. Whether to let them ride out and overtake them on the frozen road, there to cut them down by sheer numbers, or to risk it all here, disturbed his thoughts. Once on the road, they might outrun him, for he had seen with his own eyes the sleek, fast horses they rode. In here, in the bright light, with a dozen blades at his back, there was no place to run.

And so, Captain da Marolla made his choice. Now he dragged out his sword and bellowed to his men, "Two of you against the door. You others, with me!"

They came in a hedge of steel blades, throwing aside benches in their eagerness. Galeazzo Gonzaga tossed the leather cylinder behind him so that it rolled into a corner at the feet of a chestnut credenza. His blade whipped out, and he twisted his long cloak about his left forearm to form a shield.

In their eagerness, the foremost men forgot Ilarion, and Captain da Marolla lost sight of him in the press of bodies. Ilarion stood up and he whipped his own cloak outward in a flailing lash of wet wool that wrapped itself across the throats and faces of three men-at-arms. With blinding speed, his blade followed the cloak. He drove it through wool and into flesh, turned, and repeated his maneuver. Before the third man could claw the muffling wool from his eyes, the point of Ilarion's blade opened his throat.

Three men were down, and two were guarding the door. The dozen had almost been halved.

Ilarion moved as the others paused in shock at this swirl of fortune. His blade whipped out and a man screamed, clawed at his belly where Ilarion's blade had driven in under the ridged rim of his breastpiece. He caught the edge of the table and heaved it, food and beakers of wine and drinking cans. There was no gripping body-armor now to slow and betray the agility of the swordsman. He was a wind that whipped in with cold steel, and where he passed, a man gurgled thickly, clutching a torn throat and sinking to the rush-strewn floor.

Gonzaga found himself with a boot almost ankle deep in the red coals of the hearth, fighting two blades at once. Captain da Marolla, with the remainder of his men, came for Ilarion. With blade and dagger he parried their thrusts, moving slowly to one side, in a crablike movement of his legs that gave Da Marolla sudden concern.

"*Diavolo!* Watch the by-blow! He's as full of tricks as a street is of stones!"

His warning came too late. With a sweep of his blade, Ilarion caught a pair of standing floor candlestands and sent them sidewise, falling against the knees and ankles of the men who pressed him. One man dropped, and his helmet crashed to the floor. This was no time for niceties, with Captain da Marolla and his bravos tumbling and sliding in their eagerness to kill him, so Ilarion put the point of his blade into the neck of the fallen bravo.

Now there were only four men looking across their blades at him. By the hearthstone, Gonzaga was flailing wildly, tired, his swordarm numb and helpless. In a minute he himself would go down. The candlestands that had fallen gave their lighted tallows to the dry rushes on the floor, and red flames commenced licking upward. The *oste* was screaming from the kitchen doorway, alternating curses and maledictions with orders to the maids and cooks to run for water.

Ilarion found himself held in check by the swords of Captain da Marolla and his three bravos. He heard Galeazzo Gonzaga cry out sharply against pain, and from the corner of his eye he saw his body crumple to the stones that fronted the fireplace. A cutthroat paused to lift his blade and administer the final thrust, but Captain da Marolla's voice halted his downward stroke. "Never mind that one! We can finish him off at ease! This is the devil who needs attention!"

The flames themselves became Ilarion's allies. They licked up, red and bright, eating the rushes with hungry tongues, leaving little space in which to fight. The *oste* and his maids were running with wooden buckets of slop-water, throwing this across the floor, and the rising steam blinded the men-at-arms in their desperate charges.

Ilarion ran nimbly, skipping from one charred spot to another. His blade was insurance that these killers, hardened though they were, were not overanxious to run into it when their eyes were tearing from the sharp bite of smoke and steam. He slid sideways until he found the unmarked stones of the chimney hearth underfoot. With his back against the heat of its coals, he made his stand.

Captain da Marolla brought the remaining men to him into a tight little knot. "Let mine *oste* complete his fire-fighting. Then, when the room is free of smoke and steam, we'll finish the job!"

In a short while they were done, and Captain da Marolla threw his men in a fence of steel blades at Ilarion. There was no space for fancy work, no time for the *botta in tempo* or the *incontro*. It was thrust and parry, parry and bind. Steel clanged loud in the room, and here and there, blood began pinking the green surface of Ilarion's steel-lined jazerant.

And then one man who faced him screamed and pitched backward. A second fell to his knees. A third collapsed sideways on Captain da Marolla.

"The devil's come to aid me," gasped Ilarion.

He heard a laugh. Galeazzo Gonzaga crouched at his feet, a bloody dagger in his fist, grinning. He had stabbed the three in their upper thighs, between boot-tops and doublets, where they wore no armor! Now, he said, "The fools left me for dead when I only caught their blade in my cloak and screamed! And *grazia a cielo!*—the captain's call kept them from applying the death-thrust!"

Ilarion chuckled, and looked across the fallen bodies of the men-at-arms at Captain da Marolla. He said softly, "It remains between you and me." His blade lifted.

Galeazzo Gonzaga tossed his dagger high, and caught it. "I'll watch the men who are down. If they so much as stir a finger to stop you from killing this vulture, I'll spit them as our *oste* does his pigs!"

Captain da Marolla could read his fate in the hard blue eyes of this yellow-haired devil who was lifting his blade. There was as much mercy to be found in the sapphires which they resembled.

"Once I let you live, Captain," said Ilarion softly. "Only by the grace of *il gran Dio* and my own clumsiness am I alive now. The man you paid to put a crossbow bolt between my eyes almost succeeded! I'll not make that mistake again!"

"Not I!" panted Da Marolla. "It was not I. It was Paolo da Rienza who paid him, through me, to do it!"

"Who pays for this killing?" cried Galeazzo Gonzaga from a tabletop, where his dark eyes roved the floor for signs of stirring life.

"Paolo da Rienza," sobbed the captain.

Ilarion drew back and lowered his point. The captain gulped deep draughts of smoky air into his lungs. His eyes burned with the sweat that runneled his cheeks.

"Can you prove that? If I let you live, would you come with me and tell someone with your own lips what you have told me here?"

He was eager, was Captain da Marolla. He babbled by the saints above, and by the love *il gran Dio* had for all mankind, that he would do anything Ilarion wanted. He was too eager, but Ilarion was not alive to subtleties. He was thinking of Giula *la rosso,* and debating with himself that if he could confront her with Captain da Marolla, he might open her eyes to what manner of man her brother had proven himself.

And so Ilarion, not reckoning with that over-eagerness, turned to look at Galeazzo Gonzaga. Gonzaga was shouting, erupting off the bench. His right hand lifted and the dagger he had held went sailing through the air.

Ilarion whirled. Captain da Marolla stood with bent legs, his face twisted in pain and astonishment above the ornate silver hilt that protruded from his throat. He sagged, collapsing in a heap on the blackened floor.

"He'd have spitted your back with his blade," said Gonzaga calmly. "He was leaping at you with his sword up, when my dagger took him. Let it teach you caution when you deal with greedyguts like Da Marolla. He'd sell his mother for gold."

"I'd hoped to bring him to Rome with me, to face Giula da Rienza. He would have revealed how her brother plays at death with me."

Gonzaga chuckled softly. In a melee, he was no Colleoni, this dark little man, but when it came to an interplay of wits and words, he acknowledged no superior. He counseled now, "A foolish move. Her brother could claim you bribed Da Marolla. Here, let's see for ourselves."

With expert fingers, Gonzaga went over the limp form of the dead captain. He brought out a purple velvet purse that was ornamented with the crest of a golden gamecock. Ilarion had seen that crest before.

The golden gamecock was the heraldic insignia of Countess Beatrice del Gallina.

Morning sunlight formed a dappled pattern across the green-and-silver hose and doublet laid out on the big walnut bed. It splashed a pool of brilliance on the tiled floor of the bedchamber, where an Oriental rug, a rare luxury for this last year of the cinquecento, was spread to cushion the feet from cold tile. Ilarion lay under the coverlets, feeling the sunlight grow stronger across his face.

The moon had been high in the sky last evening when he and Galeazzo Gonzaga had clattered along the Via Flaminia and over the Ponte Milvio. They slowed their breakneck speed to splash through puddles in the great square below the bridge, and a mile beyond, reined in before the *palazzo* Gonzaga, a mansion of rose marble and terra cotta whose façade was set with tiny balconies entablatured in stone carvings.

Gonzaga had been exhausted from the ride, and from the fight with Captain da Marolla's cutthroats in the inn at Assisi. He had turned deaf ears to the questions that Ilarion had thrown at him, for Ilarion had galloped the eighty miles from Assisi to Rome in a welter of sick fury. For the third time he had been the target of Paolo da

Rienza. Now that he was also the target for Beatrice del Gallina, he found himself rebelling against a fate that was marking him for a coffin.

"Why is that painting so valuable? Why am I riding to Rome? What purpose of Cesare Borgia am I serving by leaving Faenza and coming here? What profit can the countess make from my death?"

These and other questions he hurled at Galeazzo Gonzaga as they pounded past Narni, toward the Tiber. Always Gonzaga pleaded haste, and when they were on the tiled floors of the *palazzo* Gonzaga, he pleaded weariness.

It was morning now. Galeazzo Gonzaga had slept a dozen hours. He would give Ilarion *della stalla* the answers today, or Ilarion would climb back into the saddle and ride for Faenza. Thus far, he told himself, he had followed Cesare Borgia with the blind obedience of a sheep. That blindness was at an end. He must know the answers to the uncertainty that showed itself in the nightmares that had plagued his sleep. With this in mind, he clad himself in the silver-and-green doublet and hose with which Galeazzo Gonzaga had provided him, and sought the nobleman at breakfast.

Gonzaga was contrite. "But certainly, Captain! The Duke assured me I was to provide you with answers to any questions you might make!"

"Why am I here, then? What is the purpose of that painting Pietro Torrigiani did of me? Why am I so important to Cesare Borgia? I'm only a stableboy, but he treats me as if I held the secret of his success in Italy in my palm! What's behind it all?"

Gonzaga laughed. The lines of tiredness were gone from his somber face, and his beard was newly clipped and curled. His black eyes were almost merry. He laid down the napkin with which he wiped his lips after each morsel of fruit and meat.

"*Macchi!* As many questions as a student might ask of Da Vinci himself! Well, I'll undertake to answer them. But in my own way!

"First, then, it is known that Venice and Florence and Milan are arming against the Duke. If those three powers throw their militias into the field, Borgia will find himself with his hands full! He must walk on eggshells daily, must our Cesare! One misstep, one display of too much strength, and the little game of teeter-totter that Venice and Florence play will be ended. The lion and the lily will be in arms against the red bull! So much for the groundwork! We come now to your part in this plan that Borgia has evolved to put himself in the driver's seat!"

Footfalls sounded in the antechamber, and Galeazzo Gonzaga motioned Ilarion to silence. A servant approached, bowing as he handed over a letter. Gonzaga broke the seals and spread out the parchment. His eyes lighted suddenly, and he smiled as he looked up.

"An invitation from Leonardo da Vinci, to visit him in his studios. Saints save us! He seems to know you!"

Ilarion told him of the afternoon those months ago when he rode from Rome, and of the *duello* in which he had saved Pietro Torrigiani and Leonardo da Vinci from the blades of the highwaymen. Gonzaga listened attentively, his eyes sparkling. If there was anything he loved above all else but slyness and a clever scheme, it was a tale of adventure. He was profuse in his compliments.

Ilarion flourished a hand. "Now I'm wondering how he knew I was in Rome!"

Gonzaga spread his palms. "Have you forgotten that Cesare Borgia is in almost daily consultation with him? Da Vinci joins the bull banner in the spring. The Duke counts on his help to reduce Faenza! What's more natural but that he should inform the master that the man who saved his life is within walking distance! And speaking of walking, let's to it! I've never met him. I'll explain those other matters later. We mustn't keep him waiting."

The Florentine was quartered in a great chamber whose white walls and timbered ceiling gave his studio almost the appearance of a monastery. But the men and women in rich robes and masks, moving here and there to assay the canvases and models, dispelled that illusion. High overhead, wide triforium were open to filter the room with fresh air and sunlight.

Da Vinci came striding from the throng at sight of Ilarion. As always, he was dressed in the latest mode, in a paned doublet and upper stocks, fitted with checkered hose. His lean, aquiline face was almost radiant in his pleasure.

"Ilarion, *salvatore mio!* It is good to see you again. Tell me, how is Pietro? As incorrigible as ever? Does he still have an eye for a well-rounded ankle?"

Ilarion laughed. "He's fine. Well-quartered at Forli, among the troops that attend Il Valentinois. As hungry and as clear of sight as ever."

The tall artist caught Ilarion by an arm and drew him away from the men and women who had turned to stare at this display of cordiality in the man they thought so arrogant. And where Ilarion went, there went Galeazzo Gonzaga, delighted to bask in this sudden popularity.

"You remember I made you a promise, there at Nepi," Da Vinci was saying. "I told you I'd fashion you a sword —the finest sword ever made! Eh? You remember?"

Ilarion's heart thudded excitedly in its rib cage. A sword from Da Vinci was better than a hundred florins! He nodded, eyes bright. "I remember, *eccellenza!*"

"Good! Come with me. And you, sir—his friend—come you, too."

Da Vinci led them into an adjoining room, one corner of which was filled by a great bronze fireplace and forge. Metal was nailed in sheets to the floor, and on this sheeting two men in leather aprons worked with bellows and hammers at a vast iron anvil. The red flames in the maw of the hearth gave the room a hellish glow. Casques and metal gauntlets, sabbatons and breastplates lay in an idle litter on the floor. Here Da Vinci wrought miracles of beauty in metal for those *condottieri* and noblemen wealthy enough to pay for his decorations.

From a rack set flush with the wall, the artist drew out a length of worn black velvet. Carefully he unwound it, peeling back the cloth.

The sword lay in a scabbard of steel enriched with red velvet, tiny silver horseheads being set in a row down both sides. The hilt was a length of tooled leather, below which a basketwork of interwoven metal bands rose from the *pas-d'âne* in a knucklebow that curved in toward the silver pommel. Long *quillons* jutted outward from either side of the hilt to guard the hand against a slash.

Ilarion caught his breath, and Da Vinci, who had been watching his reaction, chuckled in delight. "The blade, now, Ilarion. You said that was the most important part of the sword, and you're right! It's of Toledo steel, blued and shaped under my very eyes."

He drew out the steel, and it glittered with an azure sheen in the light. A tracery of horseheads was etched below the side-rings, and from these the blade swept slim and straight to its point.

Ilarion's fingers itched, and suspecting this, Da Vinci surrendered the sword to him. It glittered as he moved it. He bent its blade to a bow and released it, the sharp, high *spaang* of the liberated steel sounding like an angel's voice to his swordsman's ears.

He tried to stammer thanks, but his voice shook. He put a hand to the artist's forearm and squeezed.

"The pressure of your fingers is worth a thousand words," Da Vinci told him, moved by Ilarion's appreciation. "I've done a thousand swords in Florence, but none like this. I've slimmed the blade and lengthened it slightly. In your hands, it will be a weapon of attack and defense at one and the same time."

Though Ilarion was speechless, no such affliction bothered Galeazzo Gonzaga. He spouted a torrent of rhetoric, and nothing would do but that he take it out into the great chamber beyond the forgeroom and display it to the men and women who came crowding about. Seeing their enjoyment, Gonzaga enlarged it by relating the story of Ilarion's rescue of the master. Ilarion found himself the circle of admiring voices and bright eyes.

"Young man! Young man, attend to me!"

A lace fan tapped his knuckles, and Ilarion was confronted by a dark-eyed woman in a square-bodiced gown of heavy blue damask, hung so perilously close to the round of her bared shoulders by the split sleeves.

It was Galeazzo Gonzaga who recognized her, thrusting forward and bowing. The woman turned imperiously.

"Galeazzo, tell your friend I'm Elisabetta Colonna. I'm giving a ball tonight for the court. Bring him, with his sword. He will cause a stir."

"We will be there, *illustrissima!*"

Her dark eyes regarded Ilarion. "I've heard something of you from Giula da Rienza. Ha, you start, do you?" A little smile curved her pouting mouth. "She will be there. As will the Countess del Gallina. I think the evening should prove extremely interesting."

A ripple of laughter went through the room. Encouraged, Elisabetta Colonna touched Ilarion's chin with the tip of her fan. Her dark eyes were mocking.

"I'm going to make bets on the red or the gold! *La rosso* or the *contessa!* Which shall win you? Here, give me your palm."

Elisabetta Colonna fancied herself a soothsayer. Like many women of high birth, she dabbled in the occult, and in imagined magic. It was a time when alchemists sought to transform base metals into gold, when tiny candles were burned to honor *Dianom,* and sorcerers and wizards maintained shops to sell anything from poison to a love philter.

The Colonna finger traced a path along Ilarion's palm. Her smooth brows wrinkled a moment, and she pursed her lips. Her dark eyes widened; she stared at him.

"I see death! Death threatens from Beatrice del Gallina! Death threatens from Giula da Rienza! Whether you win the red or the gold, you are in danger of your life! May *il gran Dio* pity you, messer!"

XI

THE WORDS OF ELISABETTA COLONNA still rang warningly in Ilarion's ears as he stared out at the swirls of reds and ambers, greens and purples that mixed on the wide, tiled floor of the *palazzo* Colonna. There were gowns and tight cotehardies that left the shoulders and upper swells of women's bosoms bare, doublets and gipons that were ornate with gold thread and jewels as men vied for attention. Voices murmured, and here and there someone laughed. Candles stood everywhere, great towering tallow twists that gilded the air with brightness.

This afternoon Ilarion had smiled and tapped the new sword that Leonardo da Vinci had forged for him, as he faced the Colonna princess. A soldier faced death every day. It was his occupational hazard, he reminded her. But Elisabetta Colonna had whispered of other prophecies she made that had come true, and left him in a disturbed mood.

He had donned his black doublet and hose, and swung a fur-trimmed cloak about his wide shoulders in a feeling of bravado. His sword had brought him this far, from a stable bed and slops to a captain's rank and fame. He would trust it to see him through the treacheries that Elisabetta Colonna foretold.

So now he swaggered his blackness amid the whirlpool of colors that paraded across the Colonna floor, and used his eyes to single out a woman with red hair and green eyes, his Giula *la rosso*.

Instead, he came face to face with Beatrice del Gallina.

"*Il garzone della stalla,*" she cried. Her white fingers reached warmly to his, and then she was drawing him with her, away from the throng, under the groined stone

126

ceiling of the loggia, where scores of iron fireboxes had been laid against the cold.

"We shall be by ourselves out here, stableboy! Tell me everything that's happened since you left Rome! *Iddio!* I've heard tales of your doings. Something about Leonardo da Vinci, and a little of a drunken sot who helped you free Galeazzo Gonzaga! Tell me everything!"

She was alluring in damask and blue satin, and perfume lay in the thick mass of yellow hair that tumbled in a pearl snood to her shoulders. Those creamy shoulders were well displayed in the modish cut of her bodice. An aura of sensuality hovered over her, dancing across the red bow of her smiling mouth, shining from her eyes.

Ilarion freed a hand and fumbled at his girdle of silver plates. He lifted out a crumpled purple velvet purse, with its golden gamecock crest, that had never left his person since the ride from the inn at Assisi.

"Here's evidence of my latest fling," he told her. "Captain da Marolla had it on him when he took a dagger through his throat."

Her eyes were wide, staring down at her embroidered crest. She looked into his cold eyes and protested, in her throaty voice. "Ilarion, no! You think I— Oh, *santa in cielo!*"

"It wasn't the captain alone. He had a dozen men-at-arms with him. They cornered Galeazzo Gonzaga and myself at an inn near Assisi. It was quite a fight while it lasted. I wanted to bring Captain da Marolla to Rome with me, but he was built of the same clay as yourself. When my back was turned, he tried to knife me!"

"*Caro mio!* You insult me! Treachery and knifings in the back! Is it with that talk you show your gratitude? To me, who introduced you to Il Valentinois?"

She was a consummate actress, this *contessa*. She put hurt pride into the blue of her wide eyes, and injury in the manner of her shoulders' shrug. Her warm fingers pleaded with their grip on his hand. She moved a little nearer, that she might assault his senses in the same manner that she attacked his emotions. Her ample flesh lifted and fell against the damask that fitted her roundness like a second skin. She stood close to him.

"*Ebbene?* Don't you remember that morning I woke you out of your dreams? Have you forgotten what things I taught you? A florin to a marchetto you've held me in your dreams as I showed you ways to hold me!"

Under his breath, Ilarion cursed his memory, and the body that would not forget. This blonde witch could stir him as a ladle stirred a stew. He moved back a step, but she came after him, a devil's laughter bubbling on her wide red mouth.

"You do remember! As I remember you, *confetti mio!*"

"Madonna, I'm no stableboy, now. You saved me, then. I thought you were something out of a man's ideals! I did not know then that you'd pay a man to kill me because it suited your fancy, or your purse."

Beatrice del Gallina laughed softly. "We grow great, because we wear a captain's spurs! But it isn't so long ago that you sobbed in pleasure under my caresses. Not half a year. Suppose I were to tell your redhead the words you spoke when—"

She drew back at the anger in his face, then crowded in nearer than before, pushing him against a low balustrade of marble columns. Her soft palms cupped his face.

"There is no need for anger, Ilarion! Not with me! Listen! I bribed no man to kill you. That you found my purse was a whim of fate. I visited Paolo da Rienza at Forli. I left my purse behind me. If he gave it to Captain da Marolla, why should you suspect me?"

There was enough fervor in her words to give him pause. She was aware that he knew of the relationship between Paolo da Rienza and Captain Andrea da Marolla, and reckoned on it to add its argument to her own. She saw his indecision, and laughed softly.

"But then, you were ever the man of action! The boy who made love to Dorotea del Andriola! The boy who hid with Tea Panchesi while Borgia's men hunted the streets of Rome! Why shouldn't you jump at a conclusion when you leap at so many women?"

Ilarion asked grimly, "What do you know about Tea Panchesi?"

She shrugged a white shoulder. "I sought her out after I learned of her from Jacopo Balisandro. While you were busy fighting, I was busy learning more about the boy I sold to Borgia. I even brought your Tea to my household. She's my maid-in-waiting. But forget Tea. Think of me. Have you forgiven yourself for thinking so badly of me?"

Ilarion was no fool—but he also was no misogynist! He could not find hate in himself for this blonde *tentatrice*. He gestured, and laughed. "Almost, you convince me. So you did not pay Captain da Marolla to kill me."

She clapped her palms together. *"Va bene!* We shall be friends again! And you'll come to my chambers tonight? After the dancing? Remember, *verro mio!* The sweetest part of a lover's quarrel is the reconciliation. I am of a mood to be very conciliatory!"

He shook his head, remembering Giula da Rienza; but that he should not hurt her pride, he said, "Another time, madonna."

Her eyes mocked him. "We are become a proper soldier! Cautious in the face of an apparent ambuscade! La, I liked the man of action better!"

She put her blonde head to one side and regarded him with pursed lips. Dreamily she said, "I wonder where that man of action is hidden now? Deep down inside you, or at the surface? It's worth a little loss of pride to learn!"

He was not prepared for a physical assault. He staggered as her arms went around his back and her lips pressed to his. He lifted his hands to disengage her arms, but he discovered a wiry strength in her muscles.

It was ludicrous, and at another time, Ilarion would have laughed at himself. But the *contessa* clung to him and her mouth was a leech that robbed him of his strength. By the time he felt the strength flow back into his arms, it was too late.

Giula da Rienza stood beside her brother in the moonlight, a few steps from the arched loggia, her red head tilted proudly, her green eyes burning. Paolo da Rienza breathed deeply of his pomade ball, slim and elegant in scarlet doublet beside her white velvet gown.

"It's my fault, dear sister," said Paolo da Rienza. "I saw Ilarion come out here, but I didn't know 'Trice was here."

Giula da Rienza did not speak. She lifted her wide skirt with one hand and walked toward Ilarion. Beatrice del Gallina held him by an arm, firmly, not relinquishing her place, but she eyed the advancing woman alertly.

There was grief in Giula *la rosso,* but there was pride, too. She held out her hand. "My scarf, stableboy! The red scarf you stole from me by playing on my pity! Give it back!"

"Giula! *Cara mia,* listen—"

Her green eyes were hard. "I want no further words from you or with you, messer. The scarf!"

His hands shook as he brought it from his doublet. Something inside him was crumbling under the direct stare of this girl. Something that had been a long time

129

building in him. Once her fingers closed over that scarf, everything he had done would be meaningless. His mind went back to that first night when he had seen her face portrayed on the cameo that his swordpoint had dug from Paolo da Rienza's purse. Since then, he had been unconsciously pursuing a dream, a dream of her beauty.

"Giula, if you would only hear me—"

The bloodlessness of her face made him realize how deeply she was hurt. Her fingers trembled, and she locked them against the pride that was threatening to burst into sobs. He shrugged helplessly and released the scarf. Paolo da Rienza came forward to take her arm and turn her. But she shrugged him off and ran by herself. To add to the gloom that wrapped him, Ilarion heard her restraint burst in bitter sobbings.

"It's a shame," whispered Beatrice del Gallina. "It's all my fault! If I hadn't been so glad to see you, so anxious to plead my cause, it wouldn't have happened."

"It doesn't matter," he said slowly. It did matter, though. It mattered very much.

The *contessa* moved closer, a friendly hand on his arm. "In simple justice, she could have heard you out, as you heard me." She played on that theme, elaborating it. "She gave you no chance! Together we could have convinced her! A few words would have revealed the fact that I was only explaining a whim of fate, and that in my joy over your forgiveness, I kissed you."

He knew that she was touching on his self-pity, but what she said wounded his masculine pride, stabbing it raw. "If you'll take a woman's advice, you'd do well to forget Giula *la rosso* for a little while. Show her you're no puppet to be tugged around by her hands! Show her you can find your pleasure elsewhere, and then see her come running!"

He swung to her on that. "You think this should be my course, madonna?"

Her laughter teased him. "La, how little you know a woman! Make her jealous! She will bite her nails to think you've forgotten her. She'll manage to get that scarf back in your fingers quickly enough!"

His despair took the bait, and turned to hope. His eyes grew brighter. "Yes! There's something in that. But how can I make her jealous?"

"Dance with me! Laugh! Act as if you were Paris courting Helen of Troy!"

He slid an arm around her waist. Frustrated and angry, he was an easy prey to the plan she suggested. What right had Giula da Rienza to judge him without trial? He took the *contessa's* upheld mouth, straining her against him, telling himself that he was serving Madonna Giula as she deserved. If only she were here now, to see how little he cared! Beatrice del Gallina was right. Let her be jealous! It might prove a tonic to restore her love!

He allowed himself to be guided by the the *contessa.* His original suspicions had now been replaced by the injured pride of an unfairly maligned lover. In that spirit of injured pride he appeared to worship her as he brought Beatrice del Gallina into the great chamber that was filled with light and the music of harpsichords and lutes.

Partners were forming for the *branle,* a dance in which all participants followed a leading couple. Ilarion entered into the spirit of the play without suspecting the strange smile that flitted across the lips of Beatrice.

At the conclusion of the dance, Elisabetta Colonna summoned Ilarion and Galeazzo Gonzaga to regale her guests with stories of Ilarion's swordplay. With eager relish, strutting about the room as if his had been the hand that vanquished ten bravos and saved the life of Leonardo da Vinci, as if his were the sword that held a score of Fossate's men-at-arms at bay while Pietro Torrigiani carved a wooden key, Galeazzo Gonzaga orated at some length on the abilities and fame of Ilarion.

He was a captain now, pointed out Gonzaga carefully. He had won his rank in battle, under the eyes of Cesare Borgia himself. When Gonzaga whipped himself into a frenzy over the fact that Ilarion's blade had also saved the life of Il Valentinois before the breach in Faenza's wall, men swore hotly and women wept from their emotions. And then Gonzaga, with his facile tongue, painted a picture of the reunion that had taken place between Ilarion and Da Vinci himself, only that morning.

With a flourish, Gonzaga lifted the ornate sword that Leonardo the Florentine had made for Ilarion. He bared the blued blade, and passed it from hand to hand.

Even as the *contessa* pressed her surging heart to his arm, and whispered, *"Egli ha un cuore di leone!"* Ilarion was discovering that he was indeed the lion of this Roman court. Voices cried his name, and whispered flattery to his ears. The bright eyes of women flirted with him. Men's hands slapped his back and squeezed his arms.

He had become the darling of *duchesse* and *principesse,* the hero of counts and dukes.

Off to one side, Galeazzo Gonzaga, the man whose impassioned oratory had wrought on the hearts of these people as a catalyst works its magic on a chemical solution, watched the press around Ilarion with a tight smile. His eyes, to any observer who cared to study them, showed a deep cynicism.

He watched Beatrice del Gallina from time to time, too, did this little man with the black, curly hair and beard. He saw her eyes as they stared up in adoration at Ilarion. He noted that she clung close to him, touching him subtly with hip or bosom, to remind him always of her nearness. Remembering the purse with its crest of the golden gamecock, Galleazzo Gonzaga became concerned.

When he could, he drew Ilarion away from the press, to whisper in his ear. "Are you mad? When we rode from Assisi, you were Beatrice del Gallina's betrayed friend! I find a change in you, messer! She clings to you like a leech's cup!"

Ilarion told him of the whim of fate that had put the purse in Captain da Marolla's hands. He went on to admit, somewhat ruefully, that Giula *la rosso* had entered the courtyard at a most inopportune moment.

"Ah, so? And now you seek to drown your sorrow in the blonde *contessa?*"

"Madonna Giula will see she means nothing to me," Ilarion explained bitterly.

"*Va bene!* And if Beatrice del Gallina lied to you about her whim of fate? Will you walk so blindly into another trap? What manner of glutton for punishment are you?"

It was a thought that Ilarion had not perceived. He dwelt on it a moment, then shrugged. The fire and confidence of youth still burned in him. "You've warned me. I'll be on my guard."

Galeazzo Gonzaga shook his head. "I cannot risk it. You'll come with me. Now! We leave abruptly, and we'll let their tongues wag a little more. It'll add to the legend I've created about you tonight."

But Beatrice del Gallina had worked her spell too strongly. Desire was in Ilarion, dissolving the caution with which Galeazzo Gonzaga sought to inspire him.

"Leave now? I'm to see the *contessa* home!"

Gonzaga argued, but Ilarion was determined. Finally Galeazzo Gonzaga hissed, *"Diavolo!* There's a Ferrara stubbornness in you that's equaled only by your resemblance to those *sudiciume!*"

He paused for breath, and his hand caught Ilarion's wrist. "You'll be careful? You'll promise me that? This assignation with Beatrice del Gallina may include more than a meeting of flesh. There may be some steel, too!"

Ilarion grinned, and Galeazzo Gonzaga threw his hands high at the confidence he read in his face. "*Madre del Dio!* What can I say to this stripling that will teach him caution? I build him into a hero, and now my own handiwork betrays me! He finds in himself the ability to withstand any attack that may be made on him. At least, let me add one word more. Beware of poison! No swordsman in the world can defeat that with a blade!"

On that note, Galeazzo Gonzaga stamped off.

His place was taken by a dozen noblewomen, who crowded about Ilarion to thrust invitations on him. He was made to realize, by the carnal lights that filled their eyes, that there would be no others to attend upon them when he visited them. Fevered voices whispered of little intimacies that might be showered on the lion who had saved the great Da Vinci, of games that could be played between a woman and the man who had saved Cesare Borgia from death.

He was rescued by Beatrice del Gallina.

She swept forward with rustling skirts and a cloud of French perfume, to laugh at the women who surrounded him. She sank back against him so that, to save himself, he had to put his arm about her middle. She caught his hand and held it prisoner.

Her eyes were bold, as she whispered, "Tonight, darlings—he belongs to me!"

The bedroom in the *palazzo* Gallina was the same as he remembered it. Its bed of oak, with the four ornately carved posts and its white linens, was lighted by the gleam of a bronze floorlamp. The great table still stood before the tapestry that hung from the groined ceiling to the marble floor. The bench where he had held the *contessa* as Borgia walked in on them had not been moved.

Ilarion closed the door and faced Beatrice del Gallina. Her eyes were hungry as they surveyed him. It had been a long time since the explosive night she had shared with this youth. She was discovering, with a queer wrench, that she was starved for another experience such as that.

With white fingers, she attempted to right the disorder

of ribbons he had undone in the coach that brought them from the *palazzo* Colonna. Clinging closely in that warm darkness, she had afforded him a freedom with hands and lips that had put a seething restlessness in her body. She had intended that restlessness to work in him, but her own flesh betrayed her.

As she struggled now to lift the blue satin panels of her disordered bodice, his hands caught at hers. "This time, I play with you, madonna!"

He put his hands at her waist and lifted her, shaking her gently.

Her head hung back, and her thick blonde tresses shook free of the pearl snood that held them to tickle the flesh of her shoulders as they strained upward from her slipping brocades. She kicked at the air, helpless.

"Release me! Oh, *Dio mio!* Let me go—for just a little while! There is—I must speak with the servants—"

He dropped her so suddenly that her legs buckled, and she had to cling to him with both arms to keep from slipping to her knees. Her face was flushed, and her eyes glistened wetly. "You're a devil!" she sighed. "I'd forgotten how much of a devil you really are! I have to leave for a moment, but I'll be back. *Macche!* But I'll be back!"

She ran from the room to adjust her clothes in the safety of the dim corridor beyond the door. He heard her footsteps moving down the hall toward the iron-railed stairway at its end.

Alone, he moved to the chair beside the ormolu table. A flacon of *fior d'arancio* had stood here, last time. He turned. There was the silver maiden that Borgia had lifted to admire. He was losing himself in his memories when a footstep sounded on the corridor floor outside the door. Its sound suggested stealth. Ilarion put a hand to his swordhilt and moved on silent feet to the wall.

A woman came into the room, and for a moment, he did not know her. Her red hair was fixed in a corona of braids about her head, and her shapely figure was revealed by a tight red dogalina. For an instant, Ilarion stared dumbly. "Tea!" he cried with recognition.

She whirled, eyes wide and frightened. "Ilarion! *Macche!* Be quiet! If she finds me in here—" She shuddered, and her face alarmed him. He caught her arms to steady her.

"*Che cosa e?* What is it?"

"I had to warn you! She's going to have you killed by a

134

dozen bravos! I overheard her planning it with Paolo da Rienza. She's gone now to light a candle in a window, as a signal!"

His fingers were like steel vises on her hands. She shrank to him, whimpering. "I had to warn you. You're one of us, not like her and her kind! I'd never sleep at night, if I let you go blindly to what she plans."

He whispered his thanks, but she was too terrified to heed him. She withdrew her hands and stumbled to the door. Her eyes were wide, frightened pools below the frame of her auburn hair.

"She's coming. Be on your guard! I'll hide behind a tapestry in the hall. Don't let her see me!"

Ilarion waited until the heavy tapestry covered her, then he went striding into the hall. Beatrice del Gallina halted when she saw him. Her face clouded, and she looked beyond his shoulder into the room.

"Is anything wrong? Why do you come to meet me?"

"Such a question from an eager lover!" he mocked her.

He reached out and lifted her with an arm at her waist. He carried her thus, with her back to the tapestry where Tea Panchesi crouched. And as he walked, to distract her further, he fumbled at her dress with his hand.

He laughed away her protests. He claimed her mouth in a kiss that shook her as a reed shakes in the winter wind. He carried her past the tapestry and into the room, closing the door with his heel.

He set her down, then, and smiled into her flushed face. There was a bitter amusement in him, and a grim curiosity to lead her on, to see how far she would go to keep him here in her room, an unsuspecting victim for her assassins' daggers.

Her hands fumbled at his girdle, lifting the sword Da Vinci had made for him, tossing it carelessly aside. She fumbled at the strings of his doublet, pulling it back and down over his arms. "Why not lock the door, madonna?" he asked. "Your servants might disturb us."

"No! That is—I sent them away, with orders not to rouse us before sunup."

He smiled at her tremblings even as he evaded her reaching hands. "Why such haste, madonna? We have the night, and all the next day! I told Gonzaga I'd not be home for some little time! Your true lover is a careful workman. He does not rush blindly on."

"We do not have—I am anxious, that is all!"

He longed to whisper, "You do not have much time—before your hired cutthroats will be here with their daggers, to stab me as other daggers stabbed Alfonso of Bisceglia! You want to enjoy me once more, before I die." But he only laughed softly and caught her dress, ripping it away from the creamy skin of her shoulder.

"Last time you disrobed yourself. This time, I'll do the undressing!" He worked slowly, lingering over each kiss. She breathed harshly, clinging to him, whispering her love between urgent commands to hurry.

"Madonna has forgotten," he teased her. "It is thus she revealed herself lingeringly to my eyes, to taunt and rouse me!"

"*Diavolo!* Must you bring that up at a time like this?"

He tormented her until he reduced her to a sobbing heap that groveled at his feet. Abjectly she pleaded with him, crouching before him, veiled only in the tumbling cataract of her blonde hair. Her hands sought his legs, to tumble him down beside her.

Ilarion fought free, rising to move to the table that held a flacon of chilled *barbera*. She knelt on the floor, staring at him, shuddering.

"I do not interest you enough!" she snarled suddenly. "That redhead virgin fills your mind!"

Slowly she pulled herself up on the ornate bench where he had sat. Proudly she stood for a moment, with the candlelight playing on the satiny smoothness of her skin. With a curious smile, she shoved her hands in her thick hair and threw it back over her shoulders.

"The puling Giula! As if she could take a man that Beatrice del Gallina wanted!"

She came for him then, in a frenzied rush. He found himself thrust back by her wanton strength. She was a witchery of soft laughter and caressing hands. She grew proud and commanding at one minute, humble and abasing the next. Despite the cold curiosity with which he regarded her, he found himself matching her passion.

He was pulling her to him when he heard it.

It was the merest hint of sound, the scrape of steel against steel, muffled by cloth. It came from the corridor beyond the closed door. But it threw water over Ilarion, and with hard hands, he thrust the sighing Beatrice del Gallina from him.

She sensed the alarm that hammered in him. She twisted from the bed, reaching for a robe to throw about her.

"You fool!" she cried. "You might have died asleep, not knowing whose hand struck you down! This way, you'll be awake and screaming for mercy!"

"All I have to do is hold my swordpoint to your throat, madonna," he reminded her. "Even men hired to kill for gold would not risk your death. Who'd pay them?"

It was a thought that had not occurred to the *contessa*. She shrank back, and began to scream.

Ilarion was halfway to the table that held his blade when the door slammed open. A dozen-men-at-arms in steel caps and breastplates flooded the room. They came at him on the run, their blades in their hands, unhampered by the scabbards they had dropped beyond the door. It was the touch of a scabbard to the tile floor that had carried into the room and alarmed him.

With one hand, Ilarion sent the table flying toward the bravos. His other hand tipped his sword loose. The pause that the flying table afforded him he used to snatch up a cloak and swing it around his arm. Then he was vaulting the overturned table, his blade hammering down in a beat and thrust, and before the men could move, one of them sprawled across the table's edge, and two others were discovering themselves paralyzed before the winking point that darted at their throats.

Ilarion was a leaping flame. His blade ran red as he whirled to meet the rush of the others with blinding parry and sharp riposte. He held their blades in play with a clang and scrape of steel. Then he backed slowly, bringing them with him, so maneuvering himself that before they were aware of it, they were under the tapestry with its brocaded nymph and shepherd. A slash of his sword, and the hanging fell around their heads. Without pausing, he moved forward. His blade cut and thrust, and stifled screams heralded the success of his ruse.

But there was no chance to do more than breathe deeply. Paolo da Rienza was in the room now, and five more men with him. Da Rienza hung back, urging the five bravos on with a promise of thirty florins to the man who cut Ilarion down. Since a man could live in comparative luxury for a year on such a princely sum, the men almost stumbled over each other in their eagerness.

It was their very greed that defeated them. They were in such a sweat to blood their swords that they slipped in the tapestry crumpled on the floor. To stumble before Ilarion was to invite a deadly *affondo*.

137

Two men fell, gurgling horribly, twisting and writhing on top of the fallen wall hanging. From the corner of the room, where she stood with Paolo da Rienza, the *contessa* whimpered, "*Madre del Dio!* He's a *condotta* in himself!"

Paolo da Rienza commented wryly, "You see now why Captain da Marolla failed below Fossate and again at Assisi. He's a devil!"

The countess was becoming concerned about her own safety. She discovered that the trap she had laid for this yellow-haired captain was shifting into a boomerang. In alarm, she wrapped her robe more closely about her and stumbled toward the door.

Ilarion was ahead of her. His flashing blade shuttled in and out of those who menaced him. His *parata* and *battuta* forced an opening. He leaped for the oaken door and thrust his foot against it. As it slammed shut, he threw home the bolt.

There was a little pause as a cold chill ran down the backs of the men who faced him. Halfway between the door and Paolo da Rienza, pressed back into a walnut *cassone*, stood Beatrice del Gallina. Terror lay naked in her glittering blue eyes.

"Elisabetta Colonna prophesied he'd meet his death through me," she whimpered. "I heard it tonight at the *pallazo!* It was all anyone talked about! And now—"

The cutthroats came alive. The fact that several of their fellows lay spilled on the floor was forgotten in the vision of the thirty florins that Paolo da Rienza and the *contessa* had promised them for this man's death. They careened like a wave at the man backed to the door.

Ilarion was not there to stop them. He was moving sideways, so that his blade licked out to engage that of the end man. His sword slid into the *cavazione in tempo,* and the man screeched with a two-foot length of steel in his arm. Then as the others whirled, confused, Ilarion rushed them.

It was thrust and parry, beat and stab. The clang of steel on steel and the harsh breathing of the struggling men, the scrape of soles on the marble floor, were backdrops to the writhing form of this yellow-haired captain who fought like a darting flame. There was no surprising him. He was in front of the ormolu table one moment, the next he stood in the glare of a bronzework candlestand. And always, out in front of him, his long blue blade was a shimmer of light that was impossible to trap.

He left men in his wake as a ship leaves foaming water. A black-bearded man sprawled on his face beside a Savonarola chair. A bravo whose bald pate glittered in the light of the candelabras was clutching an arm whose severed tendons caused it to flop uselessly. Two men were moaning in the shadows over deep-slashed thighs.

And then Ilarion stood alone, and a whimpering woman and a man with fear bright in his black eyes were facing him across the width of the room. Ten bravos were down, and the others were hurling their blades from them, begging mercy.

Beatrice del Gallina moaned, "Elisabetta did not foresee this! She said I would be the means of your death!"

Ilarion said, "She said you would be a danger to me. That danger is over, *madonna la contessa!*" He glanced at Paolo da Rienza, and that fop seemed to shrink and collapse upon himself. "We are not as bold as we were in the garden a few hours ago!"

"It was a jest," sobbed Beatrice del Gallina. "I was to lure you to the gardens. Paolo would bring Giula, to find you in my arms!"

" 'Trice, for the love of heaven!" screamed the fop.

Ilarion laughed bitterly. "No need to call on heaven, messer! I'll trouble you no more. I'm going back to Faenza, where my enemy is in front of me, and not lurking in bedroom shadows and in palace gardens!"

The fop stood a little straighter. A gleam of hope flickered in his face. "You speak of troubling me no longer. I assume, then, you mean to spare my life?"

Ilarion brooded at him. He was no philosopher, to prate on right or wrong. All he knew was that he could never kill the brother of Giula *la rosso,* not even if it meant his own life as forfeit.

"And me, Ilarion?" whispered Beatrice del Gallina, leaning forward, forgetting the gaping robe.

Ilarion bowed a little. "I have already forgotten you!"

It was a gibe, but Beatrice del Gallina was beyond pride at the moment. She drew back, exhaling gustily, and fought her lips into a wan smile.

For a moment Ilarion kept them there before him, motionless, their eyes locked. And then his hand was sliding back the bolt, opening the door. In a moment, he was gone, and the echo of his footfalls faded.

Paolo da Rienza lifted his pomade ball with fingers

that trembled in reaction. He sniffed delicately of the subtle perfume. He said softly, "It is only what we deserve, when we work with fools!"

Beatrice del Gallina looked at him sharply. "You're not thinking of any more attempts on him, are you? You've seen what he can do! *Iddio!* I almost feel pity for Da Marolla! Forget Ilarion! He's promised to forget us!"

The candles guttered, hissing in pools of molten tallow. Their flames threw black shadows across the gaunt face of Paolo da Rienza, highlighting his sharp cheekbones, the cruel twist of his mouth.

"Forget him? Never! I've been as much a fool as the men I hired to kill him. All this time, there was a better way. A way that could not fail! *Madre del Dio!* What an idiot I have been, not to have thought of it long ago!"

He threw back his head and his laughter rose up like the laughter of the devil in hell.

XII

GALEAZZO GONZAGA WAS at his writing desk in the little study off the main hall of his *palazzo* when Ilarion came storming in with a thump of boots, hurling his fur-trimmed cloak and velvet cap from him. The scrape of the Gonzaga quill halted its march across the vellum that he was addressing to Cesare Borgia, Duke of Valentinois, Count of Dios, Lord of Cesena and Pesaro. It poised a moment, then came to rest on the flat-topped desk that was set to one side of the hearth whose rosetted iron fireback reflected the heat of the crimson flames.

Except for the fire and the candles in the iron stands behind Galeazzo Gonzaga, the room was in blackness. The hiss and sputter of the flames brought Ilarion to stand before them, staring down, his face hard and sharp. His eyes blazed with the fury that ate in him.

"Trickery! Treachery! A dozen men in her bedchamber to run me through!"

He could not stand against the rage that beat in him. He went striding from the flames, up and down the room, in and out of its patterns of light and shadow. There was a frustration eating in him as he sought by action to release the tide of anger that welled up against the deceits and intrigues that hemmed him in.

Wisely, Galeazzo Gonzaga let him walk his rage before he spoke, watching from beneath black brows, a wry smile on his lips. To the velvet arras that hung from iron brackets on the stuccoed wall to the table of gold and red, set with three vases of alabaster, Ilarion stalked. His fist smashed hard against his palm.

"Before that even, in the garden! A plan to discredit me with Madonna Giula! Outside Fossate and Assisi, attempts to kill me! On the battlefield before Faenza, a crossbow quarrel aimed for my eyes. *Nome del Dio!* How much can a man stand?"

Ilarion paused for breath, and Galeazzo Gonzaga spread his hands, lifting his brows high, placatingly.

"Fame brings jealousies. It is the bitterness that is usually found with the sweet. What can you do, except be ever on your guard?"

"I can go back to Faenza, to the blockade of that city from which Borgia summoned me to ride with you to Rome. There, at least, I need fear no more treachery. Da Marolla is dead. That crossbowman died on the rack under the Duke's questioning."

"There will always be other men to kill for gold," Gonzaga commented dryly.

"Nevertheless, I go. Tomorrow. At dawn!"

Galeazzo Gonzago brought his palm down hard on the desk before him. His black eyes blazed hotly, full of sudden anxiety.

"No! You stay with me. It is the Duke's command!"

Ilarion put his eyes to this dark man, as if seeing him for the first time, as he crouched there with his hand still resting on the desktop.

"You!" Ilarion snarled. "You promised to tell me why I am in Rome! Why that painting of me is so important!"

Reason returned to Galeazzo Gonzaga. The anger that had been fostered by his fear that Ilarion would ride from Rome to Faenza was draining away. He stood up and moved to the hearth, turning his back to it, letting the heat seep through his hose and doublet.

"You're right. It isn't fair to keep you in the dark. Not any longer. You should know why you are in Rome. First, however, let me say this, that Cesare Borgia and I seek to make you the happiest man in all Italy!"

Ilarion snorted and turned on a bootheel. He strode toward the door. His voice, when he spoke, was harsh.

"You mock me, *signore mio!*"

That brought Galeazzo Gonzaga away from the fire, running with awkward haste toward the marble tracery that flanked the study door leading out to the great hall. At the doorway he swung around, extending his arms. His eyes flared brightly.

"Tell me only this! What is your heart's desire?"

Ilarion regarded the little man. He could have put his hands on him and lifted him bodily aside from the doorway. Instead, he thought of Giula *la rosso* and her soft, warm mouth. He brooded there on the red beauty of her hair and on the elfin loveliness of her pert face.

Galeazzo Gonzaga snatched his thought from the air, leaning forward eagerly.

"To wed with Giula da Rienza! Ha! Is it not so?"

Ilarion shrugged. "An impossibility!"

"Not so! Not only a possibility, but almost an accomplished fact! Ah! That touches you, does it? Then be good enough to give me your attention! Stop brooding there like a Tantalus chained to his rocks. Go! Sit yourself on the settle and let me speak. And grant me your full attention!

Ilarion had discovered the spell of words that this cockerel of a man could spout. Now he was discovering that they were sending his veins into a bubble inside him. He let his elbow be caught, and felt himself turned and guided to a wall settle. He sank down as Gonzaga stood before him, hands on hips.

"A score of years ago, a baby boy was born to Ercole d'Este and his *duchessa*. His name? Hieronimo d'Este. From what we know, his eyes were blue and his hair was as yellow as sunlight.

"Ferrara was not a peaceful place, just then. There were wars and the rumors of war overreaching its *castelli* and its fields. Sixtus was casting eyes at those fields, planning on a partition of the duchy. To this end, he allied himself with Venice, and found the lion of St. Mark only too willing to do what he suggested.

"Venice hired her mercenaries and hurled them into Ferrara. Ercole d'Este—a born soldier if ever there was such a man!—went to meet them. But the Venetian *condotti* were too strong. They broke the Ferraran power at Argenta, and went storming up, smashing deep into Ferrara. Some of those *condotti* even pitched their tents in the public parks!

"It was sometime during that invasion that a band of

mercenaries broke into the palace itself. They looted and attacked, as soldiers will; they stabbed a woman and tore a squalling baby from her arms. They made off with jewels and other souvenirs of their rapine, including that baby boy.

"No man has ever seen that baby since that day. He disappeared as if the earth opened up and swallowed him."

Ilarion scowled. This bit of history interested him, in that it had to do with war and soldiery, but it gave him no immediate concern.

"Why tell me this?" he asked.

Galeazzo Gonzaga smiled grimly. "If you used your wits as you use your blade, you'd have discovered the answer to that while I was speaking. Cesare Borgia and I think you are that baby son of Ercole d'Este, the old Duke of Ferrara. You're brother to Alfonso d'Este, whom court gossip says is soon to wed Lucrezia Borgia!

"More than that! Isabella, Marchioness of Mantua, is your sister! You have for sister-in-law, my cousin, the great Elisabetta Gonzaga herself!"

Ilarion gaped unbelievingly at the little man. He had accused Galeazzo Gonzaga of mockery. Now he found himself concerned over his sanity. Something of this he bit out, harshly, as he paraded about the room.

Gonzaga gestured understandingly, *"Va piano!* Easy, easy! You go off like a bombard! Listen to my proof! Even now the Duke's ambassador, Collenuccio, has the painting that Pietro Torrigiani did of you! He is comparing it with other paintings of the Ferrara family! He has already notified the Duke that we suspect we have found his missing son. You can imagine the wave of delirium that will be sweeping Ferrara and Mantua if Collenuccio announces his decision in your favor."

Ilarion sat down on a little marble bench that was padded in quilted velvet. He was smiling grimly. "You tell me my wits are dull, but they are sharp enough to perceive the one flaw in all your arguments."

"Ah? And what will that be?"

"The fact that you hate the Ferraras as Paolo da Rienza hates me! If what you tell me were true, you yourself would have plunged a dagger in my back as I slept!"

Gonzaga scowled darkly and wrapped his fingers together behind his back.

"It is not with you that I have my quarrel. I hold you

143

blameless for what others do! Besides," and the little man sighed, "I have formed an attachment to you. It will be hard to see you go under the Ferrara roof, but even I must admit that will be better than living in a tent.

"Recall for a moment the evidence of your own senses. Who was it who allowed you to watch her strip and kiss her, believing you a Ferrara? Dorotea del Andriola! Who recognized the thick blond hair, the same breadth of bone and weight of sinew in you? Borgia himself, in your *contessa's* bedchamber, where he had come to see the blade that had beaten ten of his finest soldiers! And I, Galeazzo Gonzaga! I, who hate the Ferraras, who know them almost as I know my face, I mistook you for one of them! Is all this not proof that you bear an uncanny resemblance to them? Even your own Giula *la rosso* suspected, in the summer palace!

"Why fight truth like this? Search your own memory for further proof, if you will! Who was it fought against Ferrara with Venice? Who has his mementos of that campaign laid out before your very eyes? Well? Well?"

Ilarion frowned, and Galeazzo Gonzaga threw his hands high.

"Why, none other than your fencing master, Jacopo Balisandro! Ha! You've forgotten about him, haven't you? He fed you kicks and blows. His temper was always churly when you were around. Could it be that he hated you? Because you were Ferrara's son? Ha! Think on that a while!"

It made sense. Ilarion was remembering the hot hate in the old man's great black eye that gleamed the more malevolently, it seemed, because its mate was shrouded forever under a pad of black wool. Cuffs and kicks, yes. Perhaps old Jacopo Balisandro did hate him because he was a Ferrara. If anyone would know, Balisandro would.

Gonzaga added to his thoughts as he said, "There is a story that Ercole d'Este once had a friend, a good friend. A nobleman, of one of Italy's finest families. When Ercole d'Este wedded his *duchessa,* the story says that his friend became an enemy. The love he had hoped to win for himself was given to the Duke of Ferrara. Some claim it made that friend mad!

"When Venice marched its *condotti* on Ferrara, that one-time friend offered his services. Who can pluck the veil of the past away now, to say whether or not Jacopo Balisandro was that nobleman? But I can tell you this.

If he were, it would have been a cherished ambition to break the Duke's heart by some such stroke of villainy!

"*Macche!* To steal the son of Ferrara and raise him as a slopsboy! To kick and beat him, knowing none could aid him! *Iddio!* What a vengeance! This was no revenge to end with a blade in a man's heart. It became a living thing, day after day, to enjoy in his cruel heart the spectacle of Hieronimo d'Este serving him, mopping the slop and filth of his stables, the flagstones of his loggia!"

Ilarion sat frozen, knowing that every word Galeazzo Gonzaga hurled at him had the ring of truth. He cried out harshly, "I'll see him at daybreak! I'll learn the truth from him, one way or the other!"

Galeazzo Gonzaga shook his head. He came and sat beside Ilarion and his fingers were hard on his forearm.

"That is one thing you must not do! If he hates you as much as it seems, he'll lie to you, and twist the dagger of his hate a little deeper! You can look for no truth from Jacopo Balisandro! No, no.

"I have told you this to explain the mystery that surrounds you. But you must not spoil the plans the Duke and I have to secure you this birthright, by hasty action. Let me do the planning. All I ask from you is your presence here in Rome, and that you consider carefully all that I have told you! Dream a little, if you will, on what such a decision in your favor by Messer Collenuccio can mean to you! You will have Cardinal Ippolito and the future husband of Lucrezia for brothers! A Duchess and a Marchioness for sisters! A *rocca* for your own in the lazy tranquillity of a Ferraran valley! And with you—*chi sa?*—your lovely Giula *la rosso!*"

It was a picture to make a man dream, and Ilarion found himself dreaming, with his heart thumping inside his black doublet. And then the suspicion with which he had lived for the past few months caught him in its acid talons.

"When I am proven son of Ferrara, if I am, what will Borgia do to me? Have me killed as he had the Duke of Ganida slain? As he did Alfonso of Bisceglia? I'll be no more use to him then!"

"May *il Gran Dio* forgive you! Do you know why Borgia is troubling himself with you? Because the Estes are a most powerful family! They have connections with thrones all over Europe! Venice and Florence are friendly to them. So is Mantua and Milan! By installing you as the son of old Ercole d'Este, he causes the Duke of Ferrara to adopt a debt of gratitude. There will be good will between them. And where that good will goes, so go ambassadors like Cardinal Ippolito and Alfonso d'Este, and Don Ferrante and Don Sigismondo, your four brothers!

"He will use you to make an alliance! It is true, as I stand here! Why should you turn your back to your family because, as a by-product, Cesare Borgia wins himself powerful allies to his cause?"

He spoke with a feverish heat, this little man. He sent his voice rolling out in sonorous syllables, until the room echoed. His hands gestured, and where they went, Ilarion could almost see the scene he painted.

"You've never been in Ferrara, never heard the toll of bells rolling across its countryside at dusk. Never heard the lowing of kine as they come in from the fields. Never ridden its roads at night, with the lighted houses of farmers and merchants glowing with yellow candles.

"Picture such a life with Giula da Rienza beside you! You'll have a *castello* of your own. You may pursue your life as a captain of lances. But you'll have Ferrara gold behind you. You'll have Ferrara lances and Ferrara archers and hired Swiss pikemen to wear your livery! The Ferraras have some fame as soldiers. You'll bring them more, if you want!"

Ilarion shook his head. He put his hand to his brow and found it wet. It could not be true. These things that Galeazzo Gonzaga shouted at him were just words, coated with some magic potion that made him see the *castello* with Giula *la rosso* walking in its gardens, made him smell the odor of the fields and the crops that would be his.

"You want to be a *condottiero?* Ho! With the Ferraras behind you, you can become as rich as Federigo of Urbino at the trade!"

Galeazzo Gonzaga was an artist. His eyes studied the youth, and he held his breath.

"Is it possible?" whispered Ilarion at last. "Is it some joke you play on me? God pity you if it is!"

"It is no jest! On the word of Gonzaga!"

Ilarion came to his feet. There was a fire in his middle that choked him. He babbled of the trap into which he had stepped with Beatrice del Gallina in the Colonna gardens, and of how Giula *la rosso* had found him there.

He told him at length of the trap that the *contessa* and Paolo da Rienza had set for him in her bedchamber.

Galeazzo Gonzaga threw back his head and laughed. "When that fop hears that you are brother to Alfonso and Sigismondo, and to Cardinal Ippolito, he will get down on his knees to you! Come! As evidence of my good faith, I will go to Giula da Rienza! With my own lips, I will tell her what I have told you. I will explain that when she found you in the garden, Beatrice del Gallina was trying to lure you to your death!"

Ilarion was fresh from the sunken bath in whose soaped and scented waters he had dreamed away some of the morning hours. As he toweled himself now with animal vigor, he found his mind turning to his past, and to the memories that Galeazzo Gonzaga had churned up last night in his study. He was remembering little things, things he had forgotten months ago. The pallet of straw on which he had slept as a boy. The shape of the worn mops with which he had scoured the stones of the loggia until they shined. The great four-poster with its gilded crests that were carved into the posts themselves.

As he thought about that, his hands paused in their work, and the towel hung suspended. That crest was in the shape of the Ferrara arms! Oh, it was all adding up, all this concern and thought that Gonzaga had urged on him. He could see the hump-backed figure of the fencing master move once again, like some crablike monster, through the gloom of the cortile toward the hidden receptacle under the black stone Venus in the loggia. That was where the old man hid his treasures. Ilarion grinned faintly, recalling the times he had shivered in the night air, seeking to discover the trick of opening the statue.

"I never could find it out," he told the air around him. "*Iddio!* The times I watched him take out his jewels, and gold medallions, and the diamond bracelets and pearl pendants, to fondle them as if they were alive?"

He moved the towel more briskly, chuckling.

"I wonder what the old greedyguts is doing now? If his stableboy is as dutiful as I was?"

From these thoughts his mind skipped back to the one-eyed *schermitore* and the greed and hate that had shaped his life. "It'd be like him to lie in his teeth about me, just to balk me from the truth!" He thought of the sack of Ferrara, and the wrenching of himself from the

147

arms of a dying maidservant, to which Galeazzo Gonzaga had directed his attention. He wondered idly if that sack had been as bloody and as brutal as the sack of Fossate.

Had old Jacopo Balisandro really ripped a fortune in jewels from the Ferraran palace, to retire from the field forever? Had he actually stabbed that woman and torn a wailing infant from her arms? Was that infant himself, as Galeazzo Gonzaga took such pains to convince him? Was he, together with that ornate four-poster and the baubles under the black stone Venus in the fencing-hall loggia, just another memento of a war campaign?

He sat on a joint stool with the towel around his middle, brooding in a shaft of sunlight that warmed his golden skin, a thousand such questions flaming across his mind. He thought of the silks and satins he would have worn as Hieronimo d'Este, and grimaced, contrasting them with the rags that had covered his urchin's body as he had slaved for old Balisandro. He thought of quilted beds, and of the straw pallet on which he had grown into manhood.

His eyes went to the blade that Leonardo da Vinci had forged and molded for him, studying it as it lay on a trestle table. No Este had a blade like that! It had been such a blade that had brought him this far from the stables. Could it win him a new name, a family, a chance at a dukedom?

Gonzaga came into the bedroom then, interrupting his thoughts with a dancing anxiety that was almost comical.

"Sluggard! Lay-a-bed! Into your clothes, for love of love! Collenuccio himself is below, with a dozen paintings of the Ferraras! It is your painting, done by Torrigiani, that has fetched him. He confesses to have found some little resemblance! What have you to say to that?"

Ilarion was beyond words. He felt himself being dragged relentlessly by some cosmic whirlpool. He dressed in fumbling silence, his head buzzing. He pulled the cloth-of-gold doublet on, and drew up his yellow hose, and slipped his feet into leather shoes with a haste that brought an exclamation of dismay from Gonzaga.

"*Peste!* I can't have you go before Collenuccio like that! *Macche!* Look at the wrinkles you've put in your stock! Straighten yourself, captain! If you are to be a Ferrara, look like one!"

It was Gonzaga's fingers that put him to rights, finally, with a fluffing out of his sleeves and a tightening of his girdle of flat gold plates that made him feel like a Banchi dandy. In that mood, he went with Galeazzo Gonzaga down the wide, curving stairs, toward a library where Messer Collenuccio awaited him.

A dozen paintings stood on the floor of the library, their oiled surfaces facing the sunlight. At their entrance, a tall man, in a black gown trimmed in ermine and thrown loosely back from his doublet of somber gray, turned from his perusal of the paintings. His eyes were dark and steady under the biretta on his head.

Messer Collenuccio gasped when he swung from Galeazzo Gonzaga to the tall stripling in the cloth-of-gold doublet. For so many years that the hairs on his head were white, he had been accountant and ambassador, general adviser and almost father confessor to the Ferraras. In all that time he had seen and known all of the Este family.

On the life he loved so well, he would take oath that this man who called himself Captain Ilarion was a Ferrara. But Messer Collenuccio was no gambler. And so he put a look of dubiety on his features, and let his lower lip protrude in an attitude of mistrust.

"There's a resemblance, yes. I'd be a fool to deny it!" His eyes touched Ilarion's mouth and chin. "He looks like a cross between Ferrante and Sigismondo. He has a wider sweep of shoulder, and he's thicker in the leg. Stronger, too, I'll warrant."

"The old Duke himself," put in Galeazzo Gonzaga, "when he was at the wars!"

The Ferraran ambassador discerned the embarrassment that flushed Ilarion's cheeks. He smiled wryly. "What's your hope in the matter, Captain? How much of your inheritance do you hope to collect?"

"My parentage alone would suffice," Ilarion said stiffly. "The knowledge that there is noble blood in my veins."

Galeazzo Gonzaga broke in on that. He said, "Captain Ilarion has risen to his present rank in a matter of months. He has done services for Il Valentinois. You may have heard of them."

Galeazzo Gonzaga did not give his visitor a chance to acknowledge the fact. He plunged on into vivid presentation of Captain Ilarion's deeds in Rome and at Fossate, and outside the walls of Faenza. He concluded, "You will have observed that he is no mendicant, to take alms. He seeks no dukedom. All he asks is an opportunity to display his proofs. His ability with the blade has brought him thus far. He will gamble that it can advance him farther."

Messer Collenuccio displayed some emotion himself. He strode up and down the room, between the petrarchs set on the shelves of the inbuilt library casings. An amillary became a rest for his hand as he turned to face them. "I'll not deny Ercole d'Este is in a frenzy. It's only by my counsels that he has not come himself. If Captain Ilarion is his lost son, he will be welcomed as a member of the family, with all its privileges. But you can see my hesitation. The Ferraras want no fortune seeker foisting himself on their generosity."

Galeazzo Gonzago bowed slightly. "To think otherwise would be an affront. Frankly, Cesare Borgia is anxious to do the house of Ferrara a favor. All he asks in return is good will. No more than that."

The Ferraran ambassador nodded. "Ercole d'Este will not prove an ingrate, believe me, if this is the little Hieronimo."

Ilarion watched from the hearthstones of the towering marble fireplace. There was a fever in him as Collenuccio bent to the canvases, lifting and holding them at arm's length. From the oils his eyes traveled to Ilarion, studying him feature by feature. There came a silence to the room that was broken only by the pop of a blazing log, and its soft thump as it settled into the embers in the soot-smudged fireplace.

As Messer Collenuccio picked up the final painting, Ilarion cried out and started forward. The ambassador stared at him, and Galeazzo Gonzaga whirled.

"That picture! On the duke's doublet. That medallion he wears—"

The Ferraran ambassador leaned forward. His eyes glowed hungrily, and his breath quickened. "Yes? Yes? The medallion! What of it, man?"

Ilarion looked at Gonzaga. "I have seen one very similar to it. Perhaps it is the same one. The old fencing master who raised me as a child, Jacopo Balisandro, has it."

He told them of the black marble Venus, and the little hiding place under the stones of the loggia, and of how he lay watching the old fencing master as he fondled the jeweled treasures he secreted there. When he was done, Messer Collenuccio gaped at him.

"The medallion you mention was lost during the sack of Ferrara! It was taken at the same time little Hieronimo d'Este was kidnaped!"

For the first time since Galeazzo Gonzaga had mentioned his birthright, Ilarion felt the intoxicating wine of honest hope. The bedazed look that had settled on Collenuccio's face, the grin that split the face of Galeazzo Gonzaga, nurtured that hope into a flame of certainty. Ilarion almost danced as he came to stand with them, peering down at the medallion as the goldsmith's art had shaped it.

"The same, the same," he murmured excitedly. "You see the twisted vines about the rose? I could never forget that grouping."

Collenuccio lowered the painting. A film of perspiration beaded his high brow. "There can be little doubt, Captain! If you can produce this medallion, it will set a seal on your case that will cause me to recommend that Ercole d'Este prepare to welcome a long-lost son!"

"We will have the place searched by ducal order," announced Gonzaga. "We will have it by evening!"

But Ilarion was less confident. Where before, Gonzaga had counseled against seeing the fencing master, Ilarion now pleaded patience. "Do that, and we may lose it forever! A ducal order will be given publicity by word of mouth. There are some who might feel it rewarding to run to old Jacopo Balisandro with their tale. He would hide those baubles—or lose them—so well that we could never recover them!"

He was thinking of Paolo da Rienza. That fop would leave no stone unturned to prevent him from achieving his goal. And Ilarion remembered the hate in the eyes of old Jacopo too well to think that he would hand over the jewels to him.

"What would you suggest?" asked Collenuccio quietly.

"Let me go alone, by night. I know where he keeps the things. I will try to discover the secret by myself, without alarming him. If I cannot learn it, I shall have to go back again and again, until he opens the black Venus himself."

They spoke at length, but could find no better solution. Caution was inbred in Messer Collenuccio, and he seconded Ilarion's anxiety. To be this close to complete success, and then to lose it, was unthinkable. Since Ilarion had most to gain by discovering the medallion, he must be the one to risk its loss.

"But a fencing master!" said the ambassador, looking dubious. "If he finds you, Ercole d'Este will be in danger of losing his son twice in one lifetime!"

"On that score, let me reassure you," said Galeazzo Gonzaga, grinning. "You have never seen Captain Ilarion in action. I have!"

The house was the same. Its high-walled brick structure bulked wide beside the smaller residences around it. Narrow windows cut black rectangles along the fencing-hall wall. The worn wooden door was still black with age, recessed into the wall that fronted the cortile. Against the sky, the bare branches of an ancient oak drew traceries of black lace.

Ilarion put his hand on the door handle, and pulled.

Moonlight flooded the courtyard, coating the arches of the gallery and the brick walls of the fencing hall in silver. It looked old and familiar, and brought a twinge of memory to Ilarion as he closed the courtyard door behind him. There were the broken boards of the stable, where he had slept and worked. How often he had scrubbed down horses in the dirt yard beyond it! That stone bench before the arcade was where he had sat in the sun, trying to master the intricacies of reading and writing that Fra Matteo was teaching him.

He looked now at the black marble Venus, and the sight of the dark statue drove his blood scudding through his veins. On long, eager legs he crossed the yard, pausing to stoop and fumble around the base of the statue with shaking fingers. He probed and hunted, breathing harshly.

For fifteen minutes, he worked over the statue.

He leaned against it in despair. If he could not put his hands on that medallion, Messer Collenuccio would deny his paternity! Suppose the old fencing master had taken it, being already warned by some bit of devil's magic? A frenzy came alive in Ilarion as doubt and worry sat in him. He pushed and pulled the pedestal, but it yielded no more than the old oak might, were he to strive against it.

From beyond the arcade, he heard the slap of feet and the faint rustle of clothing. Ilarion moved quickly, withdrawing to the sheltering gloom of the gallery.

"It's old Jacopo himself," he whispered. "I'm in luck!"

The bent fencing master stomped forward on clublike

legs, his huge white head hung from the spread of his great shoulders. The black eyepatch that he wore gave his features a touch of evil that his sagging lips repeated. He fumbled in a leathern pouch that dangled from a corded girdle.

Ilarion could hear his mumbling voice in the murk of the gallery. "Lazy good-for-nothing! A dozen times I've told him to clean the pavings of the yard. Does he heed me? Bah! It's time I used the switch again!"

Even against the anxiety that was mastering him, Ilarion smiled. His successor had inherited more than a bed in a stable!

The fencing master paused by the Venus. His hand came out of the pouch with a slim needle of metal that he thrust against the stone. At the same time his fingers twisted a rose in the scrollwork around the edge of the pedestal. The black statue and the pedestal slid sideways, revealing an oval hole set in the stones of the yard.

A key! Ilarion thought in astonishment. A little needle of a key, and I never suspected! Perhaps that was because he had never before been this close to the old man as he opened the statue. Jacopo Balisandro stooped and fumbled in the brick-lined cairn. His big hand came out with a handful of jewels, necklaces, and pendants. Swaying from a rope of silver links, the medallion held Ilarion's eyes.

"He thinks to cheat me out of a fortune, does he?" cackled the old man. "Paolo da Rienza offers to buy these jewels for a hundred florins. A hundred florins? They're worth a thousand in the right hands. And old Jacopo knows where to find them."

The heart that beat in that misshapen body was unchanged. It still lived for gold, pumped by a greed that had become an obsession. Ilarion could see the glitter of the single black eye on one side of the big, hooked nose. A thick tongue came out to wet the loose lips.

And then, Ilarion moved.

Jacopo Balisandro gave a wild, weird cry. He pushed the hand that held the baubles deep into the leathern pouch. He sprang back, head leaning forward as his lone eye tried to penetrate the shadows of the arcade.

"*Chi e?* Who's there?"

Ilarion stood in the bright moonglow, straight and proud. He was no stableboy in this cloth-of-gold doublet and furred cloak to match, in the yellow hose and the

153

modish broad-toed shoes. His toque was fitted with a curling feather clasped by an emerald pin, and he seemed like one of the many dandies who came here to learn the latest swordstrokes.

"Magnificence," breathed old Jacopo, bowing slightly. "You startled me. Forgive an old man's ears. I did not hear you."

"Your ears are better than those of the lynx," said Ilarion grimly.

Jacopo Balisandro edged closer, his head hung lower than before. With his lips pursed, he stared up into the face that was so distractingly familiar to him.

"Your voice, *signore*. Your voice, and your face! They are known to me. Somewhere, at some time, I have seen them. But your name escapes me."

Ilarion drew his sword. A grim smile twisted his mouth as old Jacopo stared. "You have a blade, old one. Get it! Perhaps with a sword in your hand, you'll know me."

"Mad," muttered Jacopo Balisandro. "The man's mad! But if he wants a lesson, I'll give him one, even at this hour."

He turned and swung through the shadows of the gallery into the torchlit dimness of the hall. From a rack, he pulled down a blade and lashed the air with it. His solitary eye brooded at Ilarion, who stood in the doorway with a torch behind him, so that his face seemed that of a Nubian. Jacopo Balisandro shook his head. That gnawing familiarity was there, but he knew he had never seen this fop before.

Ilarion held up a hand. "In order that you do not fight without profit, we'll make a little wager. Ten thousand gold florins against the jewels you carry."

The breath caught in the old *schermitore's* throat at mention of such a sum. He bent forward with excitement churning in him. "No man can offer that sum, unless he be duke or prince! Where is the color of your gold?"

"There are those in Venice and Florence who will pay you. My death would insure them against Cesare Borgia allying himself with the Ferrara family, and through them with the lion of St. Mark and the red lily. Those who hate Borgia in those cities will pay you, if you kill me."

The fencing master lowered his point. "They will say I murdered you, if there is such a price on your head! I am Jacopo Balisandro, the greatest swordsman in the world! I can kill any man living, with a sword!"

"Not me," came back that mocking voice.

"*Peste!*" growled Balisandro. "I will disarm you first, to prove my word—then you shall tell me how your death will win me such a fortune!"

He flung himself forward in the *botta dritta,* counting on his powerful arm and blade to wrench the sword of this dandy from his hand. He found a lightning-like *finta de filo* turning his point, and then the golden youth was catching his steel in the *circolazione,* and his point drove in at his face. He felt the steel mark his face and fall away.

Wonderingly, Jacopo Balisandro touched his cheek. He saw the blood on his fingertips, and there was almost awe in the one black eye that he fastened on Ilarion.

"No man has even done that to me!" he whispered. "Who are you?"

"A devil," said Ilarion mockingly. "A devil out of your past to pay back some old debts!"

Balisandro grinned, and his discolored teeth showed through his sagging lips. He gestured suddenly, his greed forgotten in the surge of curiosity and pride.

"Forget the ten thousand florins! I'll fight you for the jewels alone. If you beat me, take them. If I beat you, I'll have your life!"

His blade came up and he circled the rigid figure of Ilarion. He swooped in with a stamp of feet, his blade a blur. Ilarion caught his sword and turned it with a savage *parata di picco.* The old man tried the *botta in tempo* and the *fianconata,* but the dandy turned his blade, and drove in himself.

"*Va bene!*" the old man hissed, his eye glowing. "Never have I fought one like you! *Diavolo!* Whoever taught you was a master!"

That was the last word the old man spoke. He settled grimly to his task, drawing on the years of his teaching, on the years when he had fought with mace and espadon behind the *condottieri* banners. His grotesque body was ugly and twisted, but fate had repaid him with a supreme skill at this game of ringing blades. With the knowledge heavy in him that he faced a man that might be his equal, he fought untiringly.

They drove about the dimly lit fencing hall, stamping and thrusting, parrying and attempting a dozen attacks. The blades sang shrilly. Above them, the torches hissed and sputtered. Through black shadows and pools of light they dived and whirled.

And now Ilarion was discovering that the blade before him was a devil, as others had learned the same about his own. It came from this quarter, then that, and there was no parrying it with a *battuta* or a *legamenta*. He skipped and danced, and slowly he began to break ground.

The old man pushed him back through the door and down the width of the arcade, until now the moonlight was above him, and their blades were silver lightning in the night. Once Jacopo Balisandro feinted low and came in high, and the scratch that marked his own cheek glistened now on Ilarion. A little higher, thought the youth, and his blade would be in my brain!

They pushed out to the marble Venus, breathing hard. The beat and clang of their swords made a steel diapason. Now the old man was moving in, sure of himself at last, knowing that the magic in his sword had not abandoned him.

Panic came to Ilarion. He knew that the old man was still his master. He fought as grimly, but the knowledge slowed his hand. Beyond the *quillons* of the blade Da Vinci had made for him, he watched Jacopo Balisandro gather himself for his final lunge.

Everything was lost! There was no use to fight on. He would die here on these paving stones, and never see Giula *la rosso* or his lost father. There was a grim irony in the fate that had drawn his feet back here, where he first had known life, and was now to lose it.

Jacopo Balisandro came in like a gull swooping toward the sea for its food. His foot stamped, and stamped again, but the second time his shoe slid on a pool of slops, and his blade went wide.

He tumbled, his blade wrenched from his startled fingers by Ilarion's sudden *contro cavazione*. He lay breathless, on his back, and felt the touch of cold steel at his soft throat.

"The jewels, old one!" hissed Ilarion. "You had your chance. You failed!"

"A bit of bad luck," gasped Jacopo Balisandro. "Let me on my feet, and—"

But Ilarion stooped swiftly and wrenched at the leathern pouch. He tumbled the jewels into the air, and as the medallion fell, he snatched it. With fingers that shook, he pushed the bauble out of sight in his doublet.

"You have a careless stableboy," he said. "I owe him

my life! If he cleaned these stones as I used to do, on my knees, with a brush and hot water thick with soap, he'd have saved you a fortune this night. As it is, he spared my life, and won me something I value far more."

Jacopo Balisandro clawed his way up to an elbow. His arm came out and a long, gnarled finger stabbed upward.

"You! Ilarion *della stalla!* The boy I taught to—"

The shaggy white head went back, and his laughter pealed toward the clouding sky. He gasped, "I wondered who had taught you those strokes, that defense! *Madre del Dio!* I should have known! Who but Jacopo Balisandro could have turned out such a sword?"

"Who but Jacopo Balisandro would have stolen a baby at Ferrara a score of years ago? Who but Jacopo Balisandro would have stabbed his nurse and wrenched a fortune in jewels and a medallion from her hands? And stolen a four-poster bed with the arms of Ferrara still engraved on it?"

The old man lay back, eyes wide. He attempted speech, but his breath only bubbled in his lungs. "So! That is why you want the medallion, is it? You think you're the little lost Ferrara?"

Again his laughter boomed out, mocking and maddening. His hand brushed the air. "Take the medallion! Become a Ferrara! Then old Jacopo will tell what he knows!"

He collapsed in his own hilarity, rolling on the stones, wheezing and choking from his mirth. And like this, with that laughter taunting him to the wall door and beyond, Ilarion walked away from the fencing hall for the last time.

XIII

THE MEDALLION DANGLED from the fingers of Galeazzo Gonzaga on its golden chain, swaying back and forth, its gold engraving picking up the light of the fire before which Giula da Rienza was seated. Like a pendulum it swung, almost as hypnotic in its effect as the words of the birdlike little man with the glossy black curls who cocked his head and pointed at it with a forefinger, while he declaimed on the wealth and family it would bring to Ilarion *della stalla.*

In front of a floor screen whose brocade recounted the legend of Jason and the Argonauts, Ilarion stood like a statue, a hand on the pommel of his sword, somber in black doublet and matching cloak, his black hose partially hidden by the rich leather boots encasing his long legs to mid-thigh. His blue eyes feasted on Giula *la rosso's* loveliness, and he paid scant heed to the words that babbled from the Gonzaga throat like waters over a stony brook-bottom.

They were gathered in a little chamber whose stone walls were flanked by wide walnut benches, and hung with costly draperies from the looms of Rheims. From the black mouth of the fireplace, red flames licked eagerly around a great pine log, as Galeazzo Gonzaga worked himself into a mood that was bringing tears to his over-emotional eyes.

"Our court poet, Francesco Uberti himself, would have difficulty in composing a ballad to match the truth of this great love, Madonna Giula. Imagine it! A stableboy with a gift such as his! An Achilles come to Rome! With only a sword—and the love he bears you!—he has fought a path from a stable bed to a birthright in one of our oldest and greatest families!

"When first he laid eyes on this medallion, he was a scullion. A filth! But a dream lived in him, a dream that was born when he saw your lovely features etched for eternity on a cameo his swordpoint cut from a purse on your brother's person!

"Since that happy night, his every moment has been dedicated, at times unconsciously, to you! And how has he been treated for this love?

"He has been attacked with threat of murder, not once, but many times! The swords of a score of ruffians have threatened him. A crossbow bolt was fired at his eye! He has been tricked and victimized. But through these trials his love for you has guided his steps like a beacon!"

Giula *la rosso* was not listening to this impassioned oratory. Her slant green eyes were regarding the figure of Ilarion where he stood before the screen, noting his breadth of shoulder and his length of limb, his hard, tanned face beneath the spill of blond hair that was so carefully curled and scented. He was no stableboy now, she told herself. He looked every hard inch of him the captain of lances that Cesare Borgia had made him, a soldier on leave from the front, in rich clothing that only a man of his noble blood might afford. Still, she went on to herself honestly, it was none of those things that attracted her.

Giula da Rienza sighed softly, and admitted that she was irrevocably committed to the love she bore this man, because of his very manhood and the humility in him that touched her heart.

She sat now on a polished walnut bench before the fire, her white fingers locked in a kerchief, only too well aware that this same Captain Ilarion had not removed his eyes from her face, except for that one hungry glance, of which she knew he considered himself unsuspected. In that glance he had roamed her body, seeking its thrusting curves and gentle hollows to remind himself once again of the shapeliness of this woman he adored. The gray satin of her gown was frizzled with silver work, and Madonna Giula was well aware that it was tight enough to be the explanation for the avidity she read in his hot blue eyes.

Ilarion had come with Galeazzo Gonzaga to visit Giula da Rienza on this afternoon following the night in which he had wrested the medallion from Jacopo Balisandro. In a turmoil of excitement, Gonzaga had crooned over the jewel, demanding that he go at once to Messer Collenuccio, and set it in his hands. He found unexpected resistance from Ilarion. There would be no argument on the matter. First, he must bring the medallion to Madonna Giula and display it to her. After that, he could act as his own messenger to place the bauble in Collenuccio's fingers. And so it was arranged.

The confident Gonzaga had predicted that his tongue would bend Giula *la rosso* to his will. Even if at first she were cold and distant, he would play upon her pity and sympathy, enumerating the dangers that had befallen her lover. Then he would slide slyly into a tirade against the *contessa*, Beatrice del Gallina, to give Giula a target for her anger.

As Galeazzo Gonzaga prophesied, so it proved to be.

He talked on, using his listeners' ears as a sounding board, unaware that their eyes had locked and were feeding on what they read in each other's glance. When Galeazzo Gonzaga paused for breath after an especially pleasing mixture of adjectives, he became aware that he had lost his audience. His sharp black eyes regarded them as they stared at each other. Like chickens, he thought, hypnotized by a straight line. His lips smiled and he watched them a moment, nodding with satisfaction. They were oblivious of him. Now he could be about the more serious matter of placing the medallion with Messer Collenuccio. He began to tiptoe toward a doorway that was frescoed with ivory inlay.

Ilarion felt the heat of the flames on his legs. He moved against this sudden discomfort, toward the walnut bench where Giula *la rosso* studied the kerchief in her fingers. He went to a knee, and when she freed her hand from the linen, he caught and kissed it.

Madonna Giula was discovering that it was hard to breathe. Her bosom thrust rhythmically against the gray satin that contained it, and her red lips parted to draw in the warm air of the little room. Her legs, outlined by the taut stuff of her skirt, were trembling so that she could hear the rustle of the taffeta petticoat she wore. Tears glistened on her long eyelashes.

"Hieronimo d'Este," she whispered with a sob. "A Ferraran nobleman! Oh, I think I prefer my own Ilarion!" Her hand pulled him up beside her, to the walnut benchtop. "My own stableboy who took a dream and made it come true!"

"If I did, madonna, my inspiration came from you!"

Her head bent slowly, and Ilarion kissed her, savoring the sweet warmth of her mouth, losing himself in its softness. His hands came up her back and swung her around and into him, almost crushing her in their frenzy. When he felt the pressure of her palms against his chest, he loosened his hold slightly, so that she could throw back her red head and stare with wide eyes up into his face.

Fearful that he had startled her with his hunger, Ilarion loosed her in his arms. He was keenly aware of the chasm between their stations, and the words that he had taken from the jongleurs and troubadors, and used so successfully with Dorotea del Andriola and Beatrice del Gallina, froze on his lips.

Ilarion became awkward, straightening up. He did not see the wondering glance with which Giula *la rosso* regarded him, or the quizzical little smile that twisted her lips. As her fingers fussed at the silverwork of her satin gown, her green eyes slanted sideways at him.

"You discern something in me that frightens you, Ilarion?" she asked.

He shook his head, smiling a little. How can I tell her

of the awe in which I hold her? he asked himself. Should he transform that awe to physical admiration, he had no doubt but that she would freeze, as she had when he kissed her just now.

For her part, Giula *la rosso* found herself amused at his forbearance. She thought, He imagines me an alabaster figurine that may break to his touch, should he prove clumsy! And because she was so much the tease, she added to his belief.

"You shall find me as loving as any *contessa*, Hieronimo d'Este," she whispered, her eyes lowered. She went on hastily, smiling to herself, "As soon as we are wedded, that is."

He did not notice the laughter that her long red lashes were hiding. He agreed stiffly, "Of course, madonna! It would be a presumption to think otherwise!"

Her hand lifted to his black doublet, smoothing it across his chest. "I am a maiden, unused to men and the ways of men with maids. You must be gentle and understanding with me."

Ilarion said gloomily, "According to the laws of love, of which the troubadours sang, there is no true love between husband and wife."

Giula *la rosso* opened her eyes wide. "Do you ascribe to those beliefs? That husband and wife cannot love as others do?"

Ilarion found himself wondering whether such a fire burned in her for him as he had been given to believe. There was no way of asking, he told himself glumly. He had won her hand. If she were to prove, as he was beginning to suspect, more woman of ice than of fire, it was too late to do anything about it. Still, for all of that, she would be his.

Her next words convinced him that his suspicion was fact. As her green eyes glowed trustingly up at him, and as her silken scarf hid the smile on her lips, she whispered, "Speak honestly with me, Ilarion. Isn't a pure, noble love far greater than one in which the flesh plays so great a part?"

He nodded, sighing. "You have made me very happy, *caro mio*," she murmured, and bent forward to touch her lips gently to his.

It was thus that Paolo da Rienza found them.

He came striding into the room, his face dark and gloomy. In the great square before the cathedral, he had met and had words with Galeazzo Gonzaga. He had been told that Gonzaga was on his way to visit the Ferraran ambassador with a medallion to prove Ilarion's parentage, and that following that, he would arrange for the wedding of Hieronimo d'Este and Giula da Rienza. Paolo da Rienza found his protests swept away before the other's impassioned speech. Should Paolo da Rienza persist in this hate against Ilarion, or stand in the way of this pending marriage, there might be persuasive means applied by Cesare Borgia to rid himself of this objector, permanently. The Duke played with power, for high stakes. What would one more life mean to him, if by its loss, he might accomplish his goal? Paolo da Rienza could understand that? The fop understood, and smothered his fury behind a nod of agreement.

And so he came into the room, advancing with both hands outstretched. "Sister Giula," he cried. *"Mie congratulazione!* I never suspected this man was a born Ferrara. It alters things!" He swung to Ilarion and threw his arms wide. "To you, messer, what words can I employ? I beg your consideration, your understanding! Even your mercy! What I did was unforgivable! I can only hope that your love for my sister is great enough to embrace me, her brother!"

With the taste of Giula *la rosso's* mouth still warm on his lips, Ilarion was expansive. He bowed coldly, telling himself that this was no time to bear malice.

"Hieronimo d'Este," exclaimed the fop, shaking his head. "It is like one of Serafino Cimino's poetic ballads! On my faith, I believe that your new name alone gives me clearer vision with which to view you. A Ferrara and a Da Rienza! A splendid match! One which I shall support with all my means!"

Giula started forward. "Paolo! You mean that? Honestly?"

Paolo da Rienza looked injured. He pouted and swung to Ilarion. "If my sister doubts me, what must you think? Yet there's a way to display the change that has taken hold of me. *Macche!* Of course! I will make a public protestation of my change of heart at a party to this bridegroom for all my friends. I will invite the Orsinis, the Contis, all the greatest and noblest young men of Rome! When I am done, the world shall know that next to his sister Giula, Paolo da Rienza cherishes Hieronimo d'Este the most! Is it agreed?"

Giula *la rosso* caught at straws to assure her marriage. She was eager in her delight. "You'll stay to dine, Ilarion, *caro mio?* We'll go over plans together and Paolo shall join us, to expand on his private little dinner!"

Ilarion could refuse her nothing. The doubts with which he regarded the fop still remained. He felt a hot desire to take him out behind the great obelisk, in the piazza of St. Peter's, that still lay as flat as the day they put it there, for none could figure a way to lift it, and give him a taste of the steel he had given Captain da Marolla. But this mincing dandy with the face and teeth of a starved rat was brother to his Madonna *la rosso,* strange as was the fact. And so for her sake, he dissembled his fury and his suspicion, and returned the other's bow.

It was with a wary eye on Paolo da Rienza that Ilarion went with Giula to the great dining hall. Here with silverware and crystal, on platters of china and gleaming white napery, they ate their meal. When they were done, it was Paolo da Rienza who informed them, as he pitted a peach with the point of a dagger, that he had chosen the Red Stag tavern, a hostel much in demand with the young bloods of Rome, for their proposed dinner. It was fashionable to be carried from the Red Stag in a wine-induced stupor, and would add to Ilarion's reputation, giving his martial bearing a touch of modishness. Paolo di Rienza plunged on to the manner in which the chef, Veronimo, would bake a pheasant and roast a suckling pig. "And of course," he concluded, with a wink at his sister Giula, "there will be dancing girls to while away the hours after the food is gone. Then I shall publicly announce that Hieronimo d'Este is a brother to me!"

"Not such a brother as Cain was to Abel, I trust," replied Ilarion, unable to resist the thrust.

Paolo da Rienza laughed in good humor. *"Touchè!* The point is well taken. But after our little dinner, you shall never have cause to mistrust me again!"

Ilarion spent the remainder of the evening with Madonna Giula before the fireplace in the little chamber off the mezzanine, drinking in every moment with a hunger that delighted that lovely tease. It was well for him he did, for in the days that followed, he saw little of her. There were long afternoons of conferences between Galeazzo Gonzaga and Messer Collenuccio, with himself as silent witness. His mornings were meted out to costumers who came laden with bolts of satins and velvets, their tapes whirling to measure him for cloaks and doublets. Messengers came from dawn to dusk with messages from Cardinal Ippolito, from Ferrante d'Este and Don Sigismondo, his brothers. There was even a sealed and perfumed packet from Isabella, Marchioness of Mantua.

Late one afternoon of a blustery January day, the old Duke of Ferrara arrived, with a thud of bootheels and clink of spurs and scabbard, a dozen armed retainers at his heels. He was no doddering ruin, this old soldier, but a straight and upright pepperpot, his eyes bright and still hungry for life in a tanned and lined face. In his early days, Ercole d'Este had thrown his lances against the might of Venice at Argenta, and later against the Duke of Lorraine, after Florence and Milan had become his allies. He bore the marks of his trade of war like badges.

He had not seen this little lost son since those sad days after Argenta. He paused now between the gilded wooden carvings of the Renaissance doorway, staring at Ilarion with tears running down his leathery cheeks.

Then with a cry he rushed forward and caught him in his arms. He must know all about him, the days he had spent mopping paving stones and currying horses, the nights when he had lain shivering to watch old Jacopo Balisandro at his solitary fencings. All this he must know, and further, the tale of his journeying to Nepi, on which he had rescued Leonardo da Vinci himself. Of Fossate and Brisghella, and the fighting that had taken place outside Faenza.

Ilarion warmed to this grim old warrior. It was easy to spill words before him, even to boast a little so that he might see the pride that glittered in the old man's eyes.

They talked until dark shadows crept across the room. At the end, nothing would satisfy the old Duke but that he sweep Ilarion off with him, into the bosom of his family. It required all of Galeazzo Gonzaga's talent to sway his mind. Ilarion must remain here, until the courts had ruled officially on the papers that Gonzaga and Collenuccio were submitting. True, there was little doubt of their validity, but a judgment must be passed. Until then, he must remain here. Naturally, there would be no objection if Ippolito d'Este, Cardinal of Holy Church, were to see that such a judgment were hastened along. Until then, however, Ilarion must remain here.

Ercole d'Este swept out with a promise to hurry that judgment if it cost the Ferrara fortune.

164

Fifty drinking cans pounded the bare boards of a long trestle table under the dark beams of the Red Stag tavern. Grinning servants were removing the platters that contained the bones and meat shreds of pheasant and suckling pig, hare, and lamb. Great amphorae, filled with *barbera* and *sassella, orvieto* and *frascati*, were being placed within easy reach of hands that belonged to Orsini and Farnese, Della Rovere and Savelli, Conti and Baglioni. The sons of two dozen noble houses sat here and banged their approval of Paolo da Rienza and his new friend, Hieronimo d'Este, with a roaring approbation.

Ilarion was flushed and dizzy with the wines he had swallowed in answer to the exhortations of the guests. With more than a score of grinning faces watching him, he had lifted his drinking can and matched them, swallow for swallow.

Unused to wine, his head swam. He scarcely heard Paolo da Rienza whisper to him, "Watch now, brother mine. Hai, they come!"

Through the glow of the candle flames, Ilarion could see a dozen girls gliding through the smoke and fumes onto the cleared space before the tables. They were painted and perfumed, and wore thin silken scarves about their supple, twisting bodies. Their arms curved above their heads, wriggling with serpentine grace. The fact that their scarves and nails had been tinted to match the hues of their hair added to the colorful picture they presented.

The slap of their bare feet was drowned in the sudden roar of the diners. Some stood and pelted the dancers with flowers. Others reached out to grasp soft flesh, and had to be restrained by the sharp voice of Paolo da Rienza.

"Later, *mie amici!* Let us have our entertainment!"

At another time, Ilarion would have delighted in the abandoned grace with which the girls performed. But the wine was working in him, and it was hard to focus his eyes on lengths of white legs and the willowy curves of bared torsos. His head slipped forward, nodding. He fought his rising weariness, but the table was so near! All he had to do was rest his forearms, and they would provide a cradle for his suddenly heavy head.

Beside him, Paolo da Rienza smiled, and made a gesture to the innkeeper. Two burly servants came forward from the shadows. Each caught Ilarion under an arm and drew him backward, away from the table. Paolo da Rienza waited a moment, to be certain that all eyes were glued

to the prancing women. Then he slid from his chair and
followed the servants up a narrow stairway.

XIV

ILARION FELT THE PROD of a hand shaking him. He
turned, muttering, on the pallet where he lay with dis-
arranged doublet and wrinkled hose. He tried to open his
eyes and discovered they clung as if glued. He heard the
murmur of voices. The hand came back again, to shake
him this time with renewed vigor.

The face of one-eyed old Jacopo Balisandro was bent
above him, and for the moment, Ilarion fancied that he
was back in the stable behind the hall. He rose up, blink-
ing in the torchlight.

"The stableboy wakes at last!" snarled the white-haired
fencing master. His great head bobbed from wide,
humped shoulders. "He has drunk his fill, and now sleeps
like the guttersnipe he is. Wake up, you *ladrone!*"

A hard calloused palm cracked against Ilarion's cheek.
It drove the fuzziness from his brain, the cobwebs from
his eyes. He clawed himself to a sitting posture on the
edge of the little bed. He found himself in a windowless
room whose plastered walls were hung with heavy drapes,
muffling all sound from outside. A huge oaken table
carved in quatrefoil ornamentation, was its sole bit of
furniture, outside the small bed and a single curule chair.

Jacopo Balisandro stood leering at him, and behind
him, lounging indolently against a corner of the doorway,
was Paolo da Rienza. The fop toyed gently with a velvet
sleeve while his black eyes glittered cruelly.

Ilarion said, "Where are the others? What's happened?"

It was the fop who answered. "I explained that you'd
taken a dancing girl to an upper chamber, to amuse yourself for the last time before your wedding. Our guests
found this action very commendable, and decided to
emulate your example. Fortunately, I'd provided against
the emergency with some extra women. They're amusing
themselves in the other wing of the tavern. We won't be
interrupted."

"A good thing," growled old Jacopo, striding toward
the long oak table that held a pair of blades. "I've been
waiting twenty years for this night!"

Ilarion found that his legs shook as he stood erect. The wine was still inside him, and he put a hand to the wall to steady himself. His eyes looked a question at Paolo da Rienza.

The fop grinned. "I should be on the stage, Ilarion. What an actor you find in me! How I fooled you and Giula! *Macche!* All Rome has swallowed the bait I fed it. They think me won over to your cause! None suspects that I have the lion of the hour shut up in a little room, about to die! Ah, that startles you, does it? Even at the risk of exposing my own stupidity, I must reveal that I picked poor weapons to use against you, when I had a sword at my hand all the while. I used Captain da Marolla and his bullies, then a band of hired bravos from the streets of lower Rome, to kill you. Captain Ilarion is the second best swordsman in Italy. Only the best swordsman in Italy is equal to such a task!"

Jacopo Balisandro cackled and yanked a sword from one of the scabbards that lay across the oaken tabletop.

The fop sniffed his pomade ball and went on. "Did you think for a moment I meant what I said to Giula and yourself? I hate your very soul, you *scorzone!* Before I allow Madonna Giula to wed you, I'll slip cold steel into her flesh!

"But now, there's no need for that. Jacopo Balisandro is eager for the task I set him. He hates you almost as much as I!"

The old fencing master slid forward. The torchlight was red on his naked blade. "Take the sword Da Vinci made for you, stableboy," he grinned with loose lips. "I could have cut you down in your sleep, but to do it this way—to chop you to mincemeat while you still live, and are awake to understand what I am doing—is that much more enjoyable!"

Ilarion drew his blade. His heart was cold in his rib case, and there was a faint quiver under his girdle of silver plates. He was met here for the last time with the old man, with naked swords in their hands. This time there would be no puddle of slops to spill old Jacopo. This time Balisandro would cut him to ribbons. Like a sword twisting his vitals, the thought came to him that it hurt him most now to die. Now, when he was all but accepted as Hieronimo d'Este, with a fortune and a bride awaiting him.

There was no more time for thought. Jacopo Balisandro stamped in, his blade thrusting through the shadows, and it was taking all of Ilarion's skill to skip and slide away from its darting point. He settled himself grimly, silently blessing Leonardo da Vinci the Florentine for turning out such a sliver of steel as this blade, that was so strong and yet so light, and adaptable to the slightest reflexes of his swordhand. He needed every assistance he could find.

They moved into the torchlight, the steel slithering together. The old man was bowed and humped, but his arm was an untiring thickness that moved his point from the *controtempo* into the *finta e controcavazione* without loss of motion, and followed them up with the swift and deadly *filo*. Ilarion parried and riposted, giving ground grudgingly. Once his eye saw an opening and he moved in, to be met with a coupe that missed his throat by an inch.

He knew then that the old man was playing with him. The single black eye glittered with mockery. The loose lips twisted in a scornful smile.

"Hieronimo d'Este," he said softly. "It is to jest with fate! You're no more an Este than I am, slopsboy! You want to know your real name? You're son to a tramp, a woman named Maria Bagnanino! A woman who mocked me for my one eye and my hump, and chose to wed an empty-headed adventurer. I killed him five days before you reached your fifth birthday! I went from his dead body to the house where you and your mother lived. I forced her to the bed she shared with him. I showed her what she missed by not marrying a one-eyed humpback. And then I put a dagger to her breast!"

The torches sputtered on the walls. The *slap-slap* of moving feet and the ringing clash of parrying swords filled the little room, where Paolo da Rienza bent like a statue to catch the play of steel and the leaping fury of these two bodies that sought to escape the death that hunted them in the swordpoint of the other.

Suddenly the old fencing master exploded, and the very strength of his arm beat down the blade opposing him, so that his sword came in with an *incontro* that left Ilarion bleeding at arm and cheek. As the blood welled up onto his doublet, Ilarion snarled.

"You lie like the cheap murderer you are! You speak out of the hate you have for the Ferraras! If what you say is true, you'd have come forward with your tale be-

fore! **Hate for the Ferraras and your greed for gold! Those
are your gods!"**

His pride lay raw in his one glittering eye as Jacopo
Balisandro swept in. But that same pride, that was flood-
ing him with a hot anger, caused him to be overeager to
mark the handsome face of this youth who once had been
his stableboy. His blade swung wide, and Ilarion caught
it in the *battuta,* and thrust hard. His point dug into the
fencing master's arm and came out with blood staining
its steel.

In the shadows, Paolo da Rienza almost screamed.
"*Fretta! Fretta!* Don't take any chances with the *bas-
tardo!"*

Jacopo Balisandro recovered himself. He pressed in
furiously, and his blade was a winking length of blued
steel. "Relax, your worship! It was a mistake. A mistake
I'll not make again! But I'm going to tell him some more
about himself. I want to see him squirm and grovel in
front of me, because of the hate I bear his mother! Hai!
I'll wager she's looking up from hellfire now, as I'm
about to run her only son through! Ai, I left her there
on her bed with a dagger in her *petto!* That's the last I
saw of her! But you, her son! You were screaming tears
when you'd seen what I'd done! And then my great idea
came to me! I'd bring you with me, bring you to my hall,
and make you clean its slops and dung! I'd beat and hu-
miliate you every day of your life!

"Life was good to me. It took the stableboy I hated
and made him great. A captain of lances under Cesare
Borgia! The man who saved the life of Leonardo da
Vinci! The man that all Rome is gossiping about, thinking him the little lost Ferrara! My cup runs over! I'm so
happy I could sing! I'll lay you here for them to find, and
none will ever suspect old Jacopo of killing you!"

Ilarion laughed mockingly. He retreated cautiously, his
blade entirely upon the defense, with *legamenta* and
parata.

"You lie in your black teeth, you greedyguts! You made
up the tale to tell me, not daring to reveal that you
stole a Ferrara—not with Paolo da Rienza listening! He
would have you hung for your admissions, if he thought
it to his advantage!"

He played with words even as he parried and disengaged the steel before him. Once more he must rouse up
that swift hot anger that was due to the pride that ran

like blood in the old man's misshaped body. A moment before, that pride had betrayed Jacopo Balisandro. It was his task to make it betray him just once more.

"You ravished my mother, you claim. Ha! There isn't that much manhood in you! A florin on the fact that the rest of you is as twisted and useless as your back!"

Jacopo Balisandro went mad. From birth, the hump that had disfigured him had been his weakness, something with which he must spend all his days and nights. Other young men won lovely women. All he ever won was a glare of horror or a pitying smile. And so he had given himself up to war and the arts of war and fence, and there he had made himself perfect. That he must buy the favors of women was a living cancer in his blood, for even those bought women looked away when he approached them. Now, to hear this stableboy throw up to him the misfortune that had twisted his life was too much.

He threw his arms wide and he rushed in, his blade licking out to slide past the guard that was keeping him away. His blade went in, and it sought to disengage and thrust.

His anger blinded him. He forgot that this youth who faced him had been trained into an imitation of himself. He felt his blade caught in the *circolazione* and twisted wide. Ilarion slid forward and his blade was a rigid length of steel in the unturnable *botta dritta*.

The sword that Leonardo da Vinci had forged went into Jacopo Balisandro a full three feet, its point protruding out his back. He screamed and tried to break free, and only succeeded in ripping himself on its edge.

His falling body shook the room as it hit the floor. He opened his loose lips, gulping for air. His one eye gazed blankly up at the white ceiling. His hands scraped at his bloody gipon.

Almost mechanically, Ilarion cleansed his blade on a corner of the sheet covering the pallet. He could hear the old man's choking gasp, the harsh sobbing of Paolo da Rienza from the shadows where he stood.

The dying man mumbled, "The last joke—on me! I raised the boy—in vengeance—and now that vengeance is turned against me! A jest supreme! I want to laugh . . ."

He choked, with blood bubbling in his throat instead. He lifted his great white head, his one eye rolling wildly. And then his head dropped back, to crash on the floorboards.

The door burst in, and Ilarion whirled with his blade held forward.

Cesare Borgia stood framed in the doorway, in long plum cloak and violet doublet, his powerful legs encased in boots of red Spanish leather. There was alarm in his eyes until he saw the dying man stretched on the floor, and the upright figure of the disheveled Ilarion.

Thrusting the Duke almost roughly aside, the peppery Ercole d'Este forced his way through the door to stand at Ilarion's side.

After them came a score of men-at-arms in back-and-breasts, their faces grim under their curving chapels-de-fer. Bringing up the rear was Galeazzo Gonzaga, an arm around the white-faced Giula da Rienza.

Her eyes went from Ilarion to the old fencing master on the floor, and then, with horror etched in their green depths, they turned to her brother. The fop quivered, and came forward a step, his face as white as the sheet with which Ilarion had wiped his blade. His tongue slid out to touch dry lips.

Cesare Borgia moved before Paolo da Rienza with purposeful strides, and there was something in the cold curve of his humorless smile that held the fop motionless.

"You see for yourself, Madonna Giula," said the Duke easily. "You can understand now my insistence that you come with us this evening! Observe, if you will, how your brother proclaims his friendship with Hieronimo d'Este! He fills him first with wines. Then, with your lover drunk and helpless, he brings the one man in all Italy that my blade acknowledges his superior! It is an attempt at cold-blooded murder, ranking with the other attempts that he has made."

For the first time, Giula *la rosso* heard of the duel in the inn below Fossate, and the attack at the Assisi tavern. She listened with rising horror to the story which the crossbowman had babbled on the rack outside Faenza. Shocked and sick, she turned away her head.

Cesare Borgia concluded, "*Peste!* I've ridden at the gallop from Cesena to Rome, summoned by the letters sent me by Galeazzo Gonzaga. It appears I've arrived just in time."

Galeazzo Gonzaga put scorn on his face as he regarded the shaking fop. "Did you think to bedazzle me with your words, you fool? Ilarion, yes! But he was the bemused lover already, seeing nothing but that the fact that you were brother to his madonna *la rosso!* I scented some threat in this dinner. I sent a fast messenger to my lord, the Duke!"

Ercole d'Este stamped forward from Ilarion's side, fists on his hips. "I ask the privilege of attending to this upstart, who has so many times lifted steel against my son! I can forgive him his attempts when he was not aware of his identity. But now, now that the world knows him as Hieronimo d'Este—"

The peppery old soldier was working himself into a rage. To forestall a hand that might lift and plunge a dagger into the fop's chest, Cesare Borgia moved forward. His voice was gentle, but the eyes he fixed on Paolo da Rienza were hard and bright.

"Va perdonno, illustrissimo! Allow me this pleasure!"

He moved on, and now Paolo da Rienza backed away, shrinking at his every step.

"There is a ship leaving Rome for Egypt with the tide," Borgia said softly. "It lacks a passenger. I've as good as promised the captain I'd find one for him. You understand? I am sure you will find the climate of that country so enjoyable, you will never feel the necessity of returning home! If you should decline to fulfill the promise I made the captain . . ." The Borgia shoulders shrugged, and Paolo da Rienza found them terrifying in their unconcern.

In the black shadows of a candlelighted room, Cesare Borgia moved with lithe impatience, up and down the thick Baghdad carpet that covered the study floor in the *palazza* Gonzaga. He paused to glance at an illuminated map of the Romagna on a brocade hanging, pinned there against the eyes that lifted to study it, again and again. He made a grim figure in his half-mail, a long Florentine dagger at his waist, his cloak a backdrop that trailed his stalking figure.

Once his fist hit the polished surface of a walnut writing desk, betraying the impatience that seethed in him.

He heard footsteps, and stiffened attentively.

Galeazzo Gonzaga burst through the marble doorway and paused to sweep a cloak from his shoulders, stamping the snow from calfskin boots.

"Well?" asked Cesare Borgia with furious impatience. "What news do you bring me?"

"Be at ease, *Excellenza!*" cried Galeazzo Gonzaga,

stamping forward. "Your blade is safely wed to **Madonna Giula**. He is the publicly acknowledged son of Ercole d'Este, and heir, along with **Alfonso, Ferrante,** and **Sigismondo,** to the great duchy of Ferrara! The old Duke himself made the proclamation, at the wedding banquet. Ha! You should have tasted the wines of Champagne that old Ercole imported for the occasion, the pheasant and venison that came from the hills and woodlands of Ferrara itself! *Macche!* The tumblers and mountebanks that vied for attention! It was the finest—"

Cesare Borgia chuckled.

"You rascal! You know I die of impatience, and you prate of food and merriment. The business at hand!"

Galeazzo Gonzaga threw his arms wide.

"Why this concern, Highness? Messer Collenuccio put his stamp of approval on the papers that officially proclaimed our Ilarion to be Hieronimo d'Este! Nothing remained but that old Ercole add his voice to the parchment. He did that, with a speech almost as long as the ones I make myself! *Peste!*"

The Duke permitted himself a wry smile. "And the other? The marriage of my blade with the redhead?"

"Performed by the Cardinal, his own brother. In the great Cathedral del Santo Pietro, with half Rome looking on. Paolo da Rienza could not be there—he's outward bound for Egypt! But everyone else who is anybody crowded its pillars."

There was a little pause. The two men eyed each other soberly. It was Cesare Borgia who smiled first, and Galeazzo Gonzaga took his cue from him. He howled laughter to the timbered ceiling, clutching his sides against the ache his laughter put in them. Soon the Duke joined him, and their merriment washed across the room.

"A master stroke, to pawn off our stableboy as the lost Ferrara child," babbled Gonzaga when he could speak. "None but Your Highness could have conceived it!"

"And none but your slyness could have executed it."

The Duke shook out a velvet sleeve. His face was thoughtful, brooding. "Another instance of the Borgia luck, *amico mio.* The luck that will win me all Italy. Luck, and the knowledge that wars are not won by the force of arms alone. I have thus allied myself with the Ferrara, who are friends of Venice and Florence. I have even heard a rumor that Florence plans to appoint me her Captain-General."

His control suddenly deserted Gonzaga. He laughed, bent forward, writhing helplessly. Tears sprang to his eyes and he wiped them away with a cuff of marten fur.

Valentinois smiled sympathetically. He cautioned, "Ilarion must never know! He's honest enough to repudiate everything if he learns the real truth!"

Galeazzo Gonzaga shook his head. "Neither he nor history will ever know the difference. And if I know women, his redheaded Giula will keep him too busy between the sheets for Ilarion to go questioning his fortune. No, it is an accomplished fact. Our stableboy has been turned into the lost Ferrara. No one questions it, so let it rest on that.

"A stableboy, heir to the Duchy of Ferrara," went on Gonzaga, musingly. "Oh, the delight of it! My vengeance complete at last! None suspects he is no more Hieronimo d'Este than I am. It all fit so well, even to the fact that Ilarion killed the one man who might reveal the real truth, old Jacopo Balisandro!"

Borgia laughed softly. "I counted on the fact that Balisandro had some war souvenirs of that campaign. The medallion was a stroke of luck. So much so that I have found myself wondering, if after all—"

Galeazzo Gonzaga scowled, and began slowly to pace the chamber. "If after all, he really is that lost child? I have taken some thought on that myself. Everything dovetailed so perfectly! Oh, but it would be stretching coincidence! *Macche!* Does your Excellency actually suppose we really found the lost Hieronimo? In truth? That some strange quirk of destiny greater than our efforts brought Ilarion to us as the perfect tool for our plan? The perfect tool, because he really is what we claimed him to be?"

The Borgia shoulders shrugged indifferently. His purpose was an accomplished fact. This other matter was of no moment.

"Chi sa?" he asked of history. "Who knows?"

A gurgle of wine filled the shadows of a high-ceilinged room where a man and a woman stood alone against its darkness. The marble walls were hung with drapes that were thick with gilded brocades. Above their heads, the frescoed ceilings were rich with the paintings of saints and sinners. Between two rows of silver floor candlestands was an ornate oak bed. This was the bridal chamber, a tall *camera* in the *palazzo* Gonzaga.

The magic of the afternoon and evening still held Ilarion *della stalla* in thrall. The great cathedral of Santo Pietro, whose magnificence as he had stood before the main altar with Giula da Rienza had taken away his breath, was thronged with the nobility of Rome. In a daze, as the chanting of the choir rang in his ears, he spoke the words that made him one with his lady of the cameo. Still in that spell, he had knelt and kissed the Papal ring, and moved past the tall cathedral columns out into the huge square where all Rome seemed to be gathered for the occasion.

The world was his. The dream that had begun so long ago, when he had fought with Paolo da Rienza under the bright eyes of the Countess Beatrice del Gallina, was flowering today. He was no more a stableboy but a nobleman, heir to vast fortunes and a famous name. His reputation as a swordsman was moving the length of Italy.

The gurgle of wine halted. Giula *la rosso* lifted her head and smiled at him, even as she reached for the silver cups. She was lovely in her golden gown, from which her white shoulders rose with the spotless purity of the lily. Thinking of that purity, and of the ice that lay beneath that rich dress, Ilarion sighed.

His bride!

He would have given much to swing her up in his arms, to kiss her breathless, to laugh and play in frenzied delight with her red beauty. If only he did not stand in such awe of her! If only she were less the *illustrissima,* and more the shameless, loving wife!

As if she caught his thought, Giula came forward with a faint swing to her hips, holding both silver cups. There was amusement in her green eyes as she touched one of them to his lips. She whispered, "To give you courage, husband mine!"

He shook himself, his dreams fading, obediently sipping the chilled *secco Orvieto.* She whispered again, "We are wedded now, Ilarion!"

He stood frozen, not realizing that Giula *la rosso* was laughing tenderly at him.

Her hands went to the laces on her gown of cloth of gold *à la francaise.* Slowly she tugged them loose, allowing the heavy brocades to fall.

"I'm no wooden statue to be mounted on a pedestal, *caro mio!* I'm a woman, to be loved like a woman!"

Giula lifted her white arms from the heavy sleeves and encircled his neck with them. Her green eyes grew misty as she set her mouth on his. The dreams that had come so often to disturb her slumbers would soon be pleasantly disturbing reality.

As he felt the touch of her lips, Ilarion opened his eyes wide. This clinging warmth, this soft and perfumed flesh, this thrust of hips to his, was lifting a veil from his eyes.

"I'm not made of alabaster, to be broken by a squeeze," she murmured against his mouth. "You can put your arms around me!"

It was as if she struck fetters from him with her throaty, mocking laughter. With a wild, glad cry, Ilarion *della stalla*—who was now Hieronimo d'Este, nobleman of Ferrara—lifted his wife high in his arms, kissing her as a woman should be kissed, and ran with her to the low, wide bed.

THE END
of a novel by
Gardner F. Fox